Michèle Roberts was born in 1949 of a French mother and English father. *A Piece of the Night*, published in 1978, was her début novel, and also the first work of original fiction to be published by The Women's Press. It established Michèle Roberts as a major literary writer, and was followed by *The Visitation* (The Women's Press, 1983). Michèle Roberts is now an established and acclaimed writer of poetry and prose, including her novel, *Daughters of the House*, which was shortlisted for the 1992 Booker Prize.

Also by Michèle Roberts from The Women's Press:

The Visitation (1983)

Michèle Roberts

A PIECE
OF THE NIGHT

First published by The Women's Press Ltd, 1978
A member of the Namara Group
34 Great Sutton Street, London EC1V 0DX

Reprinted 1980, 1984, 1986, 1994

British Library Cataloguing-in-Publication Data
  Roberts, Michèle
    A piece of the night.
    I. Title
    823'.914[F]   PR6068.015/

ISBN 0 7043 3830 0

Printed and bound in Great Britain by
Cox & Wyman Ltd, Reading, Berkshire

For my parents, Monique and Reg Roberts, with love and gratitude; and for the women in the writers group of which I was a member who encouraged me to write short stories and then this novel: Zoë Fairbairns, Valerie Miner, Sara Maitland and Michelene Wandor.

I should also like to thank particularly, amongst many friends, the following people, who either lent me money, or generally encouraged me, or read and criticised the manuscript, or did all three: Dinah Brooke; Marguerite Defriez; Sian Dodderidge; Anne Doggett; Stephanie Dowrick; Alison Fell; Sibyl Grundberg; Andrew Hale; Pamela Job; Monica Lawlor; James Lefanu; Sarah Lefanu; Jim Marks; Chandra Masoliver; Andy Roberts; Elizabeth Nell Roberts; Steve Thorne; Jacqueline Walton.

JULIENNE:
French culinary term
referring to a mass of vegetables
cut up into small sections and
then made into soup.

First section

There is a dead nun in the school chapel. She lies on a velvet-covered bier inside a dusty glass case surrounded by wax flowers and the stumps of night-lights winking in ruby glass containers. Sister Veronica contemplates her from the nuns' stalls behind the black wrought-iron grille. The novices are cleaning the chapel. They fight for the privilege to do so, for it is only this holy housework which enables them to enter the sanctuary, normally the chaplain's prerogative, and dust the brocade tent, the tabernacle, on the altar, that contains the Christ. The smell of floor polish mingles with that of incense, Mary Magdalene wiping the feet of Jesus with her hair.

Second section

Julie Fanchot was born in Normandy, in May, 1949. She should have been a boy, that was what they wanted, a boy with brown eyes, curly hair and straight strong limbs, a comfort to her father Julien for the diseased leg that had kept him out of any active part in the Resistance; a reassurance to her mother Claire that she had pleased her newly-won father-in-law; a reminder to her paternal grandfather of his own youth and a denial of his own death; a second-generation son for her grandmother to lavish care upon.

Claire Fanchot lies upon her marriage bed, on a hard mattress set in a high glossy wooden frame. Between fresh linen sheets her tired and aching body hides, her mind already blanking out the pain of the previous night. Above the bed, against the faded wallpaper of fields of tiny sprigs of flowers, her crucifix hangs, a branch of olive from Jerusalem threaded behind the arching body fashioned in white ivory.

Claire knows that her suffering is as nothing compared to His. She also knows that His suffering and her own have been caused by an action of disobedience and curiosity far in the past for which she is

2

responsible, every woman's second name being Eve. Her daughter reminds her of that sin, every time her mother-in-law carries the child to Claire's breast and the mouth clamps itself hungrily, passionately, to the swollen nipple and causes her pain.

August 1948. Claire edges forward towards the mirror through a sea of ferns. They wave gracefully, slowly, from the window-sill between heavy double curtains of velvet and lace so that the pattern of sun on the faded turkey carpet is intricate and always in movement; they bend their delicate fronds from brass pots placed on small tables, like lengthy fingertips catching at the trailing skirts of her dress as she glides in slow motion across the narrow room. The mirror is in the far corner, over the high grey marble mantelpiece, protected by more ferns. A bronze can in the grate spills with complicated feathery greenness springing outwards, preventing her from getting too close to her reflection. On the mantelpiece three family groups invite her closer from their plush-surrounded frames, a Limoges Virgin and Child stretch their rounded gold-streaked arms towards her. She navigates a small buttoned armchair with a frilly skirt in dimly-flowered chintz, and arrives. Leaning forward slowly and gracefully from the waist she places her gloved elbows on the only two spaces that the crowded surface of the mantelpiece allows her, the chilly marble shocking her flesh through its silk and net covering. She bends as near as possible to the glass and gazes into it.

She sees the paper of the wall behind her: a cream ground with darker, yellow stripes and bunches of pale pink and blue flowers on the cream. Between the bunches hang pictures: a female gypsy framed in gold, wearing a yellow turban and smoking a long pipe, blue tassels dangling on her shoulder. Two water-colours of the ruined abbeys of the neighbourhood, Jumièges and St Wandrille. An engraving under shiny glass of the mother and child Ceres and Persephone, a plump pomegranate passing between them.

The bed is placed along the wall beneath the window, all overtones of night smoothed away by the stiff chintz cover with matching rigid bolster that turn it into a sofa, the room by daylight into a small salon where guests sip cassis-blanc before Sunday lunch. Claire loves her aunt's room, this elegant feminine sanctuary that smells of pot-pourri and is so often held in semi-darkness, shuttered and curtained against the sun blotting the farmyard outside into whiteness. Today the shutters are folded back; through the mirror

3

Claire sees the olive-green majolica pot of geraniums on the outside window-sill. Everyone is out, helping with the harvest. One of the tasks of the women is to prepare the midday meal, long sandwiches of baguette split and filled with cheese and ham. Madame Fanchot has gone with the others, stepping across fields with jugs of cider, baskets. They lounge for half an hour under the lines of elms dividing fields, sunlight spattering their faces. Claire has stayed behind, wanting to deny the world of work. No excuse needed after she has blushed and murmured to her aunt. Her cousin Julien catches the mention of bad days; he looks at Claire with curiosity, with speculation, and she blushes again.

She has the whole house to herself, a luxury unknown in the cramped spaces of her recent childhood. She plays dolls-houses for a while, opening the great carved wooden cupboards and fingering the china and linen within, stealing a yellow plum from the black wicker basket on the cellar steps, sitting in her uncle's place at table and pounding her small fists on the gleaming top. Tiring of this, she moves a few years forward, entering her aunt's dressing-room, cupboards, clothes. The evening dress is loose on her. In the style of thirty years before it is cut low and square across the breasts in front and trails lacily along the carpet at the back.

Claire looks at her breasts in the mirror and feels a clamour in her stomach. She moves her eyes up to her face, studying its childish roundness, the crown of soft blonde hair. She sighs, she arches her neck to make it look longer, she lifts her chin to achieve a pleasing three-quarters profile, she practises a variety of smiles, haughty, flirtatious, tender, sultry. I am no longer a child, she thinks vaguely: I am a woman now, I'll show them all.

In the doorway her cousin Julien stands and watches her, his eyes moving from the tumble of lace and silk on the bed to her throat and face above the yellowing fabric that she wears.

She sees him as she gazes past herself in the mirror. His voice defines the situation before she can move.

– Already one of the family, aren't you, Claire?

Despite his lameness he moves more quickly than she between the furniture and ferns. This is his place, his mother's room, where every morning he brings her hot chocolate and rolls, reads her bits from the local newspaper, caresses her toes beneath the blanket. This is where she smiles at him and strokes his hair, Julien, my son, never mind your leg, you are here with me.

Terror and humiliation keep Claire from crying out; the shame of being discovered abusing her aunt and uncle's hospitality preoccupies her, to make her hope that whatever reproach Julien intends it will be over quickly.

But his arms are around her waist, forcing her head against his rough blue shirt and bruising her cheeks against the metal buttons. He murmurs words into her ear, words which she does not understand, in a tone which does not seem angry or reproachful. Claire squirms coyly, Julien, oh Julien, I thought you saw me only as a little girl. She is prepared for delicious flutters of the heart, for lingering kisses, she shuts her eyes and waits for the soft touch of his lips on hers, for the long handclasp and the words of respectful adoration which must follow the moment of blind passion, his mouth gobbling her neck. Her eyes fly open again as she hears him speak, hoarse and abrupt.

– This is what you want, isn't it?

He pushes her chin up with one hand so that her eyes stare into his, forced to recognise in muteness what his other hand is doing, fumbling its way through layers of lace and petticoats. He does not know the rules of courtship that she has read in novels, it appears. He is proceeding far too fast for her, but she does not know how to stop him. She is a child dressed-up in borrowed savoir-faire, which falls away from her now as rapidly as the evening frock he pushes off her shoulders with one hand. When his other hand makes contact underneath her petticoats with the hair and flesh she has never touched, she knows she has died, she cannot be connected with the horrors resident in that nameless place.

Her shudder pleases Julien, he presses her closer to him with one arm, his mouth at her ear.

– Oh yes, this is what you want, isn't it?

His certainty cannot be matched by any anger of hers, she has no words for this. If she is not to apply to herself the thundering denunciations of sin, the promises of hell from the pulpit, the sniggers of the peasant children on the farm outside, then it is better to keep silent, try to trust him, and to smile. He withdraws his hand from underneath her skirts and, still leaning against her with his body and his eyes, unbuttons his trousers, then pushes her on to the little frilly chair. Shame at his lameness, the fear of being interrupted, lend him speed and strength.

When the searing, tearing pain begins, Claire is forced into consciousness of what is happening, into guilt. It must be her fault for flirting, for leading Julien on. She cries out, feebly attempting to push him off her, the first time in her life that she has struck anyone, shown anger physically. Anger, even in self-defence, may be a sin. She knows she will not go to confession to find out. Her vacillating struggle, her little cries of no, you mustn't, serve for Julien to point her recognition of herself as female, of himself as male, and he is able to come. He gathers her into his arms, slumped on top of her on the small armchair, and kneads the soft creased flesh at the base of her throat. My little dove, my lady of the farmyard, you have no more secrets from me now, blood on your clothes, my pet, where there was none before.

Monsieur Fanchot is surprised and gratified by his son's eagerness for marriage. Noticing Claire's silence at dinner in place of her usual charming chatter, her lowered eyes, the scratch on her cheek, he concludes that his lame and girlish son is a man at last. An end to those cosy meetings with his mother, thank God, hanging about her room at all hours. He rubs his hands before he picks up his spoon and drinks, the soup slurping through his great baby moustache. Madame Fanchot sits in silence. She has noted the absence of an evening frock, the finger marks on her mirror, the moving of her little frilly chintz chair from the exact spot on the carpet it has occupied for the past twenty years. She has no pity for Claire, she thinks of future mornings, breakfasting alone.

After the feed, the baby is laid to rest in her cradle shaped like a half-barrel and slung to rock between two stout poles, the whole carved with fruit and flowers by Monsieur Fanchot years ago for his first, his only child. After Madame Fanchot's operation in the clinic in Le Havre, the cradle was stored in the grenier. For years Julien has looked at it, hung from a rafter, whenever he climbed the rickety ladder to fetch down another pot of apple jam for his mother's breakfast. Now he and his father gather around the crib, their bodies breaking the pillar of warm sunshine linking the baby to the casement window in the slanting roof. Blackness falls on the baby's face, and she begins to scream.

Claire goes rigid, her hands clutch the edges of her dressing-gown. Her mother-in-law, her teacher, has retired to her own room downstairs. The other two are waiting for her to do something; she is the child's mother, assumed to know how to quench the baby's cries. Little wailing succubus, you shall sleep, I swear it, we shall both of us have our peace. She looks with hostility at the two men, but speaks in a low tone.

6

– You can't expect a child to go to sleep if you keep on picking her up.

They accede to the authority they have laid upon her and move across to the other side of the room, where a small fire has been lit in the grate, despite the day's heat. Bending forward mechanically to spread his hands to the blaze, Monsieur Fanchot smiles, he is delighted with the child, he has always wanted a daughter, he exclaims, delighted too with Julien for having produced this marvel, willing for the moment to suppress his irritation at his son's spending so much less time on the farm since Julie's birth. It is a woman's place to feed and clean and clothe the baby; he is disquieted to find Julien so often in this atmosphere of heat, smelling of warm milk and piss, hanging endlessly over the cradle.

– Daumier says he can let us have a second tractor tomorrow, he says gently: we can begin on the top field.

– You should go, Julien, Claire says languidly: I can manage perfectly well, there is nothing for you to do here.

She does not look at either of them as they look at her. She is seated in a deep armchair, her head continually drooping in exhaustion even as she attempts to keep it upright. The chair is upholstered in pale blue brocade, glistening with sprays of flowers embroidered in silver thread. Against the pale blue is the blondeness of Claire's hair, her dressing-gown, cream-coloured. The front of the gown has fallen awry, revealing her breasts, full and hanging sideways, the nipples large, surrounded by dark circles.

Julien is angry. My wife's breasts belong to me, they are to be covered in public to indicate my ownership, that I alone in the privacy of my bed may put my hand upon them. Then, and only then, they are erotic, aroused by me and following me, desiring but obedient.

Claire sees his angry look, the twitching of the eyebrows unrecognised by any but her who has already learned the importance of reading signs correctly and acting on instruction. A mother's breasts belong to her child, at certain intervals, for a stated length of time; a hygienic interaction, a necessary task. They do not exist in a sitting-room, she understands that, available to the gaze of men other than her husband. She thinks of the night, her breasts divided between Julien and the child.

Her hand moves to close the edges of her dressing-gown. In the mirror above the fireplace, she can see the picture that she makes, a solid woman with creamy flesh enhanced by blondeness and pale blue, reclining in an armchair, two men standing opposite. They are looking at her; she sees them seeing her. A mystery painting, full of rich colour, varied texture, its intimate relaxed surface broken by tiny clues: two eyebrows twitched together, a hand clenched over a spray of silver flowers, one pair of eyes directed towards a cradle in the corner beyond the armchair. Violence bubbles behind soothing colour tones. Claire punishes Julien for the shame he has laid upon her, his love given so soon to the child leaving less for her. She will deny him the child. She repeats her words, still looking at the mirror as though to check the placid contours of her face against the brocade whirligig of silver and of blue.

– You should go, Julien, there is nothing for you to do here. I can manage perfectly well on my own.

Julie is still crying. As the two men close the door behind them, Claire crosses the room towards the cradle again. In three hours' time she will have to give her baby another feed, pose once more for her husband and her father-in-law as Ceres, as Mary. She puts her hands on the rim of the cradle and gazes at the shrunken red face, searching for any resemblance to herself and happily finding none. That mouth would suck the world dry if it could, would swallow its mother cheerfully along with it.

She watches herself, the young matron, efficiently removing a wet and stinking nappy which her nose and her fingers deny, wiping, powdering, rebinding the child's legs with a fresh square of white towelling. This is not a picture seen hanging in the galleries of art, a mother changing nappies and whispering, you little pig, you little monster, you do it on purpose to annoy me. You see only the subsequent image, a mother snatching up her child in a sudden rush of love, her resentment cast aside with her damp apron, she hugs the baby, poor little thing, what a start in life, I will love you, I will make it up to you, I swear, you shall be happy as I am not, I will do my best to be a perfect mother to you. Julie chuckles, she is delighted with herself now, with her full stomach, with her comfort, and with the warm arms that hold her safe.

Claire is exhausted, but is afraid to begin crying in case she never stops. Broken sleep every night for three months now, ever since the baby's birth, up and down to feed, rock, bring up the wind, and now cope with the beginnings of colic. Julien cannot help with any of the feeds himself. He loves to see her feed the child in the daytime; he cannot bear to hear Claire's suggestion that bottle-feeding might be easier. She'll catch up on her sleep eventually; she has little to do in the daytime, she can rest.

8

She pulls the blind across the casement window to shield Julie's eyes from the sun, and goes next door. Her dolls were never like this. She bathed and changed them only because she wanted to; when she was tired of dressing them in new clothes and playing tea-parties she shut the whole lot in a cupboard and ran outside to play in the fields. Her mother sewed the dolls' clothes, exquisite miniature frocks patterned on what the adults wore. Her father carved their furniture and made them tiny wooden-soled boots covered with fur. Remembering her parents propels Claire to the writing-desk, how can she have forgotten, she has not yet written to thank her mother for her birthday present. Three nightgowns for the baby, white cambric frilled with handmade lace, with drawn-thread work around the hem and the family initials on the dear little pocket in delicate stumpwork.

Her tiredness dissipates itself into the inkwell. She loads her pen with tears, thick and black. For three hours she is at home again, on the other side of Normandy, helping to push the water-cart to the pump, learning to make pastry in the kitchen with Jeanne, prodding the cows down the narrow muddy track to the milking-shed, beating the boys at running races, reading every book in the house a dozen times, and at the end of the day collapsing into bed demanding stories. She smiles as she looks at her mother's photograph propped on top of the desk, as she straightens her shawl and fusses at her hair. Really, Maman, that a mess your clothes are in. Dearest Maman, I miss you terribly, I am afraid it will be some time yet before the harvest is over and we can manage to get away from here and visit you. How is your back? You must take care of yourself now that I am not there to make you rest.

Five pages later, the baby writes herself back into her mother's life with cries of hunger. Claire looks vaguely at the clock on the mantelpiece, half of her still far away ten years ago. The room, she remembers, is warm, the lamp glowing in one corner, the fire crackling. On Sunday afternoons, a rare and precious time to rest, her father sleeps, her mother does the mending; Claire leans against her legs watching the fire, half dozing, cheeks scorched red. The room breathes with them, their stillness and their peace, breathes them to further contentment. Dearest Maman, I need you still. Who nurtures mothers? Who is there to nurture me now? Why are you not here to help me through this difficult time? Tell me, Maman, is it wrong to wish to feed a baby with a bottle? Sometimes to feel nothing for her? Why does my husband not understand that I must fall asleep quickly at night?

9

Her mother's tones are always calm, glossed now with chilliness. Child, you are a woman now. I do not wish to hear these things. I love my husband and my children and I do my duty to them, as I am sure you do yours. Where there is this love and duty, there is a happy family, no problems and no pain. I cannot bear to see my daughter suffering. France needs her women to be strong. Do not suffer, be good and happy, reassure me that I brought you up correctly.

Claire tears up the last two pages of her letter, throws them into the fire, glances at the clock again, and goes next door.

Third section

Few Londoners ever know where Camberwell and Peckham are, when Julie tells them she lives on the borderline between the two, her back garden the beginning of Peckham, and Mr Salmon's, backing on to hers, the end of Camberwell. But when she amplifies to the bus queue in Oxford Street today, with map directions, waving hands, enthusiasm spilling, then she is sure she can hear them exclaim: oh, *south* of the river, oh well. Oh, in that desert, that bleak endless boulevard of betting-shops, launderettes and empty cinemas, that whistling chaos of crimplene and chips, where the buses die at ten o'clock and the pubs have never heard of wine, where heaps of rotting rubbish conceal armies of wild youth armed with knives who have torn up the street-maps and corrupted the police, where the tube cannot run and the women still wear mini-skirts, and where there are no health-food shops, no elegant dogs or conversation, nothing exciting happening politically, and no good restaurants.

By Londoners, Julie means the people with whom she has had contact today north of the river, men and women, younger and older than herself, with whom she has talked in the pubs, chemists, clothes shops and newsagents around Oxford Circus, in that small circumference called the West End where that conversation, having once been held, has soon killed every other.

She met on terms of initial friendliness and ease, it seemed to her, with all these others, locked into equality over the purchase of a cotton shirt, the reheeling of a shoe. She isn't shy, she is far too old for that, she likes people, demonstrates her wit, her charm, her brains, her relish of swearing and of touch. But with her begging of love from all and sundry comes back the statement, she is sure she hears them mutter it: south, oh well. A hardening, a rejection, a definition in a language foreign to her, a distance meaning more than river frontiers ever can. What is it about her today, exile from the south, that turns them away? Perhaps the smell of last night's noisy tears still damp on her cheek? The owners of tears fouling the pavements will be fined £50. Suffering is a disgusting habit; do it in private. You will go blind from weeping, anyway. People stare at her as she tries to tell them about herself, and the conversation has to stop there, it's been ever so nice meeting her, but they are busy, must be getting back now, sorry, must dash.

She faces west on Friday afternoon, with her face to the rest of the bus queue so that she can watch the sun hang like a gobbet of blood in strings of mucus over Marble Arch, anticipating that moment when the bus, having crawled through the rush-hour traffic over Westminster bridge, will change gear, shoot under the railway bridge outside Waterloo station and instantly be sucked into the concrete maze of roundabouts before the Elephant and Castle. I'd never dream of living there; funny, isn't it; it's all a matter of personal taste of course; you must have very odd ideas of what is nice to be living there; funny creatures, women; that woman is acting in a very peculiar way; whatever made you choose to go and live south of the river of all places?

As she is never directly asked this question, Julie's answer is for herself alone. I've grown to like the strangeness and the secrecy, she hums, you do, you know. Spring is the little girls from the estate across the road wearing bikinis to the newsagent on Sunday morning; winter is sliding my hands between Jenny's overcoat and her softly-breathing shirt, hugging one another like the semi-detached houses down the street; summer is timed by Bertha, my little daughter, demanding a cotton not a woollen vest, summer is the Turkish Cypriot grocer's wife and mother sitting on the pavement on wooden chairs shelling peas into an enamel colander while the radio blares, and the crowds on Peckham Rye Common lying with each other and their candy floss and children between the dogshit and the sweet-wrappers. Autumn is the air rusting, the Town Hall chrysanthemums sour-burning up your nose and fresh school stationery in the shop windows, the library advertising do-it-yourself classes and the florid redbrick engineers-union building displaying posters about raising the old age pension. Monday is the church notice-board bearing a fresh banner about the glory of God in Camberwell and vicarage teas, stencilled exquisitely in higgledy-piggledy mixtures of gothic and roman lettering. Tuesday is going to the post-office and stopping to chat with the fat, bearded, be-sandalled photographer next door who hates the church bells tolling and prefers birdsong, he splashes insulting messages to the vicar in yellow paint on the pavement outside his shop and advertises for Russian models to pose in the nude, Natasha, he croons to passing women, come in, Natasha. Wednesday is our neighbour doing her second wash of the week, six fluffy candlewick bedspreads and a matching lavatory cover, Thursday is fresh flowers in the funeral-parlour window and taking Bertha down to the Peckham café for a treat, dripping toast eaten sitting on benches like pews on the tiled floor and the counter a quarter-mile of marble. Friday is collecting bruised fruit from East Street market off the Walworth Road, Friday at four p.m. is now, the bus picking up the women meths drinkers from their bench at Camberwell Green, wild women who clamber to the top deck and embarrass the sedate people travelling farther south by singing their songs of derision and experience. Five past four is the clump of horse-chestnut trees opposite the art school burning pink in springtime, green in summer, and the sign for Julie and the meths drinkers to alight from the bus, they to make their way to the nissen-hut refuge by the chapel on the corner, Julie to walk back to the news-stand to collect a copy of the local paper.

I like south London, she hymns in defiant silence, dragging her feet and killing time as she walks home by reading every one of the out-of-date notices of demonstrations fly-posted along the back wall of the fire station at the bottom of her street, I like it, it's got a really interesting history, I can tell you. Camberwell Green, for example, did you know that if you dug down only two feet under its surface you would come to heaps of human bones? They used it as a mass cemetery in the last war. And Ruskin, he had a girlfriend who lived around here, she jilted him, and so he moved away from the district after designing the stained-glass windows in the local church. There's even a butterfly named after this place, the Camberwell Beauty it's called. In Europe they call it the Mourning Cloak.

The iconography of streets, her streets. Her arms, folded across her breasts, hug the evening paper closer to her body. There's flaking white paint on either side of the greening stone steps Julie climbs reluctantly. The hall has looked more or less the same for years, only the top surface of the walls changing as a new layer of wallpaper is added by successive landlords. Peel back the layers for an instant history of changing décor amongst the lower-middle classes: bold geometric shapes and sludgy whirls, eighteenth-century couples under rose trellises, clumps of cabbage roses, and, far back, delicate art-deco fans in blue and gold. The five women who now live in the house have little money to spare on redecorating. It goes on repairs, the rates, the bills. They don't pay rent. Ben prefers it that way. He pays the mortgage from his house in Oxford and gets tax relief on it. His experimental commune, he calls them. They keep the house warm, dry, in good repair, and free from squatters. They are grateful to have somewhere to live, they have no legal status as tenants and will have to leave the minute Ben chooses to sell.

The walls are distempered in chocolate and cream now, done by Ben and friends ten years ago, in the days before he knew Julie, when he bought the house in London as an investment. He didn't do much to it, painted over the wallpaper and then replaced the Victorian engravings where he found them, flanking the rickety hatstand. Julie still glances at them as she hangs up her coat, ships bristling with masts battling through the monster waves of violent storms, mastiffs with heavy studded collars, gothic castle on a lonely crag, all in a row. She and the others have added some brightly-coloured touches of their own: feminist and socialist posters and pictures; drawings and paintings by the two children of the house. The floor is covered in worn brown lino, not too well-polished these days, with a strip of faded plum carpet in the middle nailed down with brass tacks running smartly to the foot of the stairs and up to the first bend. On the hall table sits a modern grey plastic telephone, a jotting-pad by its side.

Blast, I knew there were still things I had to do. She carries the notepad into the kitchen with her and puts it on the dresser while she boils the kettle and makes tea. The kitchen serves also as sitting-room, dining-room and meeting-place. It used to be a bedroom, with lace curtains and ornate pelmets; the sink and cooker look incongruous. It spills with books, plants, children's toys, pictures and photographs, notice-boards, five women's sense of style mixed cheerfully together. Julie picks up the notepad and carries it with the teapot to the table in the far corner of the room, a gate-leg covered by a circular apricot-coloured chenille tablecloth whose folds fall to the floor. Another cloth, edged with lace, from the same local junk-shop, is laid on top of it. Julie pushes both aside so that she can kick her shoes off and rest both feet comfortably on the gate-leg's bars. She sighs as she catches sight of the photograph of Jenny pinned above the gas stove. The thick creamy yellow of the walls, applied with a sponge thirty years ago to give an artistically mottled effect, has fallen off and filled her teacup. Bitter, stewed stuff. She takes a sip, sighing again, and studies the jotting-pad.

Tasks. What is to be done. Other people call it a shopping list. Julie annotates her life in desperation, little messages for all those others she will never see, will never talk to, little drawings of breasts and vulvas marching besides the cocoa, beans and marmalade. If she were a man, a famous artist, this would be called her notebook, to be exhibited in a gallery, to be studied by scholars, to be peered at with awe and fascination. Her secrets remain her secrets. She picks up a pencil and begins to tick the different items.

Clothes. All packed. Julie has bought five fashion magazines, has studied them intently to decide on the components of the current look, has spent the afternoon shopping in Oxford Street.

Passport. Collected yesterday. A grimace of disgust at the photograph, the image of self she will have to present to strangers for the next five years, but a twitch of pleasure at seeing her old name again. Julie Winterman is a Fanchot once more, husband's name exchanged for father's, what's the difference? She toys for a moment with the idea of choosing a completely new name. Julie Lovelorn, Julie Wanting, Julie Badmother. Julie Warrior, Julie Witch, Julie Earth, Julie Priestess.

Train and boat tickets, French currency. All in order.

Lover (with another glance at the photograph over the cooker). Certainly not. Jenny? Oh yes, we were in a relationship, friends, light-hearted, nothing possessive, nothing heavy. We're free, Ben used to tell me that, free to choose whom we want, what we want to do. Jenny tried to hug me goodbye this morning, Mary and Louise and Barbara waiting in the car with the children. I didn't have time to hug her, too busy, I am no longer interested, I have decided to go and nurse my mother who has been dangerously ill. Jenny doesn't need me anyway, she has begun to sleep with Barbara as well as with me. We do not believe in monogamy, our lives are exemplary, free from jealousy. I am going away, I remove myself from problems. How fortunate that my mother needs me, the others can go off to their women's liberation conference and take the children, while I depart quietly, obliterate myself in their absence.

Children. My daughter. I am in competition with Bertha these days, in need of comfort, of consolation as much as any child grazing her knee or waking, afraid, in the dark. My being a mother cancels out most possibilities of my being taken care of, my needs drown in the claims made on me by other people, now Jenny has turned from me and that brief rest has gone. There's a lot they don't know, any of them, all those years of looking after Ben, of taking care of Bertha, all on my own, hatred often of them both I pushed down with the gourmet dinners, the endless feeds, my soul leaking into chamber-pots and soufflé-dishes. He smiled at me, he promised to cherish and to provide. She smiles at me, now she is safe, a garden to play in, a house full of toys, Sam for company, four other mothers beside myself to care for her. I will abandon Bertha as Jenny has abandoned me, I will go back to Maman and reclaim my place with her, become her child again.

So many feelings batter Julie's consciousness now when she tries to think what it will be like to see Claire again that she becomes a radio station tuned in to Bedlam; words escape from the safe order of the shopping list and drift on to her tongue, locked into a pattern of terrifying nonsense with other words.

She moves hastily up to her room to avoid thinking and to catch the sunset after her bath, squatting naked on the cushion she embroidered when she was ten, blue woollen stitches chafing her knees, where shepherd and shepherdess dance happily, correctly, in a walled garden where roses bloom all year round. The sun sets rapidly, running towards the night, a yolk of liquid gold with hard gilt edges dissolving into peach. She shifts her focus on to colour, trying to understand that instead of language. If only one colour changed at a time then you would not need to bother with words, you would have the other tones to use as reference points for separation and for difference. If that is peach, that pink, that salmon and that crimson, then this one here, fading or burning, must be called plum, and in ten seconds, purple. Only the colours are disobedient, weaving together and changing each other, into each other, like the words in Julie's head, the lists and the sequences that have no beginning and no end.

She watches it all through the window, sky a hot pink like her cigarette end, a lump of sky in the room, her flesh feeling the cold sun congeal, its last rays slithering down her breasts and puddling on the floor between her thighs. Her feet grip and slide along the carpet, feeling each frayed hole, while her eyes watch a perfect fried-egg moon flip up between the pale back gardens and her hands rummage for the nightdress underneath her pillow.

Put it all back in order like the shopping list, name it so that it cannot be called terror, order it so that it lives apart from me, so that it cannot touch me. Lying on my back, arms by my sides, hands palm up on the thin white coverlet. That's what the catechism said, go to bed and think of the four last things: death, judgment, hell and heaven. Go to confession, cross yourself, and begin. My ghostly father, I wish to touch myself sinfully, in a forbidden place. I took down the curtains yesterday, so that the ghosts cannot move out from behind them to comfort me for Jenny's absence, so that the moon lies tilted on my stomach, so that my face, shoulders and arms are cool in the darkness, the air moving across my skin. The smell of lilac from the tree, however sooty, in the garden below, is raucous in the stillness.

The night chuckles; the weeds in the garden clamber through the window to keep her company, throttle her. Julie ducks her head under the bedclothes, clutches with her hands. They meet a reassuring bush, a hillock covered with softly tangling hair. Sam and Bertha, she and Jenny, burying themselves that Saturday in the dead leaves around the hollow tree on Blackheath, solemn faces regarding each other, and then the mounds of leaves exploding as women and children roll towards each other, clasp each other's bodies in their arms. She breathes out, stretches her legs, redefines her place in her own garden. Her fingers slide between her wet and parted lips, isolate her clitoris, a sharp plump bud blossoming from beneath its daytime hood. As the waves of sweetness warm, constrict, and then dissolve her body, she is, as that first time, amazed and grateful. Jenny. That first time, she didn't need to call the other by her name, who was there, sharing her breath and her amazement.

Julie twists and turns, the concentrated honey of orgasm dissipating to leave her sick and aching with the confusion of loss. Try as she may she cannot find herself within this new large space. Yesterday the garden existed to provide the fruit and flowers which were the absentees' favourites. A clothes-line between the dead stump of the tree blasted in the last war that curls with honeysuckle now, and the wooden post, notched with the children's heights each spring, was there to support sheets for all of them. Now it wags in the wind, empty. The view from the window is there only because she chose a room near both Bertha and Jenny. Tonight the view gives her back herself, solitary spectator, not daring to shift and so to change the view. Now, the alarm at seven o'clock tomorrow is the farthest horizon she can face.

Julie's confusion fills the corners of the room in the stretch of blackness before dawn that used to be filled with Jenny and herself, hands and bodies and mouths, voices protesting to the day hold off a little longer. Other people in London wake: the nuns in the convent where she went to school, opposite the Imperial War Museum, eat margarine from formica-topped tables, denying themselves for the likes of her; on the Isle of Dogs the early lorry-drivers in their parked convoys drink tea and play cards; the firemen and the factory night-shift would perhaps gladly exchange with her, let alone the nurses bleary-eyed in the casualty ward and the women derelicts in their nissen-hut refuge with compulsory bible before bed.

Heavy-eyed at eight a.m., Julie potters, making tea. Three lumps of sugar because Jenny is not there, three little cries of rage swallowed down, an added weight of grief and angry consolation, her body spreading will fill up the vacuum, the label of her lack of love and her unlovableness.

Her mouth is soured already with cigarettes, her shoulders hunched with the beginning of the day and tension, but her ears hear the plop of a letter into the wire cage on the inside of the front door. Her mind grabs gladly at the letter, toying with its possible contents. The final notice for the unpaid electricity bill. Or a telegram from Jenny: forgive me, I beg of you, I will never go away from you again.

The envelope is thick and white, some sort of heavy fake parchment. As Julie turns it over to slide her thumbnail under the flap she sees the crest in black, the motto of Ben's college: I survive. On his salary that should not be too difficult she thinks savagely, and tears it open.

The words are like fists that hit her in the face. Dear Julie, decided to sell the London house, we are divorced now so, independence, want a house in the country, weaving, pottery, goats, need to make a profit on the sale, soon, however modest, will you move out, sorry, vacant possession, sorry, yours.

At the same time, other words thump her on the back, a camaraderie so strong in its rhetoric she is reeling: brothers and sisters, struggle, state, occupy, scandal, housing crisis, squatting, solidarity, meeting.

She becomes aware of two shapes, two sets of colour: the white rectangular page headed with gothic script that she holds in her hand; a tattered square blazing with scarlet and black that is pasted on the fire-station wall. Her body, passing between the two, between last night and this morning, has connected them, and her mind waves them like flags. One piece of paper threatens to strip her naked of herself and hurl her out on to the street; the other re-armours her with collectivity to reclaim it. The faces of Jenny and her mother swing between the two; the nuns leer from the security of their cells and promise to pray for her; the meths drinkers scream that she's never spent a night out of bed in her life.

The skin on the front of Julie's body rips off like rags, the air is raw on her exposed flesh, she huddles like a foetus to escape the pain of it. She jumps back years, she sees herself hunched in the dayroom of the mental hospital in Oxford, aged twenty, rocking like a miserable child. Poor little thing, she crooned then, her arms clasped about her knees and her head bent down, poor little thing. And she shouted also: huge, powerful, omnipotent. The lines of definition others drew for her and taught her to draw were false, she was certain of that; she as she was then could see in her body all creation pulsating, the flow of energies into tides, migrations, seasons, separated from the natural world only by the gate of skin, a fragile barrier, easily ignored. On the tip of her tongue trembled words with which to address herself: girl, woman, wife-to-be. Not satisfied with them, frightened by them, unable and unwilling to find words of explanation for the patient doctor groping at her silence, she summoned other words, she rocked, she roared, and fell asleep. Now, sitting in the house on the borderline between Peckham and Camberwell, she holds her teacup tight and sees with terror the past come rushing back at her out of a hairline crack, the future flung in random clumps of tea-leaves on the cup's stained inside. You bastard, Ben, she tries to say aloud, it's not going to happen to me, this is my house, you can't throw me out like this. But familiar voices intervene, accusing fingers prodding her skull.

Poor Peckham, she should have been a boy.

Poor Peckham, cut off from her family in France.

Poor Peckham, you'll never get a boyfriend, looking like that.

Poor Peckham, not bright enough for university.

Poor Peckham, you're a saint, to care for me the way you do.

Poor Peckham, so very intense, and genius so close to madness.

Peckham, she screams to the garden stretching its summer fruit and flowers to the morning sun, poor Peckham.

Julie, she sobs, poor Julie.

How fortunate that Claire Fanchot is ill and in need of a visit. How dutiful Julie is, to nurse her mother whom she has not seen for years. How convenient that Julie is due therefore to board this morning a bus, a train, a boat, to leave the chaos of London for the well-ordered terrain of family. She will plunge back into it after the years away to find her childhood self awaiting her like a uniform to be donned, protection against anger, against pain. She is the charming little daughter, always smiling, always willing to clown, to make others laugh. She will have her revenge on Jenny, will leave her to cope, to plan. She will betray as she has been betrayed. She will run back to France where pleasing memories of the past endure, neatly ordered in photographs and on ciné-film, will re-enter the family house, the contented world of feudal relations, a prospect of inheritance, security, prosperity. She leaves the letter on the kitchen table for the others to find, picks up her coat and suitcase and walks out of the front door.

Fourth section

They have put Claire Fanchot's bed in what was once the conservatory, at the back of the house where the windows open on to the lawn and flower-beds at the foot of the mossy old walls. Claire insists that it is here she wants to convalesce, here rather than in the double bed upstairs. One eye goes out into the garden and soothes itself along the lines of plants, the other checks through the open door into the hall on the progress of domestic work.

Years ago they dined here, all the family, choosing the outdoors room to celebrate the feast of the Ascension of the Virgin into Heaven. Julie and Claire polished the heavy silver cutlery before the meal, peeled and sautéed a hundred potatoes, churned ice-cream on the back step, hammering nails into great blocks of ice held in hairy sacking and then cramming the ice splinters into the ice-cream churn. Claire's father-in-law grew cider apples in the orchard at the end of the garden, and grapes in the conservatory. Greenish metal struts divide clear and frosted panes of glass and branch into a miniature neo-gothic ceiling overhead. The vines wreathe along the ceiling, their stems hard and knotted, twine about the metal ivy-leaves suspending the gaslight in its centre. Oncle Michel stands upon his perilous and cracking chair to make a speech in honour of Claire, whose birthday it is. He seizes a bunch of grapes growing just above his ear and tosses them into the air to illustrate a point, ah, Claire, he pronounces, wonderful Claire. The children squeal at the unexpected delight and fight to catch the grapes as they fall. Encouraged by their pleasure, Oncle Michel is about to do it again when he catches his uncle's eye. Monsieur Fanchot is displeased at the unseemly waste of unripe grapes. His look bears his nephew down into his chair again. Michel picks up his dessert fork and crushes a macaroon into powdery fragments. Julie never sees him splendid and heroic again, she cannot be sure she ever has. But a memory develops for her, flavoured by the popcorn she munches in the cinema at performances of Tarzan and King Kong, of a large and hairy man swinging by one hand from the overhead vine, while with an agile jerk of his body his bare feet sweep the table clear of dishes and smear blood and red wine stains along the tablecloth.

Julie cannot believe, as she stands in the doorway, that they ever seated twenty people in what seems to her now a cramped and tiny room. The vine is long since gone; pots of cacti and geraniums provide a different green; the old straw-seated wicker chairs with their faded dark blue flowered cushions have been replaced by chairs from the salon. The room smells faintly of dust. Claire will not let Suzette Cally from the village in to clean, no, no, I am a poor sick woman turning to dust and ashes, leave me in peace, I am worth nothing any more, leave me alone. The chairs are filmy with dust, it breathes out from the carpet, from the rows of devotional books stacked on shelves above the bed, it veils the numerous small tables, cabinets, stools and cupboards that are indispensable to Claire's comfort. Her eyes slide over them each morning, counting, checking. They must not be touched or rearranged, her place is defined by them surrounding her. Most of this furniture is over a hundred years old. As well as dust, it smells of wood in various stages of decay. Wood and velvet, dust and damp and decay, their dry cold smell tickling the back of your throat.

The objects standing on the lace-covered top of her mother's bedside table are bright and modern. Plastic containers of coloured pills, bottles of red and orange medicine, packs of glittering glass ampoules nested in cottonwool, a cardboard box of tissues, rainbow-coloured. A television balances on a table at the end of the bed, a small radio beside it. The flex of an electric hairdryer coils tidily from the top of the wardrobe, another flex snakes from the wall-socket to the electric blanket beneath the bedclothes.

Claire Fanchot lies propped against many pillows so that she can sit up and more easily command a view. Julie, who is prepared for childlike frailty, is met instead by the eyes that snap with familiar determination, the hands clenched over the newspaper, the shoulders squared. Her body as she stoops to kiss her mother's cheeks is surprised. Claire Fanchot will take a long time to die, as long as those childhood summers took to pass, the warm sleepy stretches between lunch and suppertime. The child Julie hunched between the redcurrant bushes and the garden wall watches a spider with a jewelled body and delicate legs spinning a web that sways and glitters in the sunshine. The child hiding from her mother in rage shits a large and satisfying turd on the ground. When discovered, she will try to blame it on the cat.

Claire surveys her daughter critically. Julie is wearing an embroidered blouse, a full felt skirt dotted with patches, beads and bits of ribbon, black woollen stockings, clogs.

– I don't understand you, Claire says fretfully: your clothes, why must you go around looking like some sort of peasant?

A sick woman must be humoured. Julie smiles, shrugs her shoulders.

– All right then, I won't wear them if you don't like them.

Claire jerks her head in the direction of the chair beside her bed.

– Well, come on then, sit down and tell me your news. How's Bertha? How is Ben?

Julie speaks carefully.

– Bertha is fine. She's starting school next term. You know I don't see much of Ben these days, now we're divorced, I never go to Oxford and Ben's hardly ever in London. He sends you his love, and so did Jenny and everyone.

Claire frowns.

– Those people, she says indifferently: they're not family. But you never did care about the family, anyway. All those years away and hardly any letters, you couldn't care less. It doesn't mean anything to you young people. And now you've been dragged over here to sit with a boring old woman.

Her hands pick worriedly at the coverlet.

– You're not old, Julie says hurriedly: you've been really ill, that's all. How are you now, anyway? What does the doctor say?

– He doesn't tell me anything, Claire says irritably: just whispers to Julien and Suzette in the corner and tells me to rest. As though I could rest, what with no-one to run the house properly and worrying about you not looking after yourself.

– Suzette, Julie exclaims hurriedly: I didn't know she was back. I thought she'd gone off to train as a nurse in Caen or somewhere.

– She did, Claire says: but her mother's been ill, so Suzette immediately gave up her job to come back and look after her. She was coming in here twice a week to clean, but now she comes in every day to look after me and see to things.

The silent comparison hangs in the air. Julie searches for words to dispel it.

– Well, that's good, she says brightly: Suzette's used to working in this house. She knows how you like things done.

– It's not the same. I like to be there, to make sure things are done properly. I know it's old-fashioned, but that's the way I was brought up, to look after my husband and children. I can't help worrying, I lie awake at night and worry about you.

Julie denies her unhappiness, she is not going to give her mother a chance to criticise her ever again. She is strong, she can manage without approval, she will not upset her poor sick mother by starting a row.

– You needn't worry about me, she says with a tight little smile: I'm fine, I'm perfectly happy.

She takes hold of her mother's hand, realising that Claire is querulous from pain and exhaustion; she must find it hard to accept that she is being cared for. After a lifetime of serving others Claire does not know what to do with rest in her middle-age, she cannot believe that she has needs which other people will offer to fulfil. Never in all her life has she been able to express rage. She lets it seep out instead in the words of guilt.

– But you don't look well, Julie. I'm not surprised, living in that commune you wrote to me about. It's bound to be full of draughts, and I'm sure you don't eat properly, any of you, with no-one there to make sure you do.

– Oh, come on, Julie protests with a smile: we're not children, you know.

Claire looks out of the window and speaks with determination.

– That's just what I mean. It's all very well, being friends with women, but you take it to extremes. You're so idealistic, Julie, I'm sure you don't realise the dangers. I'm sure you don't mean any harm, you've got such a kind heart, but you must remember the children. Bringing them up in that sort of place, with no father around. Just for Bertha's sake, you ought to be thinking of getting married again. You can't live with your women friends for ever, you know. Supposing one of them goes off to get married, what will you do then? Jenny, for example. You can't stop it happening. It's normal, after all.

– She won't, Julie cries out in anguish: she loves me, she's my lover. She'll never leave me.

She stares aghast at her mother. It's out, the information she has spent sleepless nights wondering how to convey in the most gentle, tactful fashion, if at all. The sickroom idyll smashes; she looks around, enraged, at the trap into which she has walked. All right, mother, you asked the question, and now you know. Now let's see whether you really wanted letters from me telling you about what I was doing.

Her cruelty is confirmed. Claire lets go of her daughter's hand without moving her eyes from the window.

– Just look at those weeds in the border, she says in an angry voice trembling on tears: the minute I'm not around to oversee things, everything's let slide.

Julie clenches her lips together to stop herself from crying. It's not natural, she says to herself, you've done it on purpose, just to hurt, you're obsessed with yourself, you always were.

– You've got no consideration, Claire goes on in a shaking voice: here I am ill, and you tell me a thing like that. I knew it would happen, without a man around. There must be something wrong with you, something wrong with your hormones. You make me feel ill, just thinking about it.

– But I love women, protests Julie the monstrous child: it makes sense to me, loving my women friends. Sex is a part of that. You've got women friends, you've got Madame Mévisse, and you love her.

– I love my husband, Claire says furiously: how dare you be so disgusting? You're obsessed with sex, you young people, you know nothing about love, you've left your husband, you're bringing up Bertha in a place like that, I can't bear to think about it.

She breaks off, coughing.

– It's time for my rest.

– I'll stay, Julie suggests quickly, desperate not to be rejected: until you're asleep.

Claire shuts her eyes. Her voice sounds very tired.

– Do as you like. You always do. I'm used to it.

Julie stares at her sleeping mother in misery. On the boat coming over she had pictured herself as the perfect nurse, sponging her mother's body and tenderly dusting it with the expensive talcum-powder still in her suitcase outside; stroking her forehead gently, so gently; carefully tipping camomile tea down her mother's throat. This was the task that Julie most looked forward to: feeding her mother, coaxing, controlling her: come on now, come, another little sip, just for Julie.

Outside, the timeless noises of the summer proceed: the steady burping and cooing of doves; the braying of cows; the squawking and gobbling of hens; the barking of dogs chained up in the yard. The church bells beat against the heavy heat of the afternoon, beat up Julie's heart if she lets them. In the hot sunshine, she, like Claire, prefers to fall asleep.

In her dream Julie sees again the table set for twenty people in the conservatory, a great white cloth spread beneath the expectant faces. She sees her mother lying on the table, below hanging bunches of grapes, her eyes closed and her hands folded across her breast. She is wearing her wedding-veil and her fluffy pink dressing gown. Julie hears her grandfather sonorously intone grace, and then the family picks up its knives and forks. But it is a child who gets there first, a leaping agile child with thick auburn hair, throwing herself full length upon her mother and fastening her mouth upon her breast. The woman on the table stirs, her hands come up to caress her daughter's tangled hair, her muddy feet. Julie hears the low voice murmur distinctly, with such longing, such affection.

– Julie, I want you, Julie, I want you.

Julie smiles in her sleep and moves her cheek against the cushion on the arm of her chair, while next to her Claire moves her mouth and mutters.

– Julie, I want you to be happy, I want you to be married, safe, secure.

The nurse arriving to give the evening injection wakes Julie sharply, shocked at her inattentiveness on the first evening of her visit. The abrupt awakening coupled with the vividness of the dream jerks Julie into an outburst of angry tears. The nurse is satisfied, some filial feeling being expressed, at any rate.

– Good evening, mademoiselle Julie, she says cordially; it's good to see you here again, after so long.

– Hello, Suzette, Julie says sulkily, blowing her nose.

Claire cannot bear to see her daughter cry.

– Julie, she says hurriedly: you must need to wash. Go upstairs, darling. Rest and unpack, Suzette will look after me now. Come down again and have supper with Papa when you're feeling better, and come in to say goodnight to me. We'll have a chat tomorrow.

– You're in your parents' old room, mademoiselle Julie, says the nurse: it's less trouble that way. Monsieur Fanchot sleeps in the little salon now, down here, in case madame calls out in the night.

– He shouldn't, Claire murmurs: I don't need anything.

Julie smiles tightly at her mother from the doorway and goes upstairs, hardly noticing the unchanged details of the house, her feet remembering how to navigate the steep narrow stairs in the dimness, her hand going out unconsciously to turn the china light-switch on the landing. She battles against tears. I must not cry, I must not cry, I am strong now, I should not get upset so easily. She goes into her parents' room and lies down on their bed, sinking gratefully into the soft mattress bought by Claire a year ago to replace at last the hard one favoured by her mother-in-law. But as soon as Julie closes her eyes and lets her tense muscles relax, the kaleidoscope begins, whirling and thundering, the bed heaving up and down with her loud heartbeats like the sea. Maman, Papa, dinner. The Holy Family eats grapes while I am sent upstairs for making Maman ill.

Fifth section

At midnight Julie, aged ten, huddles with her parents and her younger brother and all the villagers outside the church. In the shelter of a buttress, flanked by altar boys bearing torches and carrying censers and vessels of holy water, Monsieur le Curé kindles the new fire, representative of the risen Christ, the flame the clock shrilling that Easter has begun. The congregation shivers in the chilly dark, the firelight flickering over their faces; they clutch tapers in their gloved hands. Inside the church again, pitch blackness blurs them, the children whispering with excitement. Enter th: huge candle on a lacy bier, the risen Christ, stuck about with flowers and nails. The light is passed from hand to hand, the kiss of peace exchanged; the choir's voice swells as the light increases.

Next day, High Mass in celebration. Wild clouds dash to and fro across the sun, sharp air pricks the skin, forsythia blooms against bare twigs, the church bells tumble and clang, filling all the air. Claire wears her new Easter outfit, navy-blue linen suit, a white blouse with polka-dots and a floppy bow at the neck, a navy-blue hat of hard shiny straw. Her feet pinch themselves into blue high-heeled shoes. She balances along over gravel, over pebbles and mud, leaning on the arm of her father-in-law. His shoes are wide, as glossy as leather armchairs, solid enough to crush the stones under his feet. He walks heavily forward, his shoulders square under his grey Sunday suit. His collar is snowy, he swings a walking-stick. He enjoys Claire leaning on his arm, he teases her about her vanity, the shoes that pinch. He strides, she teeters.

The choir soars upward, a balloon voice of triumphant joy; they are all pure, reborn like children, innocent, and loving. In their new clothes they move self-consciously and gently. Julie traverses miles of narrow red carpet, kneels at the gilded altar-rail. She closes her eyes to receive the thin white disc, which clings to the roof of her mouth. She knows she must not dislodge it with her tongue, must never chew it, for it would be the Christ she gnashes and mutilates. She may only gently suck; He will dissolve and become part of her. She rises to her feet and, eyes downcast, walks through the sacristy and back down the long side aisle to avoid forcing a path through the queue still advancing up the nave to the communion rail. Everyone is looking at her; she must assume an air of saintliness while at the same time keeping her eyes sufficiently open so that she does not trip on the frayed carpet. At the back of the church she marches past the peering latecomers and, hands still clasped together, turns again and paces up the centre aisle until she reaches the Fanchot pew near the front. She edges past her grandfather in the narrow wooden enclosure, feeling his eyes disdain her sanctimoniousness. She reaches her place and sinks on to her knees, her face between her hands. She has no need of words except to utter His name over and over again, until the incantation takes her beyond herself into a space of rapture unbounded by any physical law.

Monsieur Fanchot stands upright as he has done all through Mass. A man, he will talk eye to eye with God. It is for women, all the sighs the mumbling and the swoons. When the space inside Julie finally takes her over and she faints from longing and from lack of food, he is exquisitely tender to her, pulling down her frock so that her knickers do not show and carrying her outside. He pushes her head between her knees, and holds her till she recovers consciousness. He is irritated by her flamboyant holiness but will not say so. She is his little grand-daughter, prone, thank God, to the weakness of the flesh. He teases her: ma petite Julie, tu es tombée dans les pommes, you have fallen in the apples. Home now, for a cup of chocolate and a slice of newly-baked galette, to keep you going until it is time for lunch. Julie feels shy of him, she whispers that she wants Maman. Hurt, he turns around, just as Claire hurries through the church door full of concern, to pull Julie to her feet and assist her home, scorning the offer of help from her father-in-law. His task is to remain there, to shake the hands of his neighbours as they come outside from darkness into sun, to chat of tractors and of animal feed.

The lunch party is large, twenty-five people crammed into the little salon to sip at sweet blackcurrant liqueur and nibble tiny polished Japanese crackers, before moving next door to take their places, carefully worked out, around the table. The children sit together at one end.

Julie's chair seat is of straw. The chair is old and damaged; bits of loose straw strike up through her dress and petticoat to irritate her thighs. She shifts awkwardly from one buttock to another and finally dares to put a hand down and scratch. She has been seen.

– Julie, sit quietly, will you?

Her grandfather looks sternly at her. Her mother clutches her napkin anxiously; her technique of remote control has broken down again, she blames herself, fears further criticism of the child, which rebounds on herself. Julie looks down resentfully at her plate, and then sideways. It is all right. They have forgotten her and are talking among themselves again.

The sitting-room runs between the front and the back windows of the small dark house. Her grandfather, unofficial leader of the local Resistance in the last war in his family's eyes, knocked the original two main ground-floor rooms into one overnight in 1943, to avoid having a German officer billeted in what had been officially declared a spare room. Monsieur Fanchot is recounting a similar anecdote now, taking his time, lengthy pauses for effect, the family all laughing at the conclusion.

On Sundays and feast days they extend the table for lunch to accommodate the guests. Extra wooden leaves are brought in from the cupboard underneath the stairs and fitted into the gap created when the table splits in half and yawns. The table stretches now from the windows in the front to the windows at the back of the house; those sitting at either end have only to turn their heads to brush the sour leaves of geraniums in pots upon the windowsills, feel the thick lace curtains on their noses, extend a hand into the sun and cloud dancing on the path outside. An afternoon's walk along the stiff white tablecloth it seems to the child, the family's chairs crammed between the table and the floridly carved oak sideboards, cupboards and cabinets around the walls.

The mirror hangs on the darkest wall of the room, in the alcove next to the high stone fireplace. It is a large rectangular glass set above a small marble and mahogany side table with curly feet and reaching almost to the ceiling. Its surface is brown and spotted like her grandmother's hands, its frame a rococo froth of slowly blackening gilt. Julie contrives each meal-time to secure a seat facing it. Easy enough, since this manoeuvre also places her near the kitchen door, facilitating her female task of helping Suzette Cally from the village to hand fresh plates for every course and clear them away afterwards.

The children are not encouraged to speak during meals, unless it is to each other, in low voices that do not disturb the adults. While the men and women chatter to each other Julie kneads her bread under the tablecloth across her knees, fashioning it into little grey lumps, pleasing in their plasticity that provides a base for further sculpture. She stares into the mirror opposite her in the dark alcove. She sees the back of her father's head, and her grandfather's, and looks beyond them at her own face, at strangeness, at secret places.

Delicately, she turns the silver key and opens the twin carved doors of the largest cupboard, decorated with the motifs of the region by the village craftsman a hundred years before as part of an ancestor's dowry. Here are all the family's treasures, and, amongst them, all their secrets. Three floral dinner-services a hundred years old like the cupboard; an ivory egg-cup and spoon belonging to her grandmother that Julie is urged to use occasionally if she asks prettily, correctly; a large silver box stuffed with the letters exchanged by her grandparents during the First World War; pieces of lace from a wedding dress that then served as christening gown and burial robe for Benedict, dead in infancy seventy years ago and his pale hair gleaming still from its locket wrapped in purple silk; a battered morocco writing-case containing the household accounts studied by her grandfather every Friday night, in silence; a toffee-tin bursting with buttons cut from generations of frocks and shirts and overalls; an old box camera.

Julie opens the camera, and Tante Juliette springs out, as neat and uncreased as though she has not been lying there in the dark ever since lunchtime last Sunday, awaiting patiently Julie's pleasure.

– Well then, my little one, she says smiling: and where shall we go this afternoon?

– If you please, ma tante, the child whispers into her plate, for the arrival of a dish of mutton with piquant sauce has caused a lull in the voices around the table and Julie does not wish to be overheard: if you please, I wish to be an explorer, I want to visit the

Cave des Demoiselles, to see if that is where I came from first of all.

– Sit up straight, Julie, Claire reproves her daughter gently, and turns her back again, her anxious eyes on the possible insufficiency of sauce, her ears strained to catch the sound of china breaking in the kitchen, her mouth smiling at a joke her husband has just made.

Julie feels an agonising pain on her ankle. Claude aged five, sitting next to her, seraphic in white shorts and cardigan, is kicking out with his new white leather boots as hard as he can. An angry outburst by a child at table is unpleasant for everyone; Julie puts on the withdrawn and sulky look that so upsets her mother, and, by a mighty effort of will, ignores the pain, kicks her own feet together none too gracefully, and lands on the windowsill where Tante Juliette is waiting patiently, her little feet, so much smaller than Julie's, planted prettily between geranium pots. Holding hands, they soar together into the air and head for the west, towards the sea.

Tante Juliette lived long ago, and is dead now. This means, according to the family and to the corroborative evidence contained in the catechism, that she is an angel, with no sex, neither boy nor girl. Julie feels comfortable with her. Every Sunday they go on trips together; Tante Juliette is teaching her to fly.

Five miles away, the sea dividing France from England hurls itself upon the strip of coast called Normandy confining it, throwing up the local people's livelihood, their legends, and occasionally their bodies. Where three sections of the cliffs arch themselves into the sea at Etretat over the oysterbeds dug for Queen Marie-Antoinette by her starving peasantry, a wicked baron once lived. In his castle built upon the biggest cliff arch, he imprisoned the most beautiful of the townspeople's daughters. When he tired of them, one by one he rolled them down the cliff in spiked barrels and into the sea. The sunsets on the nights of the killings were said to have been especially fine, the blood on the rocks washed up into the sky as the pure souls fled to heaven. The place has been called the Cave des Demoiselles ever since.

The sun is beginning to drop by the time Julie and Juliette land on the beach. Picking their way over the grey pebbles, between empty lemonade bottles and discarded chocolate wrappers, and then hopping over the grey-green of mussels and the sharp fluted edges of limpets festooning the rocks, they come at last to the largest arch. Julie, who has been struggling with a decision, completes it.

– You stay here, Tante Juliette, she instructs her companion: I want to fly up there on my own. You stay here just in case there's any trouble. If you see me waving my handkerchief, then go for help. You won't be able to miss it, it's this red one with white spots.

– Julie, answer me when I speak to you, will you?

Her grandfather's voice upsets her concentration, and she falls heavily back into the lunchtime group, dropping her napkin into her plate of untouched mousse au chocolat and knocking over her glass of water tinted with red wine. Monsieur Fanchot, who has addressed to her a kindly enquiry, having noticed her silence and absorption, forgets his concern, that she may still be suffering from her faint that morning, and snorts with anger at her clumsiness. Everyone is looking at her. Unable to bear it, Julie bursts into tears. Her humiliation brings further punishment. She has disturbed a happy family party and in front of guests has demonstrated her indifference to her grandfather's words. His voice thunders at her.

– Ten years old, and you still can't control yourself. Go and fetch a cloth and then stay in your room until I call you down again.

The attention of the chief guest, Monsieur le Curé, is drawn to the unpleasant picture Julie makes, snivelling, red-faced. It is too much. She flees into the hall, hearing her mother's voice. It sounds distressed.

– Mon beau-papa, it wasn't deliberate, you know.

– That will do, Claire. The child has caused enough disturbance as it is. She needs a lesson.

Julie lies on her bed and whimpers with misery, her anger fuelled afresh by the fact that she has to cry quietly enough not to be heard downstairs. Claude made that mistake once, after a tantrum, and was shut in the coal-cellar for three hours.

The door opens. Claire Fanchot looks sorrowfully at her daughter, face down on the wet pillow. She puts her arms lightly around her.

– Julie, pet, why must you be so silly? It's not much to ask, you know, for you to sit still and quiet for a few hours.

Julie privately considers it is a great deal to ask. Her virtue at High Mass has gone unrewarded, one and a half hours kneeling to the music of an empty stomach, then the aching boredom of lunch, the impossibility of feeling at ease between cutlery, fragile glasses, silence. She does not speak now, lest she make her mother suffer more. It is their bond, their silent contract with each other, from which Julie hopes to win as reward all her mother's love away from Claude.

Madame Fanchot has brought a plate of grapes upstairs with her, the course that Julie has missed. She pops grapes into her daughter's mouth as she speaks, to confirm the child's mute acceptance of her words.

– You're over-tired, my darling. This afternoon, I want you to take a rest. Grandpère wishes to have an outing to Etretat. He's not really cross with you, it's just that he's an old man now, he's not used to children any more, not modern children, you make more noise than he can tolerate. He loves you, you know that. We'll all be back by suppertime, and you can come downstairs then, and have supper with us. You won't be lonely, Suzette is downstairs doing the washing-up while we have our coffee. But please, little one, don't leave this room, don't spoil my day for me, do as Grandpère wants, stay here and be a good girl.

No need to turn the key in the lock. Claire kisses her daughter's forehead and leaves the room. Julie's mouth is crammed with grapes. She wants to spit them out, but the locket over her heart containing the Virgin's portrait whispers to her and tells her no, the grapes are a present from her mother, and she must not make a mess. She chews the bitter pips and skin, and swallows them with loathing, the grapes that usually are her favourite food.

She lies back on her bed and stares at the mirror facing her two feet away on the door of the wardrobe. Above, the wardrobe bears a carving of a knot of formal flowers. Under Julie's gaze, it turns into an owl, and then into a hideous face, leering at her, mocking her. Julie knows she cannot leave the room. There are sounds on the stairs outside; the headless ghost is bouncing up them to the top, along the corridor as far as Julie's door. It may be dark before her mother returns from Etretat. Once darkness comes, and her mother is not there, Julie knows that the ghost will enter her room. The Virgin Mary has abandoned her; only Tante Juliette will actually appear when Julie needs her.

Julie manages to sit up. She remembers the mirror downstairs and its route into forbidden places. There are many more forbidden places in the house than simply the big cupboard downstairs. Julie's room doubles as the linen-store, its walls lined with shelves of sheets and tablecloths in snowy piles, and on Mondays the ceiling dropping sheets hung from clothes-lines and billowing like damp and fragrant tents. The wardrobe contains Claire's best sheets, her linen wedding ones, stiff and glazed by the iron and starch, with drawn-thread work around the edges and the family initials monogrammed in raised silken stitches in one corner.

The sheets belong to the bed her father sleeps in with her mother, always a fascinating place to visit in the mornings. If she has been good, and not been ill in the night, Julie is allowed to slide between the warm and crumpled sheets of her parents' bed and curl against her mother as she drinks her coffee from a blue and yellow bowl, always black coffee, Claire cannot bear the taste of milk. Julie smells the powerful night odour of her mother's skin, fits herself into the curve of her mother's breasts and stomach, soft under her nightgown, listens to her father splashing in the little curtained-off cubicle at the end of the room, hears his silence as he uses the lavatory down the passage, sniffs the scent of strong tobacco mingling with that of shit and lavender water.

Julie thinks of that warm bed, and feels her mother's arms around her again, the men and Claude are absent, there are just the two of them, as it was before her mother started trying to tell her the facts of life and Julie resolutely shut her ears. The frightening face above the wardrobe mirror gradually changes back into that of an owl, and then into a knot of flowers again. Tante Juliette does not reappear. She is lost for ever now, trapped by the wicked baron as he roams the beach. He will marry her. Julie will never marry. She hardens her heart against her aunt, fortunes of war, she mutters, and tries not to think of Juliette boxed up in a barrel of spikes.

A girl looks out of the place beyond the mirror, silent, determined, sad. She is very like Julie, but taller, and thinner. Julie gazes back at her with excitement. The girl in the mirror does not look as though she ever cries, gets angry, upsets her parents or loses her mother's love. She is hard and brave and clever, admired by everyone for being so grown-up. She tells her feelings to nobody. Only her twin sister knows what she is feeling, when they meet and talk at their secret rendezvous away from the adults.

– That's who you are, Julie says to the girl, who bends forwards and listens seriously: you are my twin sister Jules, you're even tougher than a boy.

Jules smiles at her in recognition. Julie lies back on her bed again, and begins the first of their long and perfect conversations together, which she can control, in which she can speak all the time, as much as she wishes, and no answering back.

At supper, Julie is marvellously well-behaved. She has no need to whisper to Claude, for every few minutes she can raise her eyes from her plate of boiled cod with cream sauce to check that Jules is there, beyond the mirror and the head of the family, smiling back at her. Monsieur Fanchot is relieved and delighted with the improvement in her manners. At the end of the meal he peels her a peach with his own hands.

– My little Julie, my dear little grand-daughter, you are a joy to me in my old age.

Julie smiles down into her lap, bobbing her head and blushing. He laughs, delighted with her coyness, and reaches across the table with one hand.

– My dear grandfather, she smiles at him and lowers her eyelashes as he pinches her cheek.

Now, almost twenty years later, Julien is Monsieur Fanchot. He occupies his father's place at table, sitting in the big black oaken chair, fingers tapping its polished arms as he waits for Julie to come downstairs so that they can begin dinner. Next door, in the kitchen, Suzette Cally stirs the soup. This is made every day, from the leftover soup of the day before, mixed with a fresh julienne of vegetables, stored overnight in the fridge in a tin billycan which Julien's father had in the trenches during the First World War. The soup has simmered for more than fifty years on the back of the stove, stirred by generations of Fanchot servants, feeding generations of Fanchot males. The women only toy with it, delicately handling their heavy silver spoons. Monsieur Fanchot père called his wife soupe, or else he called soupe his wife, Julie was never sure which: la mère soupe, dabbing with his large white napkin at the traces of carrots, potatoes, onions clinging to his fat silky moustache. During the war, it was his wife who sowed and harvested the vegetables for the soup; Monsieur Fanchot père lay in the trenches dreaming of it, while he drank watery chocolate out of his tin billy.

The soup boils over in the kitchen, little drops hissing on the hot enamel surface of the stove. Suzette Cally rushes at it with a red and white checked cloth, swearing under her breath so that she is not heard next door. Julien in the salon rises to his feet, walks over to the bell hanging beside the fireplace, seizes the leather thong that hangs down, beats the clapper several times against the side of the bell. Claire in the conservatory wakes with a start, her head muzzy, tears forcing themselves from under her eyelids to roll down her cheeks. Julie, slumped happily on the lavatory upstairs, sits bolt upright, remembering times past, when her grandfather rang the supper bell at half-past seven every night, regular as bowels and clockwork the family had to be in its progress to table, any latecomers greeted by the guilt-inducing sight of the head of the family with his spoon upraised from aching wrist; not until everyone is seated will the first, chief spoon be dipped in soup, the sign that everyone else may follow, must follow, must eat.

Julien has not seen Julie before now; he has been out in the fields all day. Unlike his father, he does not change for dinner; he sits in the large black chair in his dirty old trousers and baggy shirt, the sleeves rolled up. Julie is shocked at the departure from ritual, then relieved. Naughty boy, she thinks, and smiles, and kisses him on both cheeks in greeting before going into the kitchen to relieve Suzette of the soup. Suzette has not eaten, she replies, shaking her head in answer to Julie's question, but no, she will not come and eat with them. It is not her place, and besides, they will have so much to say to one another. Julie feels tired, suddenly. She marches back into the salon, holding the white porcelain tureen aloft. Julien looks up from the newspaper he is studying.

– Ah, he says: how like old times. Nothing's changed, you see? Here we are together again, with la mère soupe for dinner as usual.

Julie does not know how to answer him. She seizes on a minor point and tosses conversation back.

–Not la mère soupe. Suzette made this lot.

Julien tries again.

– I remember how you used to like wine. Let me pour you a glass.

He gets up and limps over to the big carved cupboard where the wine and liqueurs are kept. At the sight of his limp, so much more pronounced these days, arthritic now most likely, Julie's heart contracts in pity. She feels guilty; if she is unfriendly his limp and his arthritis will get worse.

Julien returns to the table, pours her out a small glass of red wine, reaches for the carafe. He is about to add water, tint the wine pale pink, when Julie covers the glass with her hand. She glares at him, removes her hand from the glass, takes a large swig.

– I'm not a child any more, you know, I drink wine straight.

– Eh? Oh, I had forgotten, Julien returns, corking the bottle and pushing it to the far side of the table: you always used to take a glass of wine like that, with water.

Julie the misbehaved child empties her glass in one gulp.

– Only because you said we had to. You wouldn't let us otherwise.

She holds her glass out to Julien.

– More, please.

She does not ask prettily, in the old way. Her father stares at her with disappointment.

– I don't like to see women drinking. You've had enough. You can have another little glass with dessert.

He uncorks the bottle and fills his own glass, raising it to her.

– Well, this is very pleasant. My little Julie, tell me about what you've been doing in London. Having lots of fun, eh? I never did think Ben was good enough for my daughter.

Julie reaches for the bottle of wine, pours herself a generous glassful, sips it slowly to give herself time to work out what to say. She can feel herself warming with the wine to his clumsy attempts at charm that once seemed the height of sophisticated gallantry. She has received her cue: this is where she smiles intimately at him, assures him of her faithful allegiance, she has always preferred older men, goodness, Papa, how well you are looking tonight. What a shame that Maman is ill in bed, you and I together again, alone, just the two of us, it's like old times. I am so much younger than my mother, so much prettier. I know how to dress well, how to pay you compliments that she has to overhear but pretend she does not understand.

I remember when you visited me in Oxford, in my first year there. You take me out to a French restaurant, you flirt mildly with me, I imagine that the men watching us from neighbouring tables do not know I am your daughter. We speak of Claire, who has been unable to come over with you, too much, she insists, to see to at home, Claude's school examinations that his mother must nurse him through. You tell me how you hold Claire on a pedestal, the most wonderful woman that you know. It was very good between you in those early days, you say. 'It' is sex, I suppose, and I suppose, with your permission, that it does not happen any more. I am wearing my best frock, I lean towards you, listening attentively. You pour me wine and tint it pale pink with water, you blossom under my compliments, why, Julie, you say, smiling and spreading your hands on the cloth, you make me feel twenty years younger. After lunch, we walk in the market, where you buy Claire a box of sweets, looking at me, we mustn't forget her, eh? When you get back to France, she punishes you for your cruelty, she flicks small barbs at you in the places where she knows they will hurt most. It is called teasing. You respond by getting furious and shouting at her. She retreats, hurt and misunderstood, to the kitchen. She writes to me, she says she worries about me. I am cruel too. I deny her descriptions of the things I know will please her: the boyfriends, the balls, the river outings. I do not tell her that I am unhappy and lonely much of the time because that means she will see me as a failure, letting her down. I write her stilted little notes, much less frequently than she would like, assuring her that I am fine, that I must hurry away now and write an essay. I have no time, I imply, for the stupid preoccupations of the farm. I am ashamed of my parents, I wish them to be more elegant, more upper-class than they are. I do not encourage them to visit me, I seize every excuse not to visit them.

– Eh? Eh?

Julien is waiting for Julie's reply, spooning the last of his soup, his eyes anxiously watching her. She understands what he means. He is getting old, she must not upset him. He needs his memories, his fantasies; after the many disappointments in his life, there is no harm, surely, in letting him go on believing whatever he wants to about her. If she tells him the truth, she risks so much: loss of his approbation, his compliments, their secret life together, her little silk-lined nesting place in his jacket pocket. She has never left him; it would be too cruel to do so now.

She gets up, and stacks the soup plates on top of the tureen, looking at Julien. Say something quickly, then run out of the room.

– Well, of course, I don't go out much these days, she temporises: there's two children in the house to look after, you know. We go out to women's discos, the pub, that sort of thing. But none of us has got much money.

– I don't know, Julien says dispiritedly: it's not at all what I wanted for you. It seems to me you're wasting yourself, Julie. After all your chances. You were such a bright little girl. Your mother was so firm about sending you to school in England. She wasn't having you spending the rest of your life in a Norman backwater, she said. If you only realised how she scrimped and saved, to do it. We hoped you'd meet the right kind of people, have an interesting life, a career, do all kinds of things.

Julie cannot bear to hear him say that she has let him down.

– How can I have a career? she asks sharply: I've got Bertha to look after, you know. It's all right for you men, you never have to bother looking after children.

She is appalled at the note of whining resentment in her voice when she talks of her daughter. She hasn't thought of Bertha at all since leaving London. She is on holiday from her, a child herself again, and glad. Julien goes on as though she has not interrupted.

– When I think of all the chances you've had, he repeats heavily:

39

I must say I can't understand you. Living with a load of women in someone else's house, when you could have a nice little flat of your own, drive a car, make some nice friends.

– The women I live with are my friends, she says sulkily: and I like the house.

She wishes to go on: and we are all extremely happy, and secure, and successful, we are all talented, we cope, we do not need your pity, your patronage. But memories fight their way in front of her. Ben's letter. Jenny sitting up in bed, wrapping the eiderdown tightly about her knees, yelling at her. Give me some space, for God's sake, Julie, I love you, but you must let me have some space. Barbara's face cool and closed. You haven't got a monopoly on Jenny's love, you know. She loves others besides just you.

Julien makes another effort.

– Well, he calls after her as she vanishes into the kitchen with the dirty plates: go on, then, tell me about this house of yours. I don't understand it, I'm sure, five of you, all women, living together like that. What's the matter with men these days? Don't you have boy-friends, any of you?

– Not really, Julie says, coming back with a casserole and dumping it down in front of her father: I think women are much more interesting.

Julien hastily serves himself and her.

– Aha. Navarin of lamb. My favourite. Claire remembered, she asked Suzette to cook it specially. We men aren't much good for anything, he jokes bravely: but we do appreciate good food.

He was so proud of himself when he got married. Julie can see the photographs on the bureau behind him. He beams into the sun, squint-eyed, the stiff new suit and the rigid posture concealing the dragging leg. The tactful Claire wears low-heeled shoes. Julie is furious with him for appealing to her sense of pity, at making her recognise his pain. He goes on inexorably.

– No real men around any more, I suppose, just middle-aged failures like your father, eh?

– You're not a failure, she says hastily: there's the farm. You run it practically single-handed. Not many people could do that.

He sighs.

– It doesn't mean as much to me as it did in the old days. Our children, that's all we live for now, Claire and I. And there you both are, living abroad.

– But you mustn't live for other people, Julie says quickly, pompously: it doesn't do you or them any good. They only resent it.

– I don't know where we went wrong, he says sadly, looking at her: we never put any pressure on you. We only wanted you to be happy. I know things with Ben weren't a success. We accepted that. Your mother suffered so much when you got divorced. But you're still young, Julie. You've got your whole life ahead of you. Not like me. I'm finished, more or less. You could have done anything, with the start you had. The way you're living now, it's a waste.

Sixth section

All the nuns in the convent bleed, except for Sister Veronica. She offered up her life at twenty-eight, her name and her hair at twenty-nine; her ovaries stopped functioning of their own accord upon her entry into the religious life. Nothing to worry about, the puzzled doctors said. Stripped by illness, stripped of illness, she truly feels no longer a woman but simply a person in Christ. Her monstrous desires have been restrained and purified; she gazes calmly at the gold goblet that the chaplain drains each morning at Mass. Her blood is thin now, her blood is non-sickening. How the others struggle, forced twelve times a year as regularly as feast-days to recognise their femaleness, all ovulating together such is the power of communality, all queueing on the third Friday of the month, the day which begins novenas and sacrifices, to receive their bulky piles of linen rags from Sister Joanna the Infirmarian who holds the keys not to heaven but to the medicine cupboard. Father, forgive me, for I have sinned. My daughter, I bless you, I forgive you. Take the name Veronica as proof of your devotion to penitence, the name of she who on Christ's journey up to Calvary stepped up to Him to wipe the blood and sweat from His face with a linen towel. On that towel she bore for evermore the imprint in blood of His holy countenance, as her reward, her comfort. Call His blood blessed, Sister Veronica of the Holy Blood of Jesus; blessed art thou, having the memory of His manhood, spent, shed for you.

Now, in the year of Our Lord 1911, Sister Veronica sits in the back parlour of the convent near the Elephant and Castle in south-east London, painting holy cards to distribute to the parish at Christmas. Memories and stories cross her mind, at the dread afternoon time of spiritual dryness, between the stroking on of pale blue water-colour and the anticipation of the bell for chapel. She feasts upon them; like an album of postcards they will furnish her with food for meditation and will enliven her confession.

She drives to Windsor on a sunny afternoon in 1889 with her rich cousins, Harriet and Vernon and Grace. The three girls are all in white, with scarlet ribbons in the little hats they wear tipped over their eyes and scarlet sashes around their tiny waists. It is a hot day; perspiration creeps into the lace between her legs despite the parasol she tilts against the sun. At Windsor Vernon unpacks a hamper in the water-meadows: hard-boiled eggs the servants have prepared for them, cold beef, fruitcake and lemonade. After luncheon, still being hot, she paddles daringly in the river. The colour in her sash runs, bright red flowing from her waist down to her knees. While the girls rock with laughter at the spectacle, Vernon is kind, giving her his hand to help her up the bank again, lending her his handkerchief to mop up the worst of it. But it is the careless and beautiful Harriet who straightens her hat for her and lends her her own sash for the journey back. When they reach home, her uncle is waiting at the front door, worried because it is getting late. While Harriet vanishes inside to practise the piano, she herself lingers with Vernon on the gravel path between the laburnum and the laurel bush. He says he hopes she has not caught a cold. He bends his face towards her, he grips his straw hat in both hands. He is about to kiss her, only then Harriet strikes up the wedding march, sweet and tinny notes muffled by the blue and pink hydrangeas underneath the open window. She is summoned by Harriet's gaiety and mockery; grateful and fascinated to be noticed by her heroine, she turns from Vernon and runs inside.

Father, I confess that I have sinned. I have indulged in memory, I have allowed personal considerations to cross my mind, I have daydreamed. Sister Veronica ceases scribbling in the little notebook given to each nun upon profession for the recording of her sins, and picks up her paintbrush again. Her body is loose and plump these

43

days, a result of the poor convent diet and insufficient exercise. Her eyes have an unchanging dull sweetness that brightens only when she sees the raw young novices passionate in prayer and scrubbing. The brightening is worth the pain it brings of recognising her own spiritual torpor, all that she can offer God after He has taken all the rest of her.

She sits at her black-stained oak desk in the stuffy back parlour with its unopened windows and the Sacred Heart bleeding over the door, painstakingly drawing pictures of the Holy Family upon squares of vellum decorated in gilt and edged in paper lace. She has completed two in as many hours. Her labour is all for love; what matters is to do it excellently without taking the slightest pride in it. Nor is her labour-time recognised in the sale-price of each card: the twopences are recorded by Mother Superior in the convent accounts, the hours of patient self-murder in a larger golden book in heaven.

Over fifty years later, the convent buildings and the convent practices are little changed. On Fridays at four, after school has ended, the lay staff, nuns and pupils attend Benediction. Regulation skull-caps are anchored to frizzy hairdos with black hairgrips, lace mantillas float on the shoulders of the sixth-formers. The service culminates in the raising of the Monstrance, the chaplain turning suddenly to face his congregation, his hands wrapped in gold brocade tossing up a great gilded sun trembling between twisted gold rays like flames and a small white disc reposing at its centre. Bodies sag on to knees, heads on to splayed fingers in blinded adoration.

The pupils make their way out two by two, in order of seniority, two by two genuflecting before the altar under the iron gaze of Mother Superior, Christ's representative and never can they forget it. A straight back and a graceful swoop of the knee are signs of holiness. Say what you like of Jenny and Julie, thinks Sister Paul as she watches them, but they genuflect so beautifully.

Once out of the dark cloisters, the school erupts into the gloomy vaulted corridors lit only by the ruby lamps twinkling at the foot of the statues of the Virgin and the Sacred Heart at every corner. Hymnbooks are flung into boxes, feet skid on the gleaming floors polished in penance by erring girls and novices. For two whole days no more bells will summon them in endless silent procession to meals, classes, chapel. The daygirls hurtle to the bus stop to flirt exuberantly with the disdainful boys from the school up the road.

Julie, at thirteen, hanging out of a bathroom window back at the convent to smell the London dusk, cannot shake off school this easily; she remains defined by her badly-cut serge skirt, her unruly hair and shiny, unmade-up face, thoughts still lingering on Sister Paul whom she has managed to see three times that day by loitering with thumping heart in the forbidden area outside the nuns' staff-room when the bell rings for the end of break. Her goddess keeps her in thrall by a curl of the lip as she hurries by.

In the bath, all kinds of sensation are possible. There is the silky feel of water all over her skin, and then, as the water cools, the shivery line above her waist that marks her body's break into the air. She lies at full length in the bath, huddled in its deep and narrow compass, every pore welcoming this new element, every particle of water drawing her in until she is enclosed by water, rocking on an endless black sea tipping over the edge of the world like a plate, a blissful darkness above and below, a softly breathing world. She opens her mouth and lets the water lap against her lips and tongue, she arches her neck and feels the water crawling through her hair.

The summer before coming to school in England, she is lying dreaming in the bath. Her mother enters without knocking. The children are not allowed to lock the bathroom door; they are there for any adult who wishes to make sure they have washed properly, have not drowned themselves. Claire Fanchot's words haul Julie gasping from her warm wet world and slap her in the face to make her breathe and cry.

– Chérie, for heaven's sake, oh, look at all the water on the floor, you're my big girl now, you're far too old to be making such a mess. Now I'll have to wipe it up. You never think of all the work you create.

Claire flops down on her hands and knees with the bit of old flannel kept for the purpose on the boiler, swabs the floor and squeezes the dirty water back into the bath. Silently furious, Julie immediately steps out and pulls the plug, refusing to help her mother, reaching for her threadbare towel.

– That's right darling, do hurry up, it's nearly bedtime, come along and I'll brush your hair for you.

If she does it slowly, gently, Julie's entire body dissolves, all feeling centred on the back of the neck. Claire rarely has time for this; tonight her duty is simply to make sure that Julie's head receives a hundred rapid strokes. Her face in the mirror is intent, considering. She speaks through a mouthful of kirby-grips.

– You're nearly a woman now. Soon you will begin to bleed from

45

your bottom. It happens to all women, but we mustn't complain. It's a nuisance, but it's God's will. There are a belt and towels in the top left-hand drawer of the little bureau in my bedroom. You needn't tell anyone else when it happens, but come and tell me. Now let's say your prayers. Hail Mary full of grace the Lord is with thee blessed art thou amongst women and blessed is the fruit of thy womb. Goodnight, chérie, I'll turn off the fire on my way up to bed.

The dark makes the room endless; Julie is pinned to it only by a red haze. The fire glows at her, two crackling bars of red light that grow and grow until they fill the room. Does it ever stop? Does it bleed all the time for evermore? What happens when I want to go to the lavatory? The room is too warm, she will explode with heat. But she dare not get up and switch off the fire herself, she must do as she is told. She lies trembling, watching the fire to make sure that the aged wall-socket does not burst into flame and consume her totally.

When at last she falls asleep, she dreams that the fire has taken hold of the whole house. Claire is seated in front of her dressing-table, carefully plucking her eyebrows, and will not take any notice of Julie's entreaties that they flee to safety. Julie runs constantly up and down the stairs to check on the progress of the fire, which is creeping upwards. Her mother remains insistently oblivious of the danger, bending forwards to gaze more closely into the mirror. At the moment of having to choose whether or not she abandons her mother to the flames, Julie wakes up, her heart roaring like a con-flagration.

It happens on holiday, when Julie has forgotten all about the possibility. In a hotel room, in a bed shared with Claude, her parents sleeping a yard away. As she wakes, she is aware at first only of a pain in her stomach, a dull ache, and a pleasant wetness between her legs, a comfortable game to move her thighs against each other and feel the smooth and slippery skin. Then, as she becomes aware of the oddity of this wetness, she remembers the sour warmth of piss in earlier beds and is shocked into shame. The hand that goes down to touch the inside of one thigh comes up again smeared red.

Claude and her parents are still asleep. Cautiously she sits up in bed, swings her legs over the side, stands up. Her centre is out of her control, a pulsing between her legs that no muscle in anus or urethra can stop sends thick blood spurting down to pause stickily about her ankles. With glued thighs she pigeons across the room to the cubicle containing the lavatory and bidet. There is only harsh brown paper to staunch the flow. With a piece of this pressed to the place from which the blood seems to appear, she hobbles back across the room to her mother's bedside.

Her daughter's hovering presence, need, wakes Claire, as it always does, years of her maternal antennae developed to function even during sleep. As she takes in her daughter's nudity, the hand clamped to the base of the stomach, the red seams on her legs, she exclaims in distress, then looks round hastily to make sure she has not woken Julien. Getting out of bed gently so as not to disturb him, and putting on her dressing-gown, she rummages in her suitcase. The gauze outfit she produces is soft and caressing, and yet bulky and uncomfortable. When Julie gets dressed and puts her shorts on she feels herself bulge before and behind. Too noticeable; she understands already that this means shame. She takes her shorts off and dons a skirt.

As she emerges from the cubicle to wash her blood-stained flannel in the sink in the other corner of the room, she hears Julien exclaim.

– She's far too young.

What shock, what loss he is feeling, she has no time to consider, her own grief and anger preoccupy her. Her mother, her father, her brother, all are awake, all see the red rag in her hand.

Maman, I'm wounded, and weeping. I hate you Maman, you will no longer let me be your child, I have proof of it now, what I have suspected for a long time, what you have tried to tell me for a long time. I would not listen, I will not listen, I do not want to know. We were attached once, physically joined to one another. Even after birth, I could still suck at you, smell you, hear you, feel you. You have cast me off, you have broken me off from your body, and the place is bleeding. I miss your arms, I want you in the old way, do not abandon me.

– Julie, for heaven's sake, and her mother is across the room, snatching the flannel from her daughter's hand, wrapping it in newspaper and dropping it into the waste-paper basket. Poor little thing, you feel it is misery now. But you are no longer a child, you are a woman. The child is joined to the mother, the woman is joined to the man. That is what being a woman means.

Julien, Claude and Julie are sent down to breakfast while Claire washes the offending parts of the sheets before the chambermaid arrives to make the beds. Julie will sleep for the rest of the holiday with her mother; her father will share a bed with Claude. Julie must now begin to lock the bathroom door against the cries and kicks of her former companion, her hurt and uncomprehending brother. Nor must she mention to her father that she is bleeding; in front of him she may only refer to difficult days, and that with a blush. She must never let him see the stained towels she brings downstairs to burn in the kitchen boiler; similarly, she must smuggle upstairs the new ones she buys. She finds this totally acceptable; for Julien she does not wish to be woman, mysterious terrifying hole stinking with blood and darkness, she wishes to remain his child, clean, attractive, charming, assured of his protection and his love. That night Julie is content; her mother sleeping only six inches away means that blood can be used after all to deny their separation.

Jenny enters the bathroom at school. There is no lock on the door; she wedges the white-painted chair under the handle and then looks gleefully at Julie.

– Tonight I am going to run away from school.

On Friday evening the convent is dark, breathing with supper smells, weariness. The eyes of the watchers are relaxed. Down the arched corridor she will glide, a shadow against shadows, blowing out each votive lamp of the Virgin after her. The clamour of cabbage and candle-wax will hide the noise of the creaking bolts she draws gently away from the garden door.

Her Saturday shoes break the film of ice formed since lunchtime over the ruts of mud in the path. The dark shapes of bushes in the garden are muffled by glittering ice; wetness hangs in the trees. Her footsteps are white on white, but her body presses itself into blackness, the squares of orange light behind her shrinking. Each bush she brushes against trembles, its stiffness bruised, drops of water tilting to run off its leaves. The sand of the path yelps as she leaves it behind second by second. The kitchen garden, enclosed by walls, is darker still. She guides herself around its edges, her hands fumbling along pear trees crucified against slimy lichen. She kicks at grass tough with frost; trickles of water clamber into her shoes.

Inside the gardener's shed she will change her clothes. A mohair skirt hugs her from hip to knee, a polo-necked jumper clings to cone-shaped breasts, a tartan bag with gilt chains flashes from her shoulder. Long black patent-leather boots constrain and caress the arches of her feet. She creates herself, an adolescent girl. She looks eighteen at least, with her back-combed hair, her face bending towards lilac-scented powder in the dark, the daytime sky torn in half and pressed to her eyelids.

As she walks through the small side door on to the street she takes small steps, her skirt chafing her knees, her high heels wobbling. She runs away slowly, to the bus stop. She will sit in a coffee-bar in the West End, waiting for Julie. The steam from her tiny cup of espresso coffee moistens her parted lips. One hand holds a silver-tipped cigarette, the other taps on the pink and black formica table-top. The juke-box glitters and thumps.

– Julie, you will come, won't you? You said you would.

Julie has been vowed here by her parents' words; she does not know she has any of her own. She is good, bright, hard-working, happy. Darkness she seeks, which is the word of God, not Jenny's whiteness and her daytime. She kneels in the chapel, sucking at love she will never exhaust. She shivers at incense, the flesh of her knees dented by the hard cold floor she kneels upon in enjoyable penance, draughts sweeping along the cloister to bang her back into straight-ness and keep her awake. It would break God's heart if she left His house, her place at His side. He is often sad, and He needs her. When He is sad, she can be sure of Him. He gives her the only rest she knows, the state of perpetually needing Him. Her world the dark-ness of the chapel; here she is absent from herself that she may know His presence, and then know herself as not-Him.

– Jenny, I can't come with you. I've got detention tonight, with Sister Paul.

Jenny and Julie have been best friends ever since they met on the first day of term two years ago. They sit next to each other at the back of the classroom, desk lids raised for a quick exchange of jokes, of forbidden novels. Secrets shared in the cloakroom, hiding together after school curled up under the stands of raincoats, the smell of damp gabardine and sweat and dried mud in the dusk. There are walls around this place, forbidding their escape, but they have built a rich world inside them. Their strength is the way they know each other, the wordless sensitivity they have grown between them; a private language constructed to express their connection with each other and their separation from the authorities: puns, quotations, riddles, Cockney. They laugh when no-one else does, because of the exquisite meanings they can give events which seem banal to everybody else. Every act, and every movement, they translate and share, looking at one another secretly, waving private flags.

Their intimacy so natural there is no need to name it or to be self-conscious. Night after night they call across the dormitory in whispers: come on, let me into your bed tonight. Midnight discussions, reading together with a torch under the bedclothes, stifled giggles at stories they tell each other, at wild flights of the imagination. They lie in bed together, bodies curled to a perfect fit, hands smoothing and stroking each other's backs. The rules in the game are not articulated, and they do not know they know them. A giggle or a squirm suffice to say: that's it, stop there, no further down.

Both of them are in love with Sister Paul, the only way they know to speak their love for each other in public, as they find they sometimes wish to do. She plays with them most delicately. Now satirical and aloof in order to net them into wit and intelligence, now warm and engaging in order then to deal them a snub, a bored look, a turned back when they become too intimate. They discuss theology and politics with her; she drops them hints about her frustration with convent life; she accepts their gifts, essays and attentions; she pretends that they are equals, delicious after-dinner companions; she never tells them anything about what she is really feeling.

– Julie, you're such a child. Still in love with stupid Sister Paul. I don't care, don't come with me then, I don't want you anyway. You're just a coward.

From the next-door bathroom cubicle, Sister Paul, bathing one of the juniors, hears Jenny slam her way out, and then the sound of Julie crying. Sister Paul stands bolt upright, gripping a nailbrush tightly in one hand. Images as bright and precise as holy cards pass across the blackness of her mind. Julie and Jenny, always together, whether in meals, chapel, or on walks; in the same class; the same dormitory. The two of them eagerly listening to Sister Paul's lessons, carrying her books, holding open the door for her, filling up her loneliness with their flattery. So tender she has been to her favourite pupils. Her feelings purely motherly, she assures herself, when she wakes in the night after a dream or finds herself waiting for a smile.

The bell for silence rings in the late evening. Those nuns not called to the completely contemplative life, the eternal loss of self through the vow of perpetual silence and sweet dissolution into secret dialogue with the lover hidden underneath the black tabernacle of the habit each nun wears, must look forward to death only at night, when the bell rings, and the most urgent of communications is broken off in mid-word. At other times, in the day, the sisters practise self-control, anticipating night, speaking only when absolutely necessary.

Mother Superior and Sister Paul understand one another's elliptical communications perfectly, sensitive after years of community life built on silence to the curl of a finger, the droop of a mouth. They pace up and down the dark red flags of the passage outside the library, arms folded into their wide sleeves underneath their scapulars, eyes downcast except for occasional sideways glances. Mother Superior swings her head like a censer to punctuate her final words.

– P.F. stands, Sister Paul, as you doubtless know, for Particular Friendships, derived from the French amitiés particulières. Just as we discourage unhealthily intense friendships between the pupils, so we frown upon favouritism shown by teachers. You have erred, Sister, upon three counts. You have failed in your duty to the girls themselves by not discouraging their exclusive relationship. You have failed in your responsibility to their parents by allowing them to waste the time they should be spending on their studies. You have broken your vow of obedience to me, your Superior, by not letting me know about this much sooner. Spiritual arrogance, Sister Paul, is a very grave fault. Doubtless you thought you had the situation well in hand. But you must learn, my dear child, to submit your judgment to mine, and to trust in me.

The Office bell begins to ring. In five minutes they are due in chapel, to join the others vanishing around the corner of the cloister. Sister Paul is cold. Draughts eddy up her wide sleeves, across the back of her neck. The draughts like whippy fingers will untie the white strings of her coif under her veil, and release her hair new-grown, longer, thicker and redder than Julie's she remembers it, a warm sweet-smelling shroud to weep behind. Her wimple with its two starched wings designed to keep her looking straight ahead at God draws in all eyes to gaze upon her face, from the white frame to the humiliation and anger suffocating within. She whimpers a little, she cannot bear the gusts whirling about her. She will achieve peace once more, she will kneel at the feet of Christ, lift her face innocent, smoothed, childlike, confess everything, relieve herself of pain, of all responsibility. Her pupils' punishment will name her comfortable again.

Julie sits on the rough edge of the shoe-boxes in the unlit freezing cloakroom, her hands ripping a lace mantilla in two. Her thoughts slide continually up to a relationship she wishes to name, but do not dare to grasp it, and so fall away again. In this darkness of unknowing she is found, hiding under a stand of smelly raincoats, by Mother Superior. The nun's triangular face splits in two, thunder issues from the lips.

– Come along, child.

Julie can do nothing but become the other's words, obedient. Only her stomach rebels, the threat of sickness clamouring. She follows the nun's black back out of the cloakroom and up the cold dark passage. She has met her mentor only twice before; that their worlds overlap now is the consequence, the indication of sin.

At the garden door Jenny stands beside Sister Paul, scowling at the floor. Mother Superior looks at all of them. After God, their first allegiance is to her. She is their mother and father both, the friend to whom they confide their conflicts and the surgeon sharply to excise them. She speaks placidly, wearing her authority with modesty.

– We have telephoned your father, Jennifer. He has cancelled a business conference in order to drive down and collect you in the morning. He is extremely shocked and grieved. He had hoped so much, he said, that we could replace for you the mother you lost when you were just a little girl. I will take you to spend the night in the sickroom. Julie, I am disappointed in you. You spend too much time alone in chapel. We must see to it that you rejoin our community life a little more. Young girls, however devout, must not neglect a healthy recreation.

Julie sits digging her fork into potatoes in the house in France. Jenny, Jenny, we weren't even allowed to say goodbye. Your eyes were sullen, you felt betrayed, you would not look at me. I knew I was wicked to let you down, such a coward not to run away with you, and so I never answered your letters, sure that you wrote only from politeness, you could not possibly love me any more. Up and down the sandy paths I walked at break-time in accordance with instructions, desperate for a companion, but speaking to no-one. The other girls laughed at me behind my back, whispered about me behind their hands. I caught the curiosity and the sneers deliberately floated across my path just loud enough for me to hear. Lesbian. That word they dropped appalled and terrified me. Evil. Repulsive. Outcast. Perverted. Monstrous. A host of hideous synonyms jangled in my brain when I tried to understand what had happened between Jenny and me.

After a week had passed in this way, I had reached my decision: I had a vocation and would become a nun. Silence, all the rest of my life in silence, it seemed most logical and desirable. I would not have to face myself one of a sisterhood of perverted monsters; I would be named again a nice young girl, a sexless being who would

52

never be loved, except by God who never goes away. At home for Christmas, I told my parents. My mother was upset, she complained I was far too young to think of it. Grandly I reminded her of the Little Flower, old enough to become a Carmelite at sixteen. I threw myself with enthusiasm into housework and washing-up, rejoicing as my hands turned red and swollen from hot water and my face was splattered with greasy water; I could offer it up, as the Little Flower had done, for all the sinners and perverts of the world. My father remarked that I should not waste my education. University first, he suggested, before I made the final choice. I agreed with him when I had thought about it, seeing myself first taste all the splendours of the world and then magnificently give them up, first prove myself perfect in the world's terms, and then in God's. Underneath my humility lurked all my rage, poured into acts of mortification which could only harm myself, not those I loved. I would become Mother Superior in time, able to punish as I had been punished, to make others do as I wanted. I lusted for power which girls and women do not have in this world; I would have it, by going beyond womanhood into sanctity, and reaching a kingdom far beyond the earth.

Seventh section

As evening approaches, the salon begins to grow dark. One by one, objects and items of furniture vanish: the photographs of the children in their silver frames, the carved wooden cupboards, the store of bottles of home-made fruit liqueurs, the lace curtains at the window, all these begin to slip backwards, their materiality lessening as they approximate to darkness and become different soft shades in the August monochrome of grey to black. Julien reconquers darkness despite his dislike of mounting electricity bills and of the moths that flutter in from the garden once the lamps are lit. He gets up from the table and presses the china switch at the side of the doorway, his fingers pull the silk cords dangling from the lampshades around the walls. His favourite armchair is once again illuminated in soft pink; his pipe, he sees, lies at the ready on the little table beside it. His after-dinner place assured, he returns to the table, where the white glare of the overhead lamp bounces off the tablecloth and demonstrates the stains left by a week of food and wine. With Claire ill in bed, Suzette forgets to change the table-linen and saves a little time from washing-day. Julien frowns at the stains, the crumbs on the table-cloth, the newspaper that some careless person has left beside his plate. He wishes that Claire were here, in her accustomed place opposite him, her back straight, her fingers neat. She would ask him about his day outside, she would be interested in the work of the farm, the work that feeds them, clothes them, shapes their conversation and their dreams. He does not understand her lengthy convalescence; he does not like the way that dinnertime suffers from lack of care, from inefficiency.

He glances at his daughter, moodily dipping her spoon into a blue china bowl of apricot purée that Suzette has dumped down before taking her leave and returning to her own home at the other side of the village. Julie does not sit up straight; she has a deplorable habit of lighting cigarettes between courses. Look at her now. She has not even waited for him to begin eating. She used to be an attractive little thing, plump, yes, but with a fresh clear skin, her hair pulled back neatly from her forehead to emphasise her large hazel eyes, her wide smile. Attractive manners, too; always interested, always understanding, ready to take his side when Claire was irritable and snapped at him. How much Julie has changed. Her hair is cut short, sticking up in spikes all over the place, her dinner outfit is a pair of jeans and a faded cotton shirt, not unlike his own clothes; her face is pale, her fingernails are bitten, her eyes are tired. She looks less like a girl than a grubby urchin. He feels unaccountably shy with her, without Claire here to complete the family group, to monitor the conversation, to fill in the awkward gaps and smooth over the jagged edges. He will speak to the doctor tomorrow about his wife's condition; he is anxious about her continuing ill-health.

Julie pushes the dish of apricot purée towards Julien.

– Here. D'you want some of this?

She does not call him Papa any more. He clutches at the dish and helps himself, spilling a bit on to the cloth. The question leaves his lips in similar fashion, unexpectedly, messily.

– Julie, do you think that Claire is getting better?

– How should I know, she says guardedly: I've hardly seen her yet. A hysterectomy, and then cancer suspected, Suzette said, well, that's really serious. You can't expect a miracle.

Julie is annoyed; her father's words push through her preoccupation with herself. She does not wish her parents to feel pain; their job is to be strong and sympathetic for their children. Here she is, a refugee from troubles of her own, fleeing back from battle to the warmth and succour they have always told her they were there to provide, and they start bothering her with suspicions of their imperfection.

– How should I know, she repeats crossly: you know she never tells me anything, she always swears she's all right, she'd never admit it, in any case, if she was in pain. And I too, Julie thinks, I too.

– She might talk to you, Julien suggests: where she couldn't to me. Women's problems, you know. I think she's been unhappy since the operation, but I don't know why.

It costs him a lot to admit this; he compensates by adopting a patronising tone. Julie uses this as the excuse to ignore his meaning.

– Well, that's what's so awful, she hurries on: even if Maman is depressed about the hysterectomy, well, I can see that she might be, well, I don't know what I can do about it. It's about being a woman in certain circumstances. Nothing she feels can change, unless those change.

Only Julie is allowed to have problems about being a woman. Julien does not understand what she is saying, but he catches her final verb.

– Well, he says in retaliation for her unhelpfulness: perhaps we'll be seeing a bit of that around here sooner than you think.

Julie looks at him sharply as he digs into his apricot. I haven't changed as much as you seem to think, Papa. I still hate change, it frightens me.

– Change? she repeats in a tight voice: what sort of change?

Julien places his spoon in exact realignment with his plate, folds his napkin and pushes it into the little linen case that Julie embroidered for him one birthday. He regrets having dropped hints; he shrinks from a flood of feminine emotion.

– You'll have to talk to your mother about it, he mumbles guiltily: she'll want to tell you, it's her place, not mine, to do so.

Panic grips Julie's heart, which begins to thump slowly and heavily in her throat, like lumps of apricot threatening to choke her. She glances rapidly around the salon, counting the chairs, the pictures, the cupboards. All are in their places, watching her. Her father too is in his place and watching her, only he is now an ageing man, no longer the dashing lover to whom she has been bound in secrecy for years. Desolation overwhelms her; she pushes her chair back from the table.

– Then I'll go and talk to Maman now.

– Don't be so selfish, Julien says sharply, from his guilt: have a little consideration for her at least, she'll be asleep by now.

Julie the thwarted child can no longer throw her food on the floor. She grips the chairback instead, stung, defensive.

– I am considerate. I'm here to look after her, aren't I? I just want to go and say goodnight to her, that's all. She asked me to, she'll be hurt if I don't. She loves me, Julie shouts: she wants to see me.

Julien snorts.

– Love. You don't know the meaning of the word. Look at your clothes, your table manners, the way you talk. Look at the way you've been living. I forbid you to upset your mother, you'll make her ill with worry.

The voice in Julie's head carries on as she goes into the kitchen to make coffee. You are unnatural, there must be something wrong with you. You are ill. You are unnatural.

Eighth section

April day in Oxford, pale golden sun blazing through its prison of thorny black trees, pillow-fighting clouds ripping the sky into banners of blue, grey, yellow. A mildness under the wind, a softness that teases you it's nearly summer. Julie sees the streets as children do, pacing along what is less a thoroughfare for cars than a landscape marked out into territories. Lamp-posts, waste-sites, derelict cars, bunkers conceal beneath their surface the doorway to another world where dons and essays growl only on the horizon. A leafless tree beckons to her, its shiny black roots sunk outside Black-friars entrance in a circle of wet clay protected by barbed wire, its branches still and yet perpetually thrusting every time she turns her back. She does not mind the tree-dance when her eyes are elsewhere; so much less pain than with the loss or change of people. The tree has caves and alleyways beneath its roots, no warning in its bland trunk of the passionate legendary world Julie describes within it. Siegfried's dragon, and Siegmund's, coil at its foot; a bridge leads from its topmost branches to the heavens, the dwelling-places of the gods; dwarfs and goblins tunnel down from it for yet more treasure. Julie remembers a painting by Burne-Jones that hangs in the museum: wet jungle green of undergrowth, roses hurling themselves upon thorns. A woman with auburn hair, a purple cloak, shelters from a rainstorm. At her side a knight bends melancholy eyes upon her feet. Julie laughing brings Ben from the other end of the gallery, exclaiming with surprise and pleasure. They drink washy coffee in the cafeteria. Ben will be King Cophetua and take her to the Swithin's ball. Julie delights in the tension of trees, their bursting reality, their place in gardens and in seasons, and the magic of them, flowering in her head whenever she needs a way out, their green tips pushing up through the carpet of her room. She sees a clump of cedars on the college lawn from her bedroom window; on her way out of college she strokes their ridgy grey-green trunks with her hand, clearing them of solitary raindrops waiting to spill. She walks towards the Bodleian, delighting in the unity of her life: an afternoon spent reading for her Chaucer essay, tucked up in the peace and leather smells of Duke Humphrey's library, and the evening dancing with a powerful and attractive man. Do well work hard and be happy, urge the parental voices in her head. She will write a brilliant essay on Chaucer's irony, she will dazzle in her golden frock, the perfect female undergraduate. Everyone, not only Ben, will praise her, love her. After this, her brother will topple from his prime place in the family pantheon.

Duke Humphrey's is the oldest part of the Bodleian and is banned to undergraduates. Julie walked in here in the first week of her first term, convinced that graduate men were so much more sophisticated than the lanky youths she danced with at the Freshers Fair, so much more delicate in their advances. She likes the bays that jut out in the long room, assuring privacy, their sides lined with folios bound in crumbling leather, the walls with their shifting medallions of colour as the sun plays through stained glass and over them, the smell of books and polish, the view from the long windows down into the little walled garden with its greening stone steps and slow-moving gardener.

She settles herself on a chair of black wood, turning it slightly sideways to face the rest of the room and afford the interested a glance at her legs, long, slender these days by dint of strenuous exercises every night, and clothed in sheer black nylon. Up, up, to the skimpy mini-skirt that barely covers her bum when she sits down. Julie will not notice if you sneak a look, however lingering, at her legs, her head is lowered gracefully over her book, her eyes devour Chaucer's story of Arcite and Palamon and their competition for the hand of Emily. As she gets more involved in her reading, her legs twist themselves around the leg of her chair, she bites her lip, she stains her cheek with biro, her nose begins to shine, she scratches at her chin. Her audience sees her grow less beautiful, more like an ordinary bluestocking, and turns its gaze away.

Emily walks in the walled garden underneath the moon. It is cut out of silver cardboard, pasted on to taffeta sewn with glistening sequins. Emily is no less thin and flat, her arms move jerkily up and down. Ah me, the day the Amazons were captured by Duke Theseus and he took my sister Hippolyta for his bride, ah me, my loneliness. A nightingale, wound-up, releases its song, a clatter of metallic notes. On cue, Emily bends to gather flowers; this is the eve of the first of May and she has arisen while it is still dark to observe the proper ritual. At the far end of the garden is a wobbly tower. Arcite and Palamon looking out from it have four round eyes. They sigh as they perceive the lovely maid; the dart of love has struck them, poor unfortunate prisoners. They do not know her name, nor she theirs; they may never meet, yet they will love her until they die. The moon blots out; just as it sinks, the sun begins to climb. The nightingale is replaced by a lark, hauled up by wires and a pulley, and made of grey cottonwool. Emily joins the lark in singing.

Julie is getting ready for the ball. She lies back in the narrow college bath, her face a white mask of slowly stiffening face-pack. She soaps herself, she piles shampoo and conditioner on her hair. Her hands shave her legs and armpits, scrub her toenails and finger-nails, splash her face with cold water to remove the face-pack. She rises from the bath, scented scum clinging to her knees. Cautiously she dabs deodorant on her stinging armpits, squirts another deodorant between her thighs. Then she creams herself, powders between her toes, seizes tweezers and plucks her eyebrows to a narrow line. She soothes her itching face with witch-hazel, then applies moisturiser. Now she is ready for the paint. First a coat of beige, to muffle the blush of her exuberant cheeks, then a dab of green rouge for the same purpose. Shiny white stuff dabbed at the corners of her eyes, to widen them, and underneath her brows. Smudgy olive-green eye-shadow on her eyelids, a line of purple in the eyelid crease, a black line drawn with a tiny brush along the outer edge of her eyelids, three coats of black mascara. Tiny black lines painted in below her eyes to resemble eyelashes, two applications of pale pink lipstick. A whisk of translucent powder to set it all and stop tiny beads of perspiration bursting through.

Then scuttling down the long draughty corridor, feet in old slippers, to her room. The dress. It slithers over her cold flesh, over the clinging nylon petticoat, the stiffened lace bra, the rigid panty-girdle holding in her stomach. She has not eaten for two days, to make sure the line is perfect. The dress is gold like a snakeskin, caressing her chilly shoulders with its harsh underside and then dropping to her feet. Sheer bronze nylons rolled up over her moist legs and hooked to suspenders. Feet pressing into gold high-heeled sling-backs that slightly cramp her toes because they are so new. She has thrown open her bedroom window so that the cold air keeps her coated cheeks from burning, stops the make-up melting, her pores from opening. The rollers plop out of her hair, releasing it in bouncing waves that tickle her ears. She back-combs it a little, in an effort to make it lie smooth and straight. She picks up a gold beaded bag, a fluffy white shawl, and is ready. She sits down carefully on the arm of a chair to wait for Ben.

The statue of Diana is plaster, rearing within the tiny temple almost to the roof. It is painted in bright colours: green, scarlet, yellow, pink, azure. The goddess wears a crown of ashleaves and a tinsel robe. Her rolling eyes are violet on cream, her hair is the crimson and white flame of purity. Emily has brought her flowers, gaudy tissue-paper, and oil and myrrh. The statue's right arm is hinged; it creaks up and down in appreciation. Emily prepares her sacrificial fire and casts her flowers at the statue's feet. She puts her hands together and drops forward jerkily on to her knees to make her supplication. Diana, goddess of the chaste, guardian of women travailing in labour, punisher of impudent men who spy on us in the bath, save me. I do not wish to marry Arcite or Palamon; I am an Amazon, and proud. But, if it be your will that one of them should win me in the tournament today, then I will accept fate, fortune and destiny.

Ben's former girlfriends, rich young women with less interest in their work than in the marriage market, always dress expensively and casually. The handbags slung over their shoulders are of the finest leather, their coats of suede. They can rely on their class for self-confidence, they have merrily gate-crashed the ball alone, no need to bother with tickets or escorts, so bourgeois, the game is to choose one when you arrive. Those academic women, the poor suburban frumps, their faces flushed from too much champagne, they cannot enter the upper classes, their style is all wrong, they try so terribly hard.

Julie knows, as well as they do, that she has failed. Everyone else floats in crepe, in velvet, in delicate cotton, in anything, in fact, but lamé, gold, I ask you, and did you see her shoes? Middle English vowels rise up like sobs in Julie's throat. It is a warm night, all the long windows are thrown open, couples dance out of one room into the other and on to the lawn. Fairy-lights giggle and sway in the trees, pale frocks trail across cast-iron benches, men fight their way in and out of the champagne tent. Ben is a gentleman, he will not tell Julie that he too knows she has failed. It is three a.m. and they are both drunk and sweaty. Julie presses her face against his white linen shoulder, her hands sticky at the small of his back. In love. She clutches him like a lifebelt. The band flows from deafening rock into a blues number, sweet, a trumpet yearning. People laugh, and clap. Gently, Ben releases himself. It is hot, he will go and find them both something to drink. It is the first of May and they must drink a toast.

Beneath a gorgeous pavilion sits Duke Theseus with his bride Hippolyta. A little further down, as befits her rank, fair Emily bends her anxious gaze upon the tournament ground. Her yellow hair is braided in a single tress stuck about with flowers, her robe is white, her fingers slim and long. The two knights astride their hobby-horses are a magnificent spectacle, their coats stiff linen painted to look like cloth-of-gold, their saddles set with glittering glass, their aspects much mustachioed and ferocious, their turbans sewn with milk-bottle tops. A brief salute to the watching throng, then their wooden lances clash to the accompaniment of shouts and mighty grunts. Arcite is wounded horribly, the lance of his opponent sticking out of him before and behind. Emily swoons, Palamon delivers an oration over his dead friend's body and comes forward to claim the fair young Amazon as his bride.

Julie is frightened. Alone on her gilded sofa, glued to it by Ben's farewell caress, she suffers the advances of one young man after another. Sliding up to her, hot breath in her face, damsel in distress, eh, come on darling, let's have us a ball ourselves, shall we? She is so shy, she enchants them, this virgin refugee from a women's college, venturing out from the library where she swoons over Swinburne and dreams over Donne but is totally inexperienced in the arts of which they speak. They will show her, they will be only too happy to help her into womanhood. They become expansive, generous, bets are laid. A bottle of champagne for the lucky winner, the first one to deflower this ice-maiden. Down with bluestockings, down with their knickers. Julie gets up and runs until she catches sight of Ben.

He has been waylaid by his best friend Charlie, grabbed by the hand and whirled on to the dance floor for a bit of fun. He is clasped in Charlie's arms, laughing. They move their hips together, up and down, round and round, sway, foxtrot and glide, pressed close to each other in a hot little communion out on the lawn under the fairy-lights where everyone can see them, stamp their feet, roar for an encore. They wiggle, they mince, broad shoulders rearing above narrow hips, their gestures, according to the applause of the audience, all perfectly observed. Julie is convinced they are doing it on purpose, to mimic her own lack of feminine grace, to demonstrate their own wit and irony.

She is running through the approach to dawn of the first of May, tinkle and crunch of feet over damp gravel, smothered laughter from open windows she passes out into the street, the smell of lilac, wet, and hanging heavy, the smell of blossoming trees; sweetness crowds along the roads in front of her, as she runs as rapid as a Fury. Back to her college room for the splash of cold water on her face, cold cream to blot out anger and pain, a cup of coffee, a valium, I shall be fine, just fine, just leave me alone, do not speak to me or I might cry and shame us both. She slinks up her corridor; no curious friend emerges.

Ben bangs on her door an hour later. He is stroking her hair, murmuring, my dear, all men are brutes, I learnt that standing at my mother's knee, come on sweetheart, cheer up, come on out and join the fun.

The May Day celebrations start at sunrise. Julie looks charming in a loose long dress, her hair waving about her shoulders, her feet bare. She pulls Ben along pavements, a spray of pink blossom in one hand, her eyes sparkling. People turn to look at her as they pass, Botticelli or Burne-Jones, they are not sure which. At the top of Magdalen tower, the choir sings its Latin hymn, unheard by the noisy revellers below blowing whistles and opening bottles of champagne. Wags dressed as jesters somersault down the middle of streets, Morris dancers gravely jig up and down. Several tourists take Julie's photograph. Maman, Papa, I've done it, I belong. At lunchtime, he will make love to me in a punt, he will ask me to marry him, the new Julie will be conceived.

The mummers line up for their final bow, Arcite, Palamon and Emily holding hands and laughing through the cracking paint. The audience cheers and claps, the clowns come back for a last encore on the hobby-horses, Duke Theseus turns a somersault and loses his golden crown, Hippolyta lights a cigarette and waves to her boy-friend in the crowd. Hand in hand, Julie and Ben turn away, Julie flushed and excited, expounding to Ben her ideas on mediaeval theatre and the best staging methods. She is carried away by her enthusiasm, it takes her a little time to notice that he is bored by what she is saying. She stops, trying to smile. It's May Day, after all, no need to get all academic.

They make their way towards the market and its cafés, to meet a group of Ben's friends for breakfast, toast spread with dripping and pint mugs of sweet coffee out of a bottle. They move slowly through the narrow streets between a crowd of people going in the same direction. Other voices sound, not the clippped tones of the upper-class English accent or the flattened vowels of the tourists, not the odd sounds of Chaucerian English, but loud voices yelling, singing. She sees the tip of a banner waving, a red flag. Craning up and for-wards to see better, she loses her grip on Ben's arm. Not over-sorry, full of curiosity about this other May Day ritual, she is swept from his side as the crowd parts, half surging into the market and the rest jolting forwards on down the street and bursting into the High.

Held up between two brawny tourists, she watches the procession celebrating International Labour Day, rank after rank of banners proclaiming the existence of trades unions, of college socialist societies, of different left-wing groups. They march along the High in rows of six abreast, arms linked, singing the Internationale and shouting at the undergraduates in their straw boaters and ribbons. Julie has always thought of lefties, if she thinks of them at all, as earnest, boring, lacking style and class. She herself is busy on her upward way; like a warrior princess she must capture a man. She has never thought of her private fight as including anyone else. She sees a group of women under a feminist banner at the end of the march. They look more or less like her, undergraduates probably, bit more scruffy perhaps. Both breasts intact, collapsible spears tucked into their handbags, obviously. She doesn't understand why they should be marching with the lefties, she doesn't know what any of them have got to do with her.

The mummers begin their second show, the painted hessian curtain is wound up above the little wheeled cart. The silver cardboard moon curls at one end. Emily, entering, knocks her head on the stuffed nightingale; the space on the cart is cramped. She is tired; she has been up since four and is in need of coffee and breakfast. Nevertheless she begins her incantation, cries to the moon, for the moon. The audience presses forward, enthralled.

Evening. Ben marches down St Giles in silence, his dry hand gripping Julie's damp one. He has no need to achieve his beauty, she thinks; he is simply a man, therefore beautiful. By his side, she is lent beauty. He will give her kisses, a gold ring, a house, security, an income, love. They will smile together at the world, her foolishness, his practical jokes. Oxford is dark, is cool, the scent of blossom touching their skin. Gold spangles of light break up black façades of walls; phrases of the Doors, harsh lovesongs, drift after them as they pass by. Inside those rooms is warmth, the smell of dope and josssticks, low lights, laughter. All those beautiful, successful, confident people Julie does not know, but whose windows she breaks with her longing eyes as she paces the streets on her own. Now she is one of them, a girl on her way to a room with a man, low lights, jazz, warmth. Others can pass by outside and look enviously at their lighted window. She will not know they are there, so happy and so lost will she be in loving.

The omniscient narrator perches wobbling on the roof of the little cart. Someone's vague memories of lectures on Norse myth have clothed him as the god Odin, an old man in a flowing cloak, long beard, a broad flat hat with one eye twinkling underneath it, the other hidden by a roguish eye-patch giving him the air of a piratical grandfather. Winking at the audience, he begins his commentary. All of you lovers, I ask this question, who has come off worse, Arcite or Palamon? The one may see his lady day by day, but from his prison must he never stray; the other escapes prison, roams on hill and shore, but see his lady may he nevermore.

Julie frowns, strikes her hands together in exasperation, whispers angrily to Ben, they've got it wrong, all wrong, they just can't do that, knit two different literary traditions together, it's completely unscholarly, Chaucer's words mixed up with figures from Norse myth, they're confusing people; it's appalling. Ben is amused, squeezing her hand. Darling it's only a play, not an examination.

Julie lies naked on Ben's low bed, shivering even though he has closed the windows and the curtains, no audience. Ben too is naked, except for a bath-towel swathed around his middle. He hops from one foot to another, one hand keeping the towel in place, the other curled over a packet of sheaths.

– Put some music on, will you? I shan't be a moment.

The Oxford Mediaeval Consort finishes a merry pavane, begins a jolly estampie as Ben comes back from the bathroom. He twitches back the bedspread from where Julie grips it at her chin and lies beside her, kissing her, then moves both their bodies on to the floor, a sheath tucked into his cheek in readiness. Diligently his tongue darts between her lips. Julie is embarrassed. Her mother and the nuns, though schooling her well in the use of items such as forks, white gloves and table-napkins, have omitted instructions on the manipulation of lips, arms, legs, cunt. These have always been kept closed, trussed-up, gingerly moved, kept out of the way lest they offend. Exposing them means asking for it: whistles, pinches, rape. Now, suddenly, they are required to explode, dance, vibrate, arch, become continents crawling with armies of desire.

She lies back, stiff not with fear but with social awkwardness. Ben, finally noticing her immobility, ceases his busy efficient caresses and looks at her.

– D'you mean to tell me this is the first time you've slept with a man?

Incredulous, indignant at the responsibility laid on him, worried he will not be able to perform in sufficiently memorable a fashion. Ashamed, she can only nod. His training as a teacher comes to his aid; giving her his most tender and encouraging smile he murmurs into her ear. Well, what a very wonderful occasion. He resumes his task. Five minutes later he flops on top of her so she assumes it is all over. Both their stomachs are wet. A tiny trickle of blood on the white rug confirms what she has not noticed: that she is no longer a virgin. Ben is kind, gives her China tea and teaches her the first five letters of the Greek alphabet. Then he dismisses her, the cinema tomorrow night perhaps, now he is tired, and anyway, she's got her essay to finish. Julie marches back to college past couples strolling damp and contented from the Cherwell boathouse. The north

Oxford gardens are heavy with pink blossom clotting the trees, touching her head, petals loading the evening air with sweetness, bushes of rain-drenched lilac bending over walls she passes by. She sits in her room, the windows open to the dark, and reads her book. Stories of heroines and saints, her rich and secret inner life, her consolation. The mummers have spoken their final invocation to Dame Nature; they roll up the sylvan-painted backcloth and stuff it into the back of their van.

Julie continues to sleep with Ben in order to discover herself, to see, through his hitherto unknown and unmet sexual eyes, the self she essentially is at the same time as the self she may become. The confrontation involved in sex is, of all those available to her, the most powerful, the most deeply personal, the most open. But at the final moment with her lover and her mirror, vision distorts: she is presented with a fractured picture of herself. Because she perceives this in wordless ways, in her feelings, in her gut, she does not know which to trust: the splintered yet separately concrete vision of herself Ben offers, or the hidden whole self that struggles to say that his vision of her is distorted and moves in fantasy. If she becomes part of his fantasy a certain security, great pleasure even, become possible, at the cost of feeling split and unknowable immediately afterwards. If she does not trust and live his fantasy, she can no longer reach out even to distorted splinters and does not know where to begin to look for herself. She locks herself into libraries, into cupboards of books, of food.

The memory of Jenny presents her with another mirror into which she is now afraid to look. The terror of positively establishing a whole self, or of discovering that there is no such simple entity, the fear of giving up the rules on how to see and discover her self, all these are greater now than the loss involved of deploying only the fantasy parts of herself. She seems to live two inches behind the front of her skin, that part of her created wilfully by herself, when she puts on her make-up, and by Ben, when he makes love to her. Certain parts of her are defined by the grass that she dents with her feet or the cushion that she hollows with her back, these have an existence both in time and space, but the breasts and cunt he briefly fondles exist only because touched at his will and through his fantasy perception of them.

Ben sits with Charlie, drinking gin and tonic. Julie, yes, she's very attractive, not an intellectual, thank God, the last thing I want after teaching all day, but she's bright, very bright, she understands when I talk to her, our conversations are really good. Oh but she worries me, you know, she's so intense sometimes, she needs me so much, she wants to make love all the time.

He picks up his glass. As though the relationship's not real unless we touch each other all the time. Those hands clutching me desperately at night, her body jerking with ferocity, her eyes closed tightly in some sort of private ecstasy or pain, or else open, and devouring me. I don't know if she comes, I'm sure she fakes it, I don't want to know.

Charlie gets up from his chair across the room. Playfully he punches Ben on the shoulder. Women.

– Come on, my lad, what you need is a drink, a game of darts. Don't worry so much. The dart-board in the senior common-room bar is painted like a woman's breast, they home in confidently to the bull's-eye every time.

Julie is never for a second free of the consciousness of what she looks like. She moves along streets holding out to male passers-by photographs of herself taken from the most flattering angle, she spends hours despairingly contemplating her face and body in the mirror; her work suffers, she does not see other people but sees them seeing her. She does not know what it is like to live inside her own skin, to look out from her body and forget it sometimes. Her body bombards her from every advertising poster and hoarding; long, lean, supple, golden, it simply *is*: passive, therefore enticing. She is a travesty of her body. She is laid out on a marble slab, chopped up and sold to the passing male public. She does not know where she resides when she looks at the sections of body spread out in front of her: head, tits, legs, cunt, bum.

Since Ben does not really touch her but only handles in fantasy the collection of items he has chosen to possess, sexual contact can continue to mean little to her. The Church's teaching can be vindicated; she is absent in sex, therefore she is doing nothing wrong. She needs to be with a man in order to be real, but she despises him, he will not trouble to look for the hidden her, beautiful perfect princess sleeping behind the thorns of silence and passivity. At night, when Ben sleeps next to her, she stares into the darkness and feels frightened. This is real, the books all say so, but I feel nothing. If I am not here, where am I? Does it matter that no-one else knows I am not here?

She has no existence yet as defined by herself or other women. In men's consciousness she remains part of the natural world, the perimeter to his centre, a pleasure indulged in, an irritant humourously acknowledged to other men, material like Jews or blacks for frightened jokes, an investment, a liability, a dream, a drug, a bandage, a responsibility, a statistic, a repository for all he fears to be. To see her as a person is to see her as a man, and manly men fear buggery. Softly, she gets out of bed, fearing to wake Ben. She huddles on the bathroom floor, remembering Jenny. A couple of lesbians in bed charm and amuse a male audience; two vaginas titillate, can't threaten. Julie learns to masturbate again, the monster girlchild sleep-walks in the playpen, safe, making love to herself; dreams of omnipotence, and of revenge.

Julie sits alone at the table, busily tracing words on the enormous white silence of the tablecloth after the dishes have been cleared away. Suzette has put on her coat and heavy shoes again and gone home. Julien sits in his crimson armchair under the pink light and sleeps behind the newspaper, stomach rising and falling in deep gusts of fatigue. Julie rests one forearm on the tablecloth, her fingernails, what is left of them, scooping and sorting other crumbs into heaps of different colours and sizes. Then she pushes a finger of her other hand through the piles of crumbs and begins to write with one fingertip on the tablecloth. Words present themselves, and phrases, as some kind of clue. Black for weddings, she writes, red for funerals. She stops, frowning at her message in invisible ink, and then continues. In his armchair Julien gives a bubbling sigh, yawns, wakes up.

   – What's that? he asks, turning his head: what are you doing, Julie?

   – Nothing. Just tidying up a bit. D'you want more coffee?

Ninth section

Julie comes out of the mental hospital after only a few weeks. People are very kind to her when she is there, and she tries to cooperate with them, smiling, swallowing her medicine. Ben has been to see her regularly, leaning patiently into her jokes and chatter, holding her hand.

It is early October, the beginning of a new academic year, her third. She treads gingerly outside the hospital; the leaves fallen in russet heaps upon the ground glitter in the sunshine like broken glass, and her hair in the car mirror is the same colour as the leaves, dried blood upon her scalp. She tries to hide this fact from Ben by wearing clean clothes for the first time in two weeks and carefully applying lipstick and mascara. The vast blue sky is far too bright, it rushes down at her. To ward it off, she experiments with a wide smile. Teeth gritted and bared. Ben smiles back at her. She closes her mouth when she feels it has been open long enough. The car has reached St Giles; Ben draws up outside college.

There is an enormous weight on top of Julie. She looks down at her lap. There is an arm lying on it, with a hand attached to one end. She has no idea how it has come to be lying in her lap, this long piece of flesh frayed out at one extremity into thin protrusions and wrapped at the other end in a piece of brown woollen cloth. The arm is heavy, it drags at the folds of the skirt covering her lap, and weighs on the thighs under the skirt. It is the hand on the end of the arm that bothers her the most, so thin, the lines and knobbles of bones and veins showing through, and the nails on the fingers chewed right down to the quick. On the third finger there is a ring, a very ugly one, a great old-fashioned Victorian thing, emeralds set in complicated frills of silver.

She decides that she does not like the hand lying in her lap, she will give it away, to Ben sitting next to her, ask him to get rid of it, open the car door and throw it into the gutter, watch the ring float along the small river flowing by the kerb, thick oily water washing over yellow, black, grey gravel. She places the hand in Ben's.

Immediately, he bends his head towards her. Like the gravel, his face is composed of tiny dots, red and black dots on a grey surface, with occasional stiff black wires sticking up, and small craters, and the long red jellybags clinging to the surface which are called shaving-scars. He rubs his face across hers, up and down, sand-papering her with a loud rasping noise that roars in her ears but which he does not seem to hear. She notices a small pimple on one side of his nose, lines cut into the webby flesh around his eyes. She wonders what he can see of her own face, this close up. Against leaving hospital she has prepared herself with creams and lotions begged from the nurses, tirelessly scrubbing, polishing, erasing. Medicines, magic potions that cure madness: if you are smeared with them, a man can approach you without crying out in horror, without seeing the snakes hissing in your hair, the teeth waiting under the hair further down. Ben is safe: Julie's skin is cool, smooth and scented, free of pimples, blackheads, moles, lines of tiredness or of stress. She sighs, and he is happy. He mumbles guiltily, his hands lifting the dead leaves and broken glass of her hair.

– Darling Julie, I'll never leave you again, I'll take care of you always.

– Darling Julie, writes Claire from France: how truly glad I am, how happy for you. You must have a restful honeymoon, chérie, take care of yourself, and not think of studying until you are quite strong again. You always were the fragile one. Not everyone is as lucky as you, to have found such a helpful and understanding husband. I blame myself, for not being able to be with you, this whole thing need never have happened. One tries so hard, to bring you up the right way. You mustn't mind my saying this, I can't help worrying about you, you always tend to go to extremes. I want the best for you, I want you to be happy, Julie, I am so happy that you have found security and love.

The letter is accompanied by a cheque. Julie spends it next day on a black 1930s suit. The junk shop in Walton Street is dark, smelling of joss sticks, mothballs, dope. Two men lounge on velvet sacks in the corner, endless legs rammed into cowboy boots, tight brocade shirts and jeans, fingers twiddling glistening black ringlets, round bright eyes watching her, full red mouths chewing their moustaches. The gaps between the ragged curtains shutting off the trying-on cubicle flash with her naked breasts, lean white arms piling up her hair, small rounded knees. She has lost a lot of weight in hospital, which makes her a success.

She parades for them in the black suit. You suck your stomach in until it sticks to your backbone, you feel the skin taut to snapping across your pelvis poking forwards, you clench the muscles of your narrow thighs. You move with delicate control, all the time feeling so light and airy that the energy inside you from lack of sleep, starvation, too much black coffee, shoots you to the ceiling. The girl who runs the shop is plumper, sandalled bare feet under an old cotton petticoat dyed screaming pink, breasts loose under a black velvet jacket fastened with a brilliant brooch. She watches her two men watching Julie, Julie watches herself being watched.

– I am going to make some tea, the girl says: you want some?

– Please, yes, oh that would be lovely, thanks very much.

The other three stare amused at Julie tripping over politenesses and skirts. She says defensively: I'll take the suit after all, I think, I need something to get married in, next week.

What a sweet funny chick she is. The two men make room for her on the velvet sack, Carla, the girl who runs the shop, squatting opposite, and they all drink tea together.

By the time the second joint is being passed around Julie is feeling nice and warm and sleepy, relaxed for the first time in weeks. The silk lining of the skirt is rough and cool on her thighs, the skirt is rucked up over her knees so that she can comfortably caress the corded seam of the cushion with her bare toes, the rasping green velvet a field for dancing in. She lays her head on the friendly shoulder of each man in turn, dreamily sniffing their skin, their hair.

The two men do not know they are supposed to be her friends, or, if they do, they offer a different interpretation. They are silent, appearing to doze, while their busy fingers crush the lace of her blouse, slide between pearl buttons, touch her breasts. Julie is not allowed to jerk away, she must be grateful for their touch. The only way that she can ward them off is with magic spells: streams of words, stories, jokes, dashes of brilliance, all learned from two years of Oxford dinner-parties. As I run, I throw down golden apples in your path for you to stumble over as you lurch along behind me. You have defined the situation as a chase, and I accept your power over me because I do not know that I have any of my own. No way to turn around and say to you clearly I do not want. If you say you want me, then in the moment of saying so you have me.

The men's fingers do not read her messages correctly, they continue touching her. Julie focuses on the other girl, sitting cross-legged opposite, and manages to call her by her name, risking much, demonstrating her fear, her vulnerability.

Carla pulls Julie to her feet. The two men mumble, put out flopping hands. Yeah, well, that's a drag.

Carla seats Julie in an old armchair with another cup of tea and decides to become her teacher. She dons an apple-green kimono, sploshed with pink flowers. Then she changes it for an orange tea-gown with silver beadwork across the front. Next, a brilliantly-coloured shawl she whirls within, staring at Julie all the while, and then a grey silk coat edged with soft grey fur. Now her eyelids are irridescent bands of purple and blue, winking at Julie as bright as neon. Carla is the queen of backstreets, sleazy femme fatale, slumped on one hip, leaning against the wall covered in rainbow-chalked graffiti. Next, she is geisha, outlined against the moon and trees, fluttering her hands and steps, her downcast eyes leading your eager ones to breast and crotch. Then she is harlequin jumping from star to star, a hectic pink on her cheeks, white-stockinged thighs criss-crossing one another. Once, Carla wore a crimplene skirt like Julie's, sensible jumpers, sling-back shoes. She learned fast, coming to the Tech and dropping out of a design course. Now Carla waits for the old ladies of Oxford to die off one by one, so that she can rummage through their wardrobes to stock her shop and other women's fantasies with huge profits on every sale. As she changes from one costume to another, she delivers a running commentary to her pupil.

Your vulnerability hurts me like razor-blades, lures them on like the smell of blood. You're crazy, yes, I like that, you're so refreshing, and so different. But with some, like these two, it's too much of an invitation. Don't talk so much; become a kaleidoscope instead, dazzling them with varied images of who you are, might be. That's your sole defence. Use your body and your eyes to act; suggest with them, a different message every day, in clothes that suit you and conceal your ugly points. Hide behind that. Wear your hair so, to be gamine, innocent and yet worldly-wise; brush it down like this, over one shoulder, to be a Fifties tart and suggest that the rape has already happened; fluff it up and droop your lips and neck to be angel of the Pre-Raphaelites, mysterious and bored. Sexiness, and confusion, that's what it's all about. Like second nature when you get the hang of it. There's something about you certainly, a sort of ignorance and gaucherie. Wear the black suit to enhance it, at the same time transforming it into a more knowing, a wittier allure. Have the black suit, and these imitation silk flowers to wear with it as a gift from me. And don't come back. You're sweet, yes, but I don't like competition.

No more than Julie does. Wearing the black suit, she walks self-consciously and gracefully along the streets towards Ben's college, thinking with complacency of all those women students of his, their carefully sloppy clothes, their confidence in their own beauty. She is as good as they are now, she awaits only the accolade from him.

Ben is delighted with her as she makes a stylish entrance, opening the door slowly, posing against it, black on white.

– Very chic, you lovely creature. But why black, Julienne? You're sad at getting married, hmmm?

She crosses the room wth tiny steps, balancing on her glittering jet heels, making him wait for the reassuring kiss. As she reaches him, he pulls her off balance so that she collapses laughing into his armchair, sending a pile of essays cascading across the carpet. He kisses her, sliding his hands up her back inside the padded jacket and tickling her, making her arch her back and squirm, kicking, giggling with delight. Just like old times, just like Papa, in those earlier innocent days, when he was my plaything, his rounded hairy stomach soft and warm from bed, his balls drooping through the slit in the front of his pyjamas, round and furry. All to be lost, as I grew up and away from him, with only shame as a companion.

As an adolescent, certainly not beautiful. My thrifty mother buys lengths of brown tweed in the Wednesday market in a neighbouring village, enough for a skirt for each of us, identical. I turn aside from smelling roughly-woven baskets full of lemons and fresh parsley, from sliding my fingers over the transparent greaseproof paper stamped in blue that wraps huge oblongs of pale butter, from hearing the cheeps of ducklings in their wooden boxes, to recognise myself again jeune fille. We go to Madame Lassalle, the village dressmaker, and her measuring-tape. Her mirror gives me back myself, blurred by puppyfat and stiff brown tweed, my eyes speechless and self-hating, the light discovering my frizzy hair, my shiny nose, my spots. I sulk, I glower, to make myself even uglier, wishing that there were someone I can blame, when there is only God there, telling me my soul is at least beautiful. My mother sighs, hurt by my ingratitude and trying not to show it, not understanding why I slouch and droop. I insert my feet in shiny navy-blue shoes, her gift to me. Stiletto heels, triangular pointed toes that emphasise the largeness of my feet, the muscles of my calves developed after childhood years of running, climbing trees, riding bicycles, doing all that boys do. Now the boys are on the other side of the street, appraising me like the cows they lead to the market. My face is burning crimson, furred with blushes and thick with fear. Whatever shall we do with you, Julie, so frowning, so uninterested in boys. Be careful, Julie, do not let them touch you or take liberties, it is up to you to see that they control themselves. Control yourself. Let go, enjoy yourself. I cover my face, I hide under greasy flesh squeezed out of a tube, a mat of powder.

I dance for you now, Ben, in your college rooms. My mouth is soft, open a little, and dark-coloured, inviting you, come closer, and come in. My shoulders are lean and wide, and padded in black cloth. Beneath this angularity, the body of a woman hides. My small round breasts do not disturb the severity of line, but you and I know they are there. My neck rises, long and white, above the blackness, my face is open to inspection, uncluttered by long hair, arching from side to side, to offer you a view of careful flesh and bone, my angles clean and clear. My eyes are huge, green in this light, encircled by shadow, two soft holes of darkness. Such delicacy, such vulnerability.

Who am I? A pretty boy in drag; a woman sexily boyish. A woman trying to be everything, protected by ambivalence from ever having to say I am. A woman donning the only image offered her of femaleness and beauty, and then hating it, terrified of male responses to her body. I dance alone, conscious of your eyes, and those of all men, on me. Here, in the safety of music, I may move my breasts and hips as I never let myself in bed with you, gliding, shaking, my own patterns of movement, my own rhythm. Only never touch me, do not force yourself inside me. Come closer, admire

me, recognise my sexuality, but on my terms. You call this flir-
tatiousness, cock-teasing, but I am only trying to survive a power-
battle.

Now I have found a man, or rather, I have let a man find me.
Select me. Therefore I must be beautiful after all. I must stay
beautiful or else his eyes will wander. He is kind, tells me to take
care of myself. I translate: get enough sleep, apply creams and make-
up, watch my weight. He wishes I would be more natural, like his
other women students with their taut breasts and straight silky hair;
still, I am learning fast. He takes care of me, pays the bills, buys me
books, makes love to me as often as he has the time. My dependence
on him worries him, he says. He likes women who live from their
own centre, who are strong and do not bother him with tears and
with reproaches, who are weak and need protection and guidance,
who do what he wants. I cannot show my weaknesses, which
terrify me; I cannot ask for love. I bitch, I sleep badly, I cry alone, I
eat too much. My misery reproaches him; he has taken on a lot in
taking me on. He feels guilty, he has his problems too. We are to be
married in two weeks' time.

Their wedding is held towards the end of the Michaelmas term.
Over a hundred guests, mostly friends of Ben's whom Julie has not
yet got to know. But there's no need to be scared any more, to fear
the allusions she cannot understand but pretends she can, the
awkward gaps in conservations when she struggles for something to
say, her charm too heavy like make-up in summer and falling awry.
Now her French nationality, her newly-won silence, the black suit,
are all in her favour. Ben, you old dog, they all say, digging him in
the ribs, leering at her and making speeches and kissing her smack-
ingly on the mouth. Not with my wife, you don't, and Ben is reacting
on cue, an arm on her waist, and they all laugh in admiration, good
old Ben, he's got himself a nice one there, eh?

As the crowd of men clustering around her and Ben disperses and
moves away, Julie disengages her arm from that of her husband and
resumes her progress around the room to talk to her guests, moving
with awkward elegance, smiling until her lips are stiff, shaking
hands over-heartily, trying desperately to remember faces, names.
She is conscious of wanting to go and sit in the Ladies by herself for
a while to recover, but knows that that would never do. Her mouth
is dry; she turns as she reaches the top of the room and looks around
for a waiter and more champagne.

She sees her husband, far away from her, huddled in a corner with a young woman, talking earnestly to her, heads together, looks intertwined. Jealousy flares so violently that as Julie grips her hands together she splits her black lace gloves. Cautiously, she looks again. Memory clambers out from where she has locked it away in a cupboard of old school books, shakes itself like a sleepy beast, pads downstairs and out into the sun. The curve of a cheek, the plane of a shoulder-blade, the movement of the corners of a mouth trembling into a smile, all these signs collide, knot together to form a pattern spelling out a name. Jenny.

Ben never talks about the people he meets away from me, the other friends he makes. He never wants to. Tells me I'm being inquisitive and jealous if I ask, possessive, incorrect. Now he's here with Jenny, he's dug up my past, my treasures and my bones, and is coolly bundling it all into a sack for his own private museum. My face sets like cement into a tolerant smile. How delightful to meet an old friend again on one's wedding day. Only someone is trampling over my face, heavy boots gouging into my eyes, so that my skin turns into crazy paving. I am lost, don't know what I'm feeling. The more that those two whisper together, the less there is of me, no more secrets, no more private past. Keep a grip on myself. If I remain silent and watch, something horrific will happen – what? If I stay silent, the three of us will blur into one another, blood and guts and bones spilling all over the floor. Keep smiling, eyes on my glass, on Aunt Chrissy's hat. Jenny has seen me watching them, she is moving this way, to be kind to the poor little bride, to include her in a tête-à-tête. Let Ben only put his arm around me again and he will be once more the husband I love; no room for anybody else for either of us.

Her voice sounds just as it did when she was circling the room being hospitable to her new relations.

– Jenny, how lovely to see you. What a surprise.

Jenny looks back at her, hands nervously lighting a cigarette and eyes shyly coming to rest on Julie's face.

– I don't know what to say. I'm completely overwhelmed.

– You seemed to have plenty to say to Ben, Julie says lightly: he's very charming, don't you think?

– I don't know, Jenny says with a sudden understanding grin: I only met him a couple of days ago. You're marrying him, presumably he's delightful.

Jenny always used to know what Julie was getting at, when she was clumsy, fumbling for words, hiding her meaning under layers of politeness. In the old days this was part of the delight of being with her: the word-games, the play, the teasing, with Jenny snapping triumphantly at whatever Julie concealed. Now that Julie moves in a difficult world with a glass wall between her and other people, it feels more dangerous. Jenny is monstrous, with x-ray vision and grabbing hands. Julie slides away from her with the ease of practice.

– What are you doing now? Where are you living? It's been such a long time since I've heard from you.

A silence that you never tried to break, Jenny thinks: and you're instructing me now not to tell you anything that you don't want to know.

– Well, she tries: I've just got a job teaching in London. I was telling Ben just now, I'm looking for somewhere to live that's big enough for me and several friends.

– What do you teach?

– History.

– Oh. Well, you and Ben must have had lots to talk about, teaching the same subject. It must be fascinating.

– What about you though, Julie? What are you doing now?

– Oh, well, I've been terribly busy organising the wedding. I couldn't be bothered finishing my degree, I was so fed up with institutions. I'm not working or anything at the moment, I've got too much to do in the house, redecorating, all that. You know.

To Jenny, Julie looks like a little creature peering out of a hole in the ground, big eyes ringed round with black makeup, paws throwing pebbles at her.

– You've changed so much, she blurts: I wouldn't have recognised you if Ben hadn't pointed you out.

Julie looks back at her. Jenny has changed too. She has cut her hair short, which suits her. The schoolgirl plumpness has vanished; a tall, lean body has emerged, an open bony face. Only the eyes are the same, humorous, inquisitive; and the hands with their long flexible fingers. She exudes attractiveness, self-confidence, and these qualities overwhelm Julie, filling her with envy as they always did in the past.

– I still don't know why you're here, she says rudely: I never thought I'd see you again.

– I came up for the Ruskin workshop for history teachers a couple of days ago. I'd seen the notice of your marriage in the paper, and then I met Ben at the workshop. A friend of mine introduced us. He suggested I come to the reception, he thought it would be a nice surprise for you.

– He could have warned me first, Julie says with difficulty: it's been a bit of a shock.

– I know. For me too. I'm sorry, Julie, it was stupid of me to do it like this. I should have rung you.

Julie smiles at her in a sudden rush of warmth and gratitude.

– It doesn't matter. I'm really glad to see you.

– Me too.

They stand looking at one another, newly cocooned in the old affection, unwilling to break it with words which are about newness, difference, change.

– You look fantastic, Julie says.

– You too.

– Come on, let's go and find something to drink.

Taking hold of Jenny's hand, Julie drags her over to the buffet to collect a bottle of champagne and then towards a couple of white iron chairs, sweeping off the black hat and the veil with one hand and tossing them aside with her ruined gloves. She pours champagne, she chatters, willing them both to get drunk fast, to experience nothing but pleasure. She drains a couple of glasses too quickly, and tries to refill Jenny's as well as her own.

– Take it easy, love, Jenny says with a smile: we've got plenty of time.

Julie feels rebuffed now that she has decided on total love. Jenny remains obstinately outside enchantment. Julie must be some kind of monster, to want so much. When people withdraw from her, she knows, in the silence, that she is a vampire.

– Sure, she says angrily: we've got plenty of time. Another seven years or so and we could meet for a cup of tea.

– I don't mean that. Couldn't I come and see you again? I'd like to. Can I come and visit you when you get back from your honeymoon?

Ben is approaching them. Julie fluffs out the skirts of her party voice.

– We'd love to see you again. We're not going away on honeymoon, though. Far too old-fashioned.

Ben is collecting her hat and gloves from where they are strewn around the little white table. He glances at the nearly empty bottle of champagne and then at Julie.

– It wouldn't, he remarks austerely, have done you any good to rush around on a honeymoon anyway, not in your condition.

This is a game we play. He tells me off and I coax him back into good humour. Then we know we love each other. I note anxiously the sulky set of his mouth, but this time, I am impatient.

– Oh, darling, stop fussing, for heaven's sake.

She turns airily to Jenny. For some reason, far too petty and obscure to bother with, she hadn't wanted her to know.

– Hadn't you noticed? I'm pregnant.

– Is that why you're getting married?

Julie is scarlet with anger. Remembering Jenny in class at school, hand raised. Please Sister, why is communism evil? What is sodomy? Why do I have to go into the senior dormitory just because my periods have started? Why can't we talk at meals? Why is abortion murder, Sister? Even remonstrations from Mother Superior are of no avail.

Ben knows the answer to the question, but does not want it said in public. He pulls Julie's arm through his and moves her forward.

– Come on, darling, time to go. See you, Jenny.

Not for the first time that day, Julie wishes that her mother were here. She would do all the correct things, weep, embrace me, recognise me at last as grown-up, a woman, give me advice on how to handle being married. Madame Fanchot's severe attack of bronchitis has forbidden the attempt. Julie's knocking heart warns her not to think of France, the last weeks of the summer term, the bad essays, the first row with Ben, the telegram from France announcing her grandfather's death and funeral, the hand holding the razor to shave her legs in the bath hovering nearer and nearer her wrist dangling in the warm soapy water. Having timed events accurately, she is found. She goes into the Warnford because there is nowhere else to go. College is closed; her grant has run out, she cannot afford digs, she is not well enough to find a summer job. Ben writes to her mother to say that Julie is too ill to come to France for the funeral. She shrinks from those who call themselves her friends. Unless you are strong, confident, unafraid, better to hide. You can hide anywhere, outside under a great spreading cedar on a college lawn, sweet chilly grass waving about your ankles, a hundred faces turned towards you, aware as you are of the rings on the third finger of your left hand, an insurance, the best of all, against failure and disgrace.

– Are you all right?

This is an instruction. Better smile.

– You were right, love. Too much champagne. I'll be all right.

She remembers the next gesture in the ritual. Unpinning the small garden of flowers she wears in her lapel, she raises it in one hand and looks around. Jenny's bare short-haired head rears above other women's floppy hats. Deliberately, Julie hurls the bouquet straight in her direction. She misses her aim, but only slightly: the silver-wired stem of the flowers hits Jenny on the eyebrow so that her eyes, darkened by blood that smells of flowers, do not see Julie and Ben borne by the crowd across the quadrangle into the waiting car.

Dinner has to be cleared away and washed up immediately. Ben moves more easily between points that are precise. While Julie dons an apron and leans over the sink, Ben wanders about the sitting-room, straightening any details out of place. Hardbacks are arranged by author, if novels, and by subject, if non-fiction, on glistening white wood shelves; the contents of a small stationer's shop are laid out on the desk's bare and polished surface; two large filing-cabinets restrain any clutter in a life neatly conceptualised and pigeon-holed. The record-player is new, large and expensive; a small table is crowded with expensive tropical plants. The walls, paintwork, and fitted carpets are white. No objects, no pictures.

Julie comes back in from the kitchen, disturbing the whiteness with her clamouring black suit, the white cushions with her body as she drops heavily on to the sofa. This is my home. She picks up the whisky bottle from the table by the sofa, pours herself a large drink, catches Ben's eye, downs the lot. From the muddle of the afternoon must be salvaged somehow the reassurance that they want each other. It's not difficult; you quickly learn what to do, what to say or not say, when to sit still and let him approach, when to seduce. He is looking tense, sitting over there fiddling with the record-player. Usually he likes her to make the first move. She goes over to him and sits on the floor at his feet, puts her head in his lap, moves her face and mouth across his hardening penis. His arm comes round her and he hugs her to him. She knows she must not speak, she must not look at him, or he will turn to stone; he prefers his sex in silence, she embarrasses him with her loud cries. Julie un-zips his fly, brings out his penis, begins delicately to suck, her lips and tongue sliding, caressing, bringing him to the pitch of excitement so that he will assert himself, push her back on the floor, remove their clothes, and enter her.

This achieved, the next anxiety is whether he will touch her as she wants, whether he will wait to come until she does too. Cradled by his body sprawled sideways across hers, she grips him with her legs, levering until she is in a position to move forwards and backwards over his penis, feeling it slide over the hood of her clitoris and pull her lips, rub over the entrance to her vagina with each thrust, floating in rhythms of omnipotence, her mouth licking his ear, her hands stroking his back, her feet caressing his. Ben grunts faintly, comes, and flops on top of her. He buries his head in her shoulder, panting, and muttering that he is sorry. Julie clasps him tightly.

– It's all right, it doesn't matter, it was lovely.

Ben disengages and rolls over, his head turned away. That's that, we've done it, now we can relax and be friendly again. He gets up and goes over to the record-player and puts on a record, dusting the needle with care, adjusting the turntable delicately. He comes back, lies down again, puts his arm around Julie and cuddles her, his other hand stroking the silken flowers discarded on the floor beside him. This is what he likes, and what Julie has learned to like, close, and yet not too dangerously close. He closes his eyes and sighs, listening to the complicated interplay of jazz instruments floating over in exquisite syncopation from the other side of the room.

Julie's clitoris and vagina thump. I am holding a dead man in my arms, stiff as a log of wood. I am the Pieta Mother, allowed to hold a man as long as he is dead, as long as all I do is nurture him.

– Ben, please touch me. Here, like this.

She moves his hand away from the silk flowers, places it over her cunt, inserts his fingers between her wet and parted lips, lets him feel the swollen clitoris, the soft and silky flesh around it. She holds his fingers, moving them up and down, round and round, at the same time massaging his penis to life again with her other hand. His guilt forces him to do what she wants. He enters her again, stroking her clitoris with one hand as he thrusts. Julie immediately begins to writhe with pleasure, calling out, and kissing him.

Julie is full, is round, as warm and contented as a world. She swims around him, sucking at him with her lips, he is giving her all that she wants. She is no longer simply herself, she loses herself in him, they glide against one another, into one another, merge. Her coming will be her greatest demonstration of her openness, her total trust in him.

Ben's hand aches. He cannot always keep it on Julie's clitoris, which feels so small, so hidden. He is swimming in dark water, in darkness, towards further darkness. Dark is endless, he is lost within it. Darkness is his death, the further that he goes he is losing himself, losing all control. She will swallow him up and devour him, her terrifying darkness. He jerks his head away from Julie's lips, his penis out of her cunt, rolls over, sits up, and puts his head on his knees.

– I'm sorry Julie, I'm sorry, but I can't, it's so mechanical. I don't want to have to touch you like that, I want to be spontaneous, not some kind of orgasm machine.

My loss of you is my death, when you go I go also, I must not be angry with you and drive you even further away. She speaks with difficulty.

– My God, you don't make it easy for me to be spontaneous.

– I'm sorry love, I'm sorry.

Julie gets up, plucks the bedspread off the back of the sofa, swathes herself in its white folds from head to toe. Her neck is cold; she draws the fabric over her head and winds the ends around her neck. I am alone again, it is so much safer. I have let myself be seen as sexual and I must take the consequences, cover myself and protect him from my rapaciousness. I am harpy, vampire, monster and whore. I am pure, silent, ice-cold and virginal.

She goes into the kitchen and makes them tea, stuffing her anger down with slices of bread and peanut butter, eaten standing behind the kitchen door so that Ben will not see and be worried. She munches greedily until she feels sick and has to rush back through the living-room into the lavatory to throw up. Ben hears her and comes and stands over her, gently holding her head. No way she can shout at him to go away, he would not understand. Ben with his arms around her supports her up the stairs to the bedroom, tucks her in. He sits beside the bed, stroking her forehead.

– You poor old thing, being ill on your wedding-day. Get some rest. We mustn't forget the baby. We must take good care of you both.

She remembers the questions that have dogged her all afternoon and evening.

– Ben, why did you invite Jenny to the wedding?

– It's obvious, surely, he says: you haven't seen each other for years, I thought it would be a pleasant surprise.

He sounds as smug as a wizard performing a complicated trick. His next trick is to measure out Julie's sleeping-pills from the bottle on the bedside table.

– Come on, Julienne, sweetheart, you're supposed to be getting some sleep.

She lets him raise the glass of water to her lips, swallows the pills obediently.

– What were you talking about for so long? she persists: I want to know.

His hand ceases to stroke her forehead and lies flatly, heavily across her eyes.

– Nothing much. I was suggesting that if she needed somewhere to live in London with her friends she could move into the house in Peckham. It was a mistake to buy it in the first place, and now that the Fergusons have moved out, it'll deteriorate fast. I might as well have some new people in who'll look after it.

The sleeping-pills are already beginning to work, so that Julie's answer is faint.

– But I thought you were going to sell it as soon as the Fergusons moved out. You always said it was such a white elephant, such a responsibility.

His voice swims back to her as she falls into a black pit of sleep, gently pushed there by his hand covering her eyes.

– I've changed my mind, that's all. Jenny seems a nice girl, I'd be glad to do her a favour. The market's depressed at the moment, anyway. No point trying to sell just now.

How fortunate for Julie that the sleeping-pills are working so fast. She has no time for an angry retort, she does not have to face an angry response. She is a piece of the night, broken off from it, a lump, a fragment of dark, lying in her marriage bed, her husband's hands and the pills healing her rift with the night, sliding her into the dark, into the quiet.

Tenth section

The Fanchot house is the size of a large cottage but is called a house to separate it from the tumbledown and even smaller cottages the farm labourers live in. Sunlight picks out the cracks, the flaking paint on window-sills. With Claire ill, no-one has thought to water the geraniums; their grey-green stems wither above dry earth. Julie slumps on the bench outside the conservatory window, the sun pressing her on to the baking iron seat, her bare heels scuffing dusty concrete. The garden walls are braced by pear trees. Between them flowering shrubs and creepers speak the different seasons, forsythia and narcissus in spring, and now, in August, the hanging crimson bells of fuchsia. As a child, and fanciful, she called them ballet dancers. Imagination made them bend and whirl, her own legs long and delicate as their slender stamens beneath their dark red petals like silky frocks. Then at age eleven she saw herself through Claude's affectionate jeers, a hulking great girl, strong enough years ago to help their father build a tree-house and to raise water from the well. Claude played in the tree-house with her, rocking on the narrow platform through all weathers, sun and wind, shadow and leaves rushing and rustling, hidden from the grown-ups, and with their own supply of windfalls to cook on Julie's toy stove.

It is Claude aged six who brings the dolls with him up to their airy retreat. He arranges them in a row, pulling their dresses straight, and counts them: Marie-Baptiste, a creature all plastic and taffeta but affectionately held; Beccassine the silly servant girl with her green felt boots, soft button nose and no mouth; the twins Claudine and Claudette with china heads and red stuffed sacking bodies; Madame Zeppa from the Cameroon with crisp white turban and frilly skirt. Julie lies on her stomach dropping apple pips through the cracks between the planks. In ten years, twenty years time, she proposes, we shall have thirty apple trees of our own, and all our friends can come and live in tree-houses with us. A race of children sprung from us, our food mud pies stuck all with violets, our covering the old grain sacks from the grenier. Hours that summer spent dozing above the ever-moving leaves, a clear view over the cows in the field next to the garden, the distant church bells quartering the hours with rolling chimes. Sometimes they hollow out a cave in the hedge and crouch there listening to the slapping of cow jaws; or they hide underneath the redcurrant bushes in the front garden, mouths open, hands causing the sharp translucent fruit to pop off its wiry stem. But the summer ends; school and household tasks pluck them back again, and Suzette Cally is scornful of the mud pies stuck with cornflowers that are presented for her inspection. Look, Suzette, at the delicate bowlshape of my sculpture, the nest of green moss in its hollow, the passionate blue of my flowers. Mes enfants, I have spent an hour I can hardly spare to prepare your goûter, the tartines soaked with last year's plum jam, the large bowls of weak café au lait. Come, and eat, and leave your foolery.

Suzette Cally now issuing from the kitchen door clouds Julie's memories with wet sheets; their hot soapy smell shoots prickling up her nose. Guiltily she rises and hurries across the lawn. Suzette dumps the wicker basket of steaming laundry on the well, disused now, a wooden cover screwed across its top and plants with grey furry leaves like rabbits' ears swarming around its base. Suzette's mouth is full of pegs, bright modern plastic ones, not the wooden ones they used to buy from gypsy women passing through. Slowly, gravely, Suzette and Julie begin to sort the washing: table-cloths pearled with embroidery white on white, three generations of women sewing trousseaux all their girlhood through; the double bed sheets with silky monograms; the counterpanes Julie learned to hem in hours of sulky boredom timed by neat rows of spots of blood where the needle regularly caught her finger. The women fling the damp washing over the line, take one side of a cloth in each hand and step forwards and backwards with it, facing each other across the line, their faces hidden by damp and billowing sheets, arms raised in the air to separate the two sides of the cloth hanging over the line, and then lowered to bring them together again, their movements ordered, gracious, despite the weight of linen, a pavane of counterpanes.

In the Oxford house we had a washing-machine, Ben gave it to me for my birthday one year, libérer la femme with Moulinex, he teased. We kept it in the basement, a squat god crouching on the concrete floor, leaping up and down when I pressed the switch to activate it and fed it torrents of dirty underwear. Ben always looked so clean and elegant; it was the Monday god, and I, its acolyte, who disposed of dirtiness in secret in the basement. I wanted to walk into his lecture-hall where he bent a serious face above the soft white collar I had ironed, I wanted to drag my groaning linen basket with me, to smother his rhythmical periods with my staccato pillowcases shrieking of orgasms missed, to flap my sheets in his face. I wanted to tumble my unscholarly evidence all over his desk, women's domestic labour I wanted to scream, how about that for stains on your academic purity? In the event, I left him quietly, and without fuss. I went on a Tuesday, after I had done the ironing, so that he would have a whole week to work out how to use the washing-machine.

– Suzette, I'd forgotten how much you have to do of this, all our washing as well as your own, every week of your life.

I've seen your doll, Beccassine the silly servant girl. I'm like her, I suppose, all large feet and no mouth. Yes, madame, no, madame. I'm clumsy sometimes, when I've slept badly and no time for breakfast if I'm to get to the boulangerie on time to collect a fresh loaf for your breakfast. I tread my mud across your coloured tiles and make more work for myself. I loiter outside in the sunshine talking to the men come to collect the rubbish in their shining aluminium lorry, just for a minute, I say, my ears pricked for your upraised voice. I am tired and I have few words, my defences silence and stupidity.

– Eh bien, mademoiselle Julie, you get used to it, I suppose.

– Suzette, you haven't told me, how's Madame Cally now? Is she any better?

Suzette shrugs before she pegs the last sheet on the line.

– No better, no worse. The doctor says she needn't go into the clinic, that's something at least, she's all right at home with me looking after her. You should come and see her, mademoiselle Julie, you've plenty of time to spare and you were a favourite of hers in the old days.

– All right, all right. I'll come over and see her this afternoon.

Julie is red-faced, defensive, as she stares at Suzette. The maid smiles back at her, holding the red and yellow linen bag of pegs.

– It'll do you good, mademoiselle, to get out of the house for a bit. Now I must go in, there's lunch to do.

– I'll come and help, Julie says hurriedly. Approve of me, accept me as dutiful, pretend I still belong. Let me be a child again, making pastry men, licking the bowl, getting in your way while you peel vegetables.

Suzette cocks an ear.

– Is that your mother's bell? She'll be needing her medicine. In you go, mademoiselle.

The sulky child glowers, drags her feet over to the conservatory door. Stop, pat my hair, pull my skirt straight, put on a smile, resolve to be charming, cheerful, calm.

– Maman, for God's sake, what on earth are you doing? Of all the stupid bloody things to do, get back into bed, you'll kill yourself.

– I will not have dirty words used in my house, Claire manages to gasp: control yourself.

She is on all fours, grunting with effort, her greyish-blonde pigtail flooding across her back over the crocheted white shawl and the frilled cambric nightgown Julie considers mothers should wear in bed. Her knees have taken her as far as the rug in front of the chest of drawers where she keeps her household documents, and her hands are outstretched, one clutching for support at the padded edge of her prie-dieu, the other reaching towards the lowest and largest drawer.

– Leave go. What I am doing is none of your business.

Julie hesitates, then slackens her grip. She remembers kindly nurses clutching her back as she makes a dash for the locked doors of the ward. She remains squatting by her mother's side, her arms around her, gently supporting her. Claire understands this, and relaxes her own muscles, sighing, and allows herself to be shepherded back to bed. Once there, she falls back heavily against the pillows heaped up behind her which Julie leans over to thump into plumpness again. She waves away the proffered medicine glass.

– No, I don't need that. The doctor said I don't need that one anymore. He says I'm much better.

Julie sits down by the bed.

– What did you want, then? Can I get it for you?

– The photograph album, Claire says sulkily: the big grey one, I wanted to look at it again.

The album is a fine one, covered in grey leather that gleams as polished as pearls. The inside boards are covered with grey watered silk, and the marker is a twisted grey cord that ends in a fat silky tassel. The pages are stiff grey cartridge paper, with sheets of thin tissue paper laid carefully in between. The photographs are stuck in with scalloped black tabs at the corners, and underneath every glossy square Claire has pasted a slip of white paper with a legend inscribed on it in curly brown script.

Julie jolts forward.

– My God, I'd forgotten all these.

Claire flicks over the pages of the album, holding it propped on her knees.

– You see? she repeats continually, in a pleading tone: you see?

Julie studies the photographs indicated by Claire's pointing finger braced with three rings: engagement, wedding, eternity. Happy family groups laugh back at her, mouths pausing between bread and wine and cheese to grimace at the camera. Bunchy cotton frocks, baggy trousers, hair shaved up the back of the head, plump arms, feet bare or wriggling in sandals. Rows of children astride tree-trunks, donkeys, esplanade walls. Circles of adults raising their glasses in a toast at café table after dinner table after picnic table. Everybody smiles, laughs, eats, drinks, and it is summer all the year long. Julie peers at the little pasted legends. Etretat, Fécamp, St Valery, Honfleur, Caudebec, Bolbec, Criquetot L'Esneval, windy pebbled beaches scoured by the sea, long lines of elms, straight roads travelling through dust to infinity, planes and poplars marching alongside. The hedgerows are creamy with cowparsley, threaded with yellow and purple flowers, wheat billows and rolls in the orange fields of the little sunny valley. Every village, every small town with its spire, its florid Mairie, its scrawled-upon urinal, its glittering gravel roads in the fine August rain. Bowls of pâté in the charcuterie windows, flanked by speckled potted plants, the glass and gilt and baking bread smells of the boulangerie, the cheerful orange and blue plastic buckets in the quincaillerie. And the family smiling, smiling through them all.

– Yes, we were happy sometimes, Julie says slowly: I tend to forget that.

– All the time, Claire corrects her, pressing further photographs on her attention: we are a happy family, we are lucky to have had the times we had. Look at this one, and this.

There are no photographs of children crying, of adults arguing, of people sleepless at night, of people worrying. Julie flicks on to the album's final pages, searching for something.

– But what about the photos of Peckham and Camberwell I sent you? she asks: where are they? Why haven't you stuck them in as well?

– Oh, I don't know, Claire says vaguely, sipping at a glass of water: I don't know what happened to them, I must have put them down somewhere, I don't remember where.

– But you can't have lost them, Julie protests: I sent you a whole lot, the house, me and Bertha, Jenny, the others, I wanted you to have them to keep in your album.

– Why? Claire asks bitterly: you don't care about the family, you think it's dreadful, you think we brought you up all wrong.

– I don't, Julie bursts: it's not your fault, I don't mean that when I criticise the family as an institution –

She breaks off to hand the glass of water back to her mother, who has started coughing again.

– You're so cruel, Claire whispers: where did I go wrong? If I could start all over again, perhaps you would turn out differently.

– I don't, Julie manages to say: want to be different. I'm happy as I am.

– I know you're unhappy, Claire continues: living in that house, no money, no security. I'm so worried about you.

– Why don't you come and see me then? Julie says sharply: I've asked you to, several times. I've got a nice house to live in, a family, you could come and see for yourself.

Claire goes into a paroxysm of coughing. Julie digs her clenched fists into the pockets of her skirt, willing herself not to feel guilty, to hang on to anger.

– You're so cruel, Claire gasps again: of all the hurtful things to say –

– You've been to see Claude once, Julie reminds her: why not me?

– It's too far, Claire says: too expensive, a trip like that.

– Too dirty, Julie explodes at her: my house is, isn't it? Full of lovely dirty women having a good time, and with a room each all for themselves, and not feeling they have to clean up all the time, and sharing the housework and cooking, and having time to themselves, and a good time in bed. You'd like that too, wouldn't you? I've got something you haven't got, and you hate it, it really frightens you –

She stops, shaking in terror. Tears pour down Claire's cheeks.

– Go away, Claire whispers: leave me alone.

– It frightens me too, Julie sobs: I'm not used to it, I'm not supposed to have a good time.

– After all I've done for you, Claire weeps into the pillow: to have to listen to you talking like this.

– I love you, Julie says with a mighty effort: but I get angry with you as well. Can't you understand that?

– I never feel angry with you, Claire says, drying her eyes: I just feel so hurt at the things you say. I tried so hard to be a good mother to you. It hasn't been easy. And then you just turn round and say everything I did was wrong. I suppose I didn't love you enough, that's why you go in for these ideas. I failed you.

– Feminism's about mothers, Julie says despairingly: it's about backing them up –

– You could have fooled me, Claire says with great bitterness: as far as I can see, you hate everything that I believe in.

She lies back against her pillows.

– I don't ask for much. I'm tired now, I need to sleep.

Julie gets up from her chair, picks up the photograph album from where it has fallen on to the floor. She bends down to kiss her mother, wanting desperately to put her arms around her, to be comforted, to be told that bad children can be kissed and made better again. Claire's cheek is icy, she lies with her eyes tightly closed, the lines and the furrows in her forehead tightly marked. Julie lingers at the door, trying to think of something to say, some lie, some bright comment that will name them easy good friends, all rifts healed. No words come. She goes out, carrying the album, and up to her mother's room on the floor above.

The outside of the Oxford house was warmer in autumn, Virginia creeper colouring and softening its ugly gothic contours. In black and white, on glossy celluloid, it stares at her, bleak, and austere. Ben took the photo; Julie cannot remember what she was doing that day, hiding behind the curtain perhaps, and refusing to smile as he fiddled with light meter and lens. She flicks over the pages hurriedly, noting with pain the clenched set of her mouth, the legs plonked awkwardly on garden path or college lawn, her body hidden under clumsy and unattractive clothes. Surely I wasn't always like that, she thinks desperately, there have been times, there must have been, when the expression on my face was open, soft, when I held Bertha easily and smiled at her, when I ran lightly up the stairs two at a time, when I dug the flower garden, when I played netball at school. Jenny. Her fingers are touching the end pages of the album, turning over the loose photos wedged in there. One of Jenny and herself, taken by one of the nuns, she can't remember which, at a half-term holiday at school. They stand beaming against a concrete fence, their arms around each other's necks, dressed in identical pleated skirts, looking for all the world like a pair of twins. She picks up the photograph and juxtaposes it with the view of the Oxford house. That is the house as she remembers it, glowing with Virginia creeper ruddy in the light of early afternoon, Ben outside in the front garden taking photographs, herself persuading Bertha into sleep in the room at the back upstairs. And then Ben's voice calling Julie, Julie, I'll look after Bertha, come down, Jenny's here, come down.

Eleventh section

As they go down the steps of the Oxford house, Julie reaches for Jenny's hand and squeezes it.

– First time I've been out without Bertha for ages. Since the last time you were here, I should think. And you come so rarely. Four visits in three years!

– Can't you get babysitters? I should have thought you and Ben had loads of friends who'd come and help out.

– It's not worth it, Julie says vaguely: now Bertha's older, she's a lot more demanding. It's more trouble than it's worth. You get home and you find that she's been allowed to eat all the wrong things, or to have all her toys out at once and the house is in a complete mess. I can't be bothered any more with all the upheaval, it's easier to stay in.

Jenny squeezes her hand in return and looks for an easier topic.

– Do you remember the walks at school?

– Course I do. I used to fight to walk next to you.

Looking at Jenny, Julie experiences what she always desires to feel: an uncomplicated rush of love. It fastens like loops on to things which can be possessed: the stiffness of Jenny's dufflecoat, navy-blue wool encircling her white throat; her boots plonking with splashes of enjoyment through sodden messes of squelching leaves. Julie cannot enjoy in silence; words must intervene, to stop her from being over-whelmed by pleasure and vanishing into it.

– But you're right. I should do this more often, come out on my own. Makes me feel like a child myself again.

– What about me? Do I have to be mother?

– No. We'll be twins. No parents, just us, running away from home for a good time.

Sky is the blobby blue of a child's water-colour box of paints, the trees wet clear streaks of black. Against, balloon clouds pull. Julie's words are paper boats she launches across ponds.

– Look. The fair's even got an apple-fritter stall. Let's have some.

They walk, munching, teeth stinging on the hot apple mush underneath the crisp outside smearing sugar on their lips. Happiness boils over like fritter fat; you can eat standing up, outside; you can talk with your mouth full; you can eat whatever you like. Any moment now the Virgin Mary will untie her silken girdle, smile reproachfully, regretfully, and lash them. But with daring Julie shouts and Julie sings, kicks at great heaps of fallen leaves. Intent-ness on each other is the thread that draws them through the crowd and always reconnects them, whether they pause at different stalls or merge separately with the bright sea of people washing up and down the street. Arm in arm, and then breaking contact to swoop on a new discovery, Jenny, Jenny, come and see what I've found. They heap presents on one another: gilt rings set with sparkling glass gems; sugar mice; windmills of coloured plastic whirling on sticks; sprigs of heather. Julie recognises people that they pass: other dons' wives mostly, set into family groups and looking curiously at her, arm linked into another woman's, hair and smiles blowing across her face, free hand clutching a carrier bag bursting with toys and trophies. They hurl wooden balls for coconuts, drop rings over spikes to win dolls frothing with tinsel and net skirts, highly glazed ashtrays, baubles of feathers and tin; they shoot for the bull's-eye, ride on the swings.

The organisers of the fair, conscious of the fashion for nostalgia, have acquired a replica of an old steam roundabout with wooden horses sailing up and down. They pay a small fortune for tickets and scramble on. Swoop and soar, swoop and soar, hanging on to a wooden mane with one hand and with the other grabbing for the tassel bobbing above their heads which, when caught, gives them a free ride next time round. Julie is drunk on the motion of rocking;

94

she turns round and shouts to Jenny galloping behind her above the din of machinery and the blare of old-time music.

– We used to go to the fair as kids, years ago, in France. They never had one of these, only the modern sort.

– Wait till we go on the bumper cars. They're the best.

Julie's stomach lurches out of its comfortable rhythm with her horse. When the roundabout slows down all too soon and they get off, she follows Jenny's back in silence, inching their way nearer to the large scaffolding and canvas structure housing the bumper cars. Where the pillars supporting the roof meet the horizontal beams parallel with the floor, there are tacked between them at intervals triangular sections of plywood painted with designs as bright as rainbows. Eight pictures of romance, boy and girl with swelling parted lips, he with black and curling hair, open floppy shirt, tight breeches, his hand always on her arm and his eyes on her flushed cheeks and startling pointed breasts bursting from her low-necked peasant blouse. They pose endlessly around the floor, by rustic fence and windmill, in front of snowy crags, by waterfalls in flowery meadows. Come on, come on, you'll like it when you try it. Their living counterparts are not so different, a noisy crowd of youngsters who strut and push and giggle. Jenny is making for the booth at one side to buy a handful of the plastic discs that operate the cars. Desperate, Julie clutches at her arm.

– Jenny, I don't want to.

– Why not? What's up?

– Because I'm scared, Julie mutters resentfully: I know I'm being stupid.

At the fair in France, the bumper-cars were the big draw. We would go to the fair after dinner, an unheard-of treat for us children to stay up that late and to be out after dark. The men seemed different, they wore their heavy overcoats against the summer night, they treated us like grown-ups, whirling us off for rides, glittering. All the farm labourers were there, in their best blue suits, hair wetted and slicked down. All the usual barriers of class were gone, I was scared of them looking at me, making jokes to each other.

It was the time of the harvest festival. All the men used to celebrate by getting a bit lit up. My father took me on the bumper cars, he was sure I would enjoy it. Everyone on the floor bumped us as much as they could, la jeune Anglaise they kept shouting, they'd grab at my sleeve as they jerked past, and then swing round and hurtle towards us again, to bump le patron and his anglicised daughter. I skated shuddering from one side of the floor to the other, terrified, between their control and my father's. The sides of the car were cut so low I thought I'd break my arm every time we were hit. And Papa kept turning us around so that we'd hit them back, that was the whole point of course. He was so happy, his bad leg didn't matter any more. La jeune Anglaise, all the farm labourers shouted, every time that they hit us.

– It's not fair, Julie starts sobbing: I didn't want to go away to school in England, it wasn't my fault they spent all that money on me. They didn't want me with them any more. It's not fair, whenever I'm in France they all peer at me like some kind of animal in the zoo, and whenever I'm in England they all mutter to each other oh well she's French of course, that explains it. The bastards, all of them, they don't let me belong anywhere.

Jenny puts her arm around Julie. It's such a noisy exuberant atmosphere, it's all right to cry in it, nobody is taking any notice of Julie weeping stormily into the stiff wool of Jenny's dufflecoat.

– We won't go then, that's all right with me.

– You're just saying that, Jenny, you want to go really.

– Don't be daft, I'm saying that I'm not going to drag you on the bumper cars if you don't want to go.

Jenny hugs Julie. It's all right, see? You can cry if you want to, you will not drive me away. Julie can't bear this much acceptance, she feels obliged to stop crying. She turns her head on Jenny's shoulder, sniffing, her lips meeting the soft whiteness of Jenny's neck.

– Come on then, Jenny says: let's go and have a drink instead.

– Hang on a minute, says Julie snorting on tears and mucus: let me blow my nose.

Her eyelids are swollen with violence. She stuffs her handkerchief back into her pocket and picks up the carrier bag, carefully pushing back its spilling contents. Bertha will like to have their spoils to play with.

– All right? Come on then.

The pub is even more crowded than the fairground. Pints of beer are flung backwards and forwards across the marble-topped bar between tap and mouth. The pub is small and warm, crimson plush wallpaper, radiators going full blast. They balance, pressed against each other, exchanging shouted telegrams above the din.

– I hated going away so much. That bloody Channel, I must have crossed it a million times.

– You never told me before. Why ever did they decide to send you away to school in the first place?

– It was my mother's idea. She said an English education was the best. She used to fight with my father about it. She said I'd have more chances that way. It's funny, what it really came down to was that she didn't want me to marry a Frenchman, she had a real thing against them. She was so pleased when I married Ben, she'd always wanted to be a teacher. The English were gentlemen, she used to say to me.

She glances at Jenny, whose face is interested, waiting to hear the next bit. Julie's not used to telling people about herself, she doesn't expect they'll want to listen. She's relieved, she thinks, when two women, pushing towards the bar from behind them, stop when they see Jenny and touch her on the arm.

– Hey, I didn't know you were still in Oxford. What're you drinking?

Their warmth rapidly includes Julie not only as Jenny's friend but as herself; all fight their way over to a window alcove with a fresh round of drinks, to stand squashed up against each other and the burning radiator. Julie treads on a man's foot accidentally in passing. He looks up at her and smiles, no harm done, then as he sees she's with a bunch of women he raises his glass in mock alarm and jokes to his friend. Kate, Hannah and Jenny don't notice him, they are deep in a discussion of the conference they have all just attended, assuming Julie's interest and participation but not halting the animated flow of their conversation so that she can join in. She stands clutching her beer like she used to do at parties, listening to words whose meaning she cannot understand, feeling stupid, hating them. She has not even asked Jenny what the conference was about, she recognises, she has not had time for ideas for a long while now, she has submerged gratefully under the claims of wifedom and motherhood. Now these women are claiming her as their audience, expecting her to speak with understanding of topics she knows nothing about. Rage boils, the word lesbian hits her and she glares at them. The man next to them hears as well, he surveys the little group of women with heightened attention.

Kate, mistaking Julie's response for eager interest, speaks to her, enabling Julie to snap back.

– I don't know. Anyway, I'll have to be going. Time to put Bertha to bed.

– But you said Ben was going to, Jenny protests: he was going to put her to bed, and have dinner ready for us at seven. What's up?

– Nothing, Julie says stiffly: you haven't got children, you wouldn't understand. I can't leave Ben on his own to cope with Bertha, she might start crying or something.

Julie might too. She looks resentfully at the other three, at their ideas from which she feels excluded.

– Come on, Jenny exclaims: you've been telling me all day about how lovely it is to be away from Bertha for a bit, and now you've suddenly decided she'll die without you. Give Ben a chance, he'll never learn about looking after children otherwise.

Jenny's raised voice amuses the men standing next to them. One of them puts his hand on Julie's sleeve.

– Calm down, darling. No need to get upset.

– Naughty girl, says the other man, winking: having a night out with the girls, are you?

She looks from one to the other of them, flustered, smiling placatingly, not wanting to annoy them by rejecting their abrupt entry into the conversation.

– Plenty more fish in the sea, the first man suggests to Julie, enjoying her confusion and the blush which makes her prettier than usual: don't worry about your lady friend. Come over here and have a drink with us.

– We're not interested in talking to you, Jenny says impatiently: leave us alone, will you?

– I'm not talking to you, the second man says angrily: I'm talking to your friend here. Come on, darling, give us a smile.

Julie obeys weakly, not knowing what else to do. She is amazed and frightened when Jenny, Hannah and Kate join in.

– Leave us alone, will you?

– We're not talking to you, d'you mind?

– For Christ's sake, will you go away?

The men grow sulky and cross, their faces reddening, hands clenching their pints of beer.

– What's the matter with you, then? jeers the first: can't get a man, can you?

– Stuck-up bitches, the lot of you, joins in the second: why don't you stick with your own kind?

Julie can't believe her ears: the charmers of a moment ago have turned nasty, their venom directed against her as much as the other three.

– Silly cow, says the first man to her: you don't know what's good for you.

– Oh for God's sake, Jenny says angrily: I'm not listening to any more of this. Come on, let's go somewhere else where we can talk without being interrupted.

She puts down her drink, picks up her coat and marches out. The others follow her, Kate and Hannah sighing humorously as though they were used to such encounters, Julie amazed that they do not shake with grief at the epithets which follow them out of the pub. It's the farmyard, the zoo, the gallery of freaks she appears suddenly to inhabit. The others are smoothing down their ruffled feathers, cawing with laughter. Julie struggles into her coat and wraps it around her. They find another pub down the street. Two rounds later, safe once more, with these women who suddenly are her comrades, her friends, she is emboldened to demonstrate her appreciation of their performance.

– Let's go back to my place, she suggests diffidently: we've got plenty of drink. Ben won't mind. My husband, she explains to Kate and Hannah: is cooking dinner, I'm sure there'll be enough for all of us. I told him I'd be back at seven. It must be way past that now.

They are skilled enough to translate: please behave, please don't be outrageous, he's very nice really, just a bit shy. Cheerfully, they link arms and move off down the street. Jenny has regained her equilibrium, she teases Julie about the reputation for drunkenness and pub brawls of a respectable don's wife. Julie thumps her, it's nearer the truth than you think. Ben's face at the front door is angry at first, where the hell have you been, dinner's ruined, then as he sees Julie's mascara smudged from her tears earlier in the evening, he shows nothing but concern. Jenny, what's she been doing? As the other two women enter his vision and his house, he looks first surprised and then completely blank as Julie explains that these are friends of hers and Jenny's and she is bringing them back to stay the night, they can easily catch trains to London in the morning.

When Julie mentions feminism for the third time in ten minutes Ben pushes his chair back from the table.

– I've had enough, thanks.

And off over to the other side of the room, past the acre of soft white rug where his daughter still grazes happily outside the paddock of grown-up talk in her own concentration on woolly toy, past the bookcases containing besides most of the major works of Marxist historians a not inconsiderable number of books and offprints of articles produced by himself over previous years, past the TV set to the long easy-chair beside the stereo. Legs stretched out, headphones on, body relaxed, the rest of the room cut away to silence, music binding his ears, a language he knows and can think and feel within, jazz bounding his self in safety, syncopating his brain, giving it order and coherence.

His wife is at the other end of the room with those other three. They've been huddling like that all evening, little pools of excited chatter in the kitchen making great clumsy sandwiches to replace his blackened chops; in the bathroom making full use of fresh soap and clean towels after two nights of sleeping on church floors during the conference; on the sofa, cheerfully tipping back the last of the duty-free whisky. All these places he cannot enter. When he approaches and tries to be friendly, after all Julie hasn't seen Jenny for a while and it's only natural they have a lot to talk about and he will do his best to be polite to Jenny's friends though God knows what she sees in them so hostile and unattractive, well, whenever he approaches, they break up their little huddle, draw him in with interest and attentiveness, pity more like, pretend he is one of them. But their little circle has changed, he drops into it heavy as a stone, rocking them with the ripples of his difference and his words. He'll never find out what they talk about without him, he isn't good enough at sneaking up on them unawares.

Look at them now, four witch heads bent together under the lamp and around them darkness. He turns the stereo up to drown their muttering that beats at his heart like fists. They have been brewing and hissing all day, Julie, Julienne stirring them up, showing off, puffing all the accomplishments boiling over in that bloody huge family of hers, and swimming, swimming on new ideas. They are plotting now, those four, drowning him in their bottomless cauldron of woolly subjectivity and hateful sloppy jargon, it is for his own good they tell him that his soul shall be sandpapered and his psychology darned. They are laughing. Christ. He lays aside the headphones, gets to his feet, marches over to Bertha and sweeps her yelling up to bed. It's far too late for a three-year-old still to be up, Mummy'll be up later, I'll read you a story tonight.

He is not completely wrong. Julie has been talking about him, only she feels that it is she who is drowning. In this atmosphere of female warmth and support there is nothing to stop her cracking up completely, letting go once and for all the dazzling personality she has worked at constructing over the years like a master jeweller.

– I still love him, I don't want to stop loving him. What would I do if I did?

She clutches for support at the other three women, unable to stop talking, spilling her personal life like a vegetable soup that simmers from day to day on the back of the stove, the soup stirred by generations of Fanchot women. Suddenly realising that she is starving she feeds herself to the others, she ladles out the soup as though it is the last before winter comes, she presses second helpings upon them, which they accept. She is aghast at the mess of words she spills on the floor. The others are making no attempt to wipe them up, they do not stop her by calling her intense, they are simply leaning forwards, listening.

– Well, I knew I'd be home late, you know what parties are, you can't be sure what time they'll end, so I'd told Ben not to wait up. He usually does, maybe he was hurt I didn't want him to bother, I never thought of that. Well, I crept up the stairs, and then I threw up on the landing. I'm not used to drinking so much, well, I suppose I felt like getting drunk really, I'd had such an awful week with Ben and Bertha both being ill, and someone had brought whisky along as well as wine. So I crept about clearing it up, trying not to make any noise, except I knocked the mop over and that must have woken Ben up, and then I had a shower and went into the bedroom, really tired, you know, all I wanted to do was to fall into bed and sleep it off. And then he said get out. I thought he couldn't mean it, and I did feel a bit guilty, so I crept into bed and just lay there, and then I touched him, wanting him to hug me to show me he didn't feel cross, and then he pushed me so hard that I fell out of bed on to the floor. So I came and slept down here. He was so ashamed in the morning, he didn't want to talk to me, he stayed in bed until it was time for Jenny to arrrive for the weekend. You can still see the bruises – look.

The other three regard the elbow and knee that she displays to the soft lamplight. Hannah stretches out her hand and gently strokes a bruise already turning purplish-yellow.

– You ought to keep bathing it in cold water. Does it still hurt?

Julie snatches her hand away.

– No, it's fine. Don't fuss. I'm not a baby.

Suddenly she does not want to hear any more. No more dangerous sympathy, no thought-provoking criticisms of her situation. She stands up and crosses the floor unsteadily towards the drinks cabinet. She faces them, the empty whisky bottle swinging from one hand.

– Anyone for another drink? No? Then I'll make up your beds and we can all go to sleep.

She does not want them to help her, she will not let them; she dashes about, opening linen cupboards and bringing out piles of snowy sheets despite their protests that they can sleep on blankets, she hauls mattresses, she lays out clean towels. After bidding them goodnight, she lounges at the door.

– Goodnight, you lovely lesbian ladies, she drawls in a camp voice, giggling: don't do anything I wouldn't do, will you?

Jenny looks at her.

– Why don't you sleep down here with all of us? It'd be nice.

– I couldn't do that, Julie says quickly: Ben would be too upset.

On her way to bed, she remembers to look in on Bertha, tidied away from adult conflicts and now curled up asleep, the blanket thrown back, most of the contents of her toybox in the bed with her. Julie bends down to straighten the cover and kiss her daughter's sleeping face. Her own bedroom is dark, Ben's breathing sounding regularly. As she gets into bed and lies down, his voice surprises her.

– You've been drinking again, you terrible woman.

She curls up to him instantly, seeking love and reassurance, joking nervously. At once his hands seize her, seeking to know whether she will reject him or not. She is filled with an ache of loss for the three women downstairs, the words left unsaid; an ache of regret for her own dishonesty. She lies rigid, incapable for once of pretence. As he rolls over away from her again, she catches the words he whispers. Frigid. Lesbian. And she remembers Jenny's words from earlier in the evening: Julie, you are not just a victim. You are a strong woman, you make decisions all the time, you have an effect on people. Don't be so frightened of that. And lies awake, dry-eyed, fighting her anger down, the anger which maims, it seems to her, which damages those she loves.

Twelfth section

Claire Fanchot is preparing for sleep in her bed in the conservatory. Julie is lying in her parents' bed upstairs, in the little room with the sloping ceiling. The bed is wedged into a corner, canopied by the faded sprigs of flowers on the wallpaper. Parallel to the walls, along two sides of the bed run shelves, comfortably within reach. Julien Fanchot's grandfather was an amateur book-binder. Shelves of nineteenth-century volumes march, dictating Julie's dreams all through her childhood: works on natural history and theology by Jesuit scholars in a boarding-school now defunct, school prizes awarded for good attendance and Christian devotion, lovingly bound by their recipient in later years in ugly bindings of half-calf and marbled boards. Other works date from the early years of this century: a uniform edition in publisher's cloth stamped with gilt letters conceals the many adventures of Sophie, naughty girl and heroine for generations of Fanchot daughters struggling between parental love and authority. Between are other objects whose positions have not changed as long as Julie can remember, whose surfaces and shapes she can summon anywhere. A florid bronze and marble inkwell, a small mahogany barometer decorated with gilt curlicues, a set of cider-cups, old and wide-handled, painted in different colours, pink and yellow and blue. Tonight these objects do not comfort her, their security on the shelves, their place unchanged, mocks at the chaos whirling in her life, her head.

Darkness chews the edges of the room, sucking away the washstand, the wardrobe, even the walls. Julie knows she must use the only instruments she has at hand. The first, her parents' room, the second, their bed, the third, great weariness. Sleep, then. You accept that it can happen there, in dreams. You can forget them afterwards if you wish, keep them as a cupboard of escape-maps, or you can remember them, open yourself to yourself, contemplate the wishes and the conflicts that you find intolerable. She slides between the tightly tucked-in bedclothes. Coarse linen sheets glazed finally to smoothness by years of wash and starch and iron, cold on her flesh. Her mother's family initials sewn into one corner brand her cheek.

She is too busy with thoughts to fall asleep, she is too terrified to face them, waking.

She stares ahead at the walls she cannot see. Darkness has always meant loss, been absence. Larger than me, outside me, threatening to enter and devour me so that I too am lost. I struggle to stay visible in darkness. As I do so, I must face the fact that it is peopled with horrifying presences: ghosts, the devil, vampires. Darkness, loss, my mother, Jenny, the house.

I will enter darkness and explore it, before it overwhelms me and I go mad with terror, and lose Jenny, Maman, the house, for ever. Others travel to the East, to map it and explore and bring back booty, explanations. I choose a different voyage, out into the yawning black shed at the end of the farm courtyard to shovel coal and face the horror lurking behind the door, all hands. I will go upstairs to the attics where there are no lights and rummage through old suit-cases, turning over old letters and school exercise books, trying not to notice how the candle flickers, giant shadows lurching on the wall. I will go down into the cellars, past the back door where the intruder hovers, the butcher with his gleaming knife upraised, past the cupboard where my fingers brush over unrecognisable and terrifying surfaces. That game we used to play at Christmas, sitting in the dark. My father acts the ghost of Tutenkhamen, wrapped in a white sheet, his voice sepulchral. He passes to us objects we cannot see. This is the liver, the eye, of Tutenkhamen. A cold brussels-sprout, a peeled grape, domestic items transformed by our imaginations. The grown-ups squeal with self-indulgent fright, Claude and I shudder, haunted for weeks afterwards.

I remember going home from school for Christmas. We are put to sleep in the afternoon of Christmas Day, we need a rest after being up so late at Midnight Mass the day before. Coming home from Mass in the dark, by car, a special treat in winter weather. The trees pale cardboard cut-outs sucked backwards in an endless strobe, same white telegraph pole a hundred times, the headlights filled suddenly with a bird smashing silver blood on to the windscreen. Blackness on the road may be pits, or merely shadows, the car drowns a thousand times between cobblestones. Back home there is black pudding to eat, pigs' blood in a sausage mixed with herbs, roast goose to tear apart with delicate silver forks. The struggle not to fall asleep afterwards, in order to catch the Père Noel creeping up the stairs with presents. I hear my mother's voice clearly, on the stairs, a whisper carrying a giggle and an intimacy I do not wish to catch, Julien, sssh, your great boots, for Heaven's sake, you'll wake them up. Sleep, to drown curiosity. Next day, the rest before the evening meal and party. Odd, to be in bed in the daytime, my lack of a nightgown demonstrating that it is not night. The eiderdown chilly on my bare arms reminds me of my bare flesh. I move my limbs experimentally against the bedclothes, understanding that nakedness can contact other surfaces beyond itself. Free time, not necessarily to be filled with eating, walking, playing to order. Like the charms of illness, the bed freshly made, orange juice as much as I wish, my mother sensitive doors away to my despotism. Sitting up with me to tell me stories, wiping my vomit and kissing me better, enchanting me with her smell and her nearness, foregoing on my behalf her bed, her sleep, her husband. My desires are not fulfilled even by this; I become a sleepwalker. At the door of my parents' room a ghost with a face as round and white as a moon, a breast, forbids my entry. And afterwards bobs endlessly, without a head, up and down the stairs.

Julie sits up in bed, heart banging. Switches on the bedside lamp, grabs for a cigarette. Take it easy, go at your own speed. There are other nights beside this one. Let yourself remember things because you want to, because you've decided to.

The weekend mornings are the best times. Before they'd decided to send me away to school. My mother in her pink woolly dressing-gown, her beautiful deep-set eyes surrounded by smudges of tiredness, lines in the soft skin. Her hair is rumpled and uncombed, her body relaxed. We eat biscottes together, smearing them with the apple jam my father makes. I am allowed tea, some of her precious store

brought by visitors from England, weak, with a generous splash of
boiled milk. Every cup of strong yellow tea at convent school
reminds me of that, the milk tasting so different, and my mother
there, open and accepting, there all for me, before it is time for her
to bath and dress and become a farmer's wife once more, the flesh
straightened under an overall, the mouth painted into a bright
smile, the eyes careful and hard-working again. So much work for her
to do, despite the help of Suzette Cally, housework, laundry, mending
and sewing, the preparation of hefty meals to oversee twice a day for
the ravenous farm labourers. I sulk when breakfast is over at being
made to help with the housework, it is the work of women, not mine.
No praise for my reluctant labour, and Claude freed to play outside
after he has performed his one task of stacking wood at the side of the
fireplace.

It takes me over an hour to dust the salon, all the curlicues of
carved wood adorning the furniture, the complicated legs of chairs,
the surfaces clotted with ornaments and photographs, all fragile, to
be moved one at a time and then put back. I travel slowly, angrily
swiping at dust. I have circled this room a hundred times, at first
patiently, seeking an exit somewhere, anywhere, between two soup
tureens, behind the firescreen, through a mouse-hole in the shabby
skirting-board, and then faster, my legs entangled in lace curtains,
my mouth smothered by sofa cushions, my eyes poked out by
knitting-needles, until I am shooting from one wall to another,
violent with panic, my bruised and torn flesh smearing blood along
the striped silk wall-paper, along picture-rails, underneath silver
photograph frames. When my mother enters, exhausted from the
kitchen, she is grieved at my sullenness. Running her finger through
the gouts of blood, patiently she commands me to begin all over
again.

Julie gets out of bed, perhaps all she needs is a piss, the physical
relief will let her sleep. Once up, she cannot let herself go back to
bed. It is too far, too dark, to venture to the lavatory down the
landing, she uses the china pot kept behind a flowered curtain at the
other end of the room. As she emerges from the little cubicle still
smelling of lavender-water, she catches sight of her reflection in the
glass-fronted wardrobe, haggard, glassy eyes staring, a couple of
pimples on her forehead. To escape herself, she wrenches the wardrobe door open, so that the mirror swings out of sight against the wall.

The cupboard contains her mother's clothes. Suits and dresses
crowded on racks; hat-boxes; rows of shoes. The smell is rich: moth-

balls, her mother's scent, a carton of Gitanes kept for special occasions. Julie sniffs guiltily, remembering former times in childhood when she sneaked up here, to crouch on the wardrobe floor under the swinging coat-hangers and their silk and cotton burdens. Like the church festivals, allied to them, her mother's clothes divide her daughter's year, neatly as the parish priest's vestments and no less splendid in Julie's eyes. The dark blue woollen frock worn at Christmas-time, the black and white polka-dotted nylon swirl for family marriages in summer, the long bunchy yellow cotton skirt that means July and trips to the patisserie to buy pink and green ice-creams; the two tweed skirts, one brown, one green, that alternate throughout the working winter months; the cotton shifts sprigged with flowers that cover the body labouring in summer. The evening dress. Julie suffocates again within its stiff purple and silver folds. Smoothing them, she remembers the night once a year when her mother used to go to the Farmers Ball with Julien, her arms and shoulders bare. The child helps her mother dress, tongue protruding with effort as she hooks up the back of the boned bodice, powders the neck and shoulders with a swansdown puff and dusts them down, sprays scent behind the ears, pins the flowers at a becoming angle on the corsage, holds out the purple and silver shoes. Claire stands at the top of the stairs for a moment, then she bunches up her skirts in either hand and walks carefully down, the dress billowing back at her in the narrow space. Julie notices how red her mother's elbows are, and is angry with her for not being an unflawed beauty; she cannot understand why her mother wears the same frock year after year. But she sniffs her scent, and looks at her arms and shoulders above the tight brocade, and hands her her long silver gloves, her little silver bag, her short fur cape smelling faintly of mothballs with two claws dangling over Claire's breast. Julien is proud of Claire, so proud; delicately, he takes her arm and lays it on his, before ushering her through the door and handing her into the battered 2CV Citroen as though she were the harvest queen herself.

Next to the plastic-covered fur cape in the wardrobe is a black suit, an old-fashioned one, that Julie glances at and passes quickly by. A blue smock patterned with grey flowers, in which Julie buries her face, overcome with sudden desolation. She understands that much, that her mother is away from her, downstairs, even though the room up here is filled with her: her battered pale blue leather writing case and address book; her stack of ancient copies of *Le Temps des Femmes* preserved for their sewing and knitting patterns; her missal with silver flowers embossed on the cover; her inlaid jewellery box containing her Norman cross, paste diamonds slung from a black velvet ribbon. All these objects name Claire insistently as Julie does not wish her to be named; as mother also of Claude, as wife of Julien, as worker, as private person who lies awake sometimes and thinks her own secret thoughts.

If Claire rings her little bell, it will mean that she too is awake, in need of comfort and companionship. Perhaps she has rung the bell already, without being heard. Julie opens the bedroom door, pads barefoot down the stairs, the worn stubbly carpet sliding against her soles. The door to the conservatory is shut; no chink of light shows beneath it. But from inside, from behind the closed partition and the fastened catch, come voices, those of Julien and Claire.

Julie is sitting on the bottom step of the stairs, fists clenched in her lap, head bent and eyelids tightly shut. This is how she travels on her journey through her past, hunched, and miserable, and mainly on her own. Memories of a baby crying in a dark room, and it is late, nobody comes, nobody comes. She has been abandoned; she screams, growing more and more terrified of her anger that nobody can help her to quench because they are so terrified of it themselves.

If I cannot be a saint, so perfect that I need never suffer or know the pain of loss, then I will be the Devil. I cannot be trapped any more into feeling lack of my mother or anyone; I have another personality at my disposal. I am clothed in silver and purple, my nails are long, my face is loathsome, sprouting with ugly hairs and blossoming with scars and rashes. I am decadent and superb, rotten with ill-health, too many cigarettes, the wrong kind of food, jumping with caffeine and alcohol in my blood, unkempt and filthy. Nobody dares to name me woman, for I am dangerous and powerful. I can make others go mad too, just by desiring them. I cause storms and migraines, I turn milk sour, I am both the ruined harvest and the shameful blood that sickens cattle. I am the witch whom you call your crazy daughter. You tell me I am mad; I tell myself that, every time I weep, my face blotched red, every time I scream to touch the silk of your breast and lay my head there. Ben understood that I was the crazy woman, loved and feared at a distance. I did not harm him, I warned him about myself, and he understood. He gave me words with which to define myself: socialist, incorrect practice, finds sex difficult. From him I learned again what I had always suspected: only I can give myself what I want, solitude, silence, sleep. Now I need nobody. Do not dare to love me: I am dangerous, I wound, I maim. I am wounded, I am maimed, I am lost, I am lonely.

Julie wrapped in her bedspread breaks all the rules of years ago, sits on the stairs and cries softly outside her mother's room. The nice girl, the bad mad girl cries all through the night, she cries herself awake, towards death, towards remembering.

Thirteenth section

Julie's husband's great-great-how-very-great aunt is a legend in the family. Travelled alone in south-east Asia she did, alone meaning no man, for she had her companion with her, Miss Amy Sickert, who handled the money, organised the lodgings and in the photographs looks understandably harassed. Julie's ancestor by marriage, let us call her Harriet while remembering all the greats that go before, stares forward splendid and grim. She is one of the foremost travellers and anthropologists of the country, of the age. She knows exactly where she wants to go and gets there majestically by junk or palanquin.

Julie will be travelling as do lesser mortals, on the bus. She too is on a voyage of discovery, she is brave and full of confidence, she is facing the streets as a woman on her own, she is a little crazy with freedom. In fact she is in flight from her husband and is wishing for a divorce; she has sold Aunt Harriet's Balinese ring that goes to the eldest son's wife of each generation, and is abandoning herself and her child to a women's commune in south-east London. The first fact upsets Ben, the second and third outrage him as she intends them to.

The Oxford bus station is a series of railed-in enclosures like cattle pens, bounded by the backs of pubs, the bleak façade of the cinema, a hot dog stall. Buses hurtle in and out of narrow parking-spaces, passengers dodge to and fro and bunch in shivering queues as the March wind collects the city's refuse and chucks it at their ankles. Julie's luggage, three suitcases and a clutch of paper carrier bags, sags at her feet. Her daughter Bertha, nearly four, sucks with determination at a gristly hot dog, a peace-offering and a bribe offered by the guilty Julie to keep her quiet. In her hands Julie holds a fat book bound in leather, the journal written by Miss Amy Sickert during a voyage with Harriet to Siam and Laos, rescued by Julie from her in-laws' attic and rejected by her husband as material unsuitable for a monograph. Julie has not cared till now to recognise her loneliness. She eats Miss Amy Sickert's confidences with her eyes, her hand restraining Bertha from falling off the kerb and her ears pricked for the wheezing engine of the bus. This, she reads,will be my private journal, for my eyes alone. Elsewhere I take notes at Harriet's dictation; here I shall be able to fulfil my need to record my own observations, with no fear of ridicule of spelling or of style.

The samlor is made of tin, brightly painted. It hurtles up the newly-built Sukhumvit Road and around Patumwan Circle. On either side the klongs of Bangkok slap, brown waters giving back rich smells of garbage and fallen flowers to the damp and sticky dusk. Harriet and Amy, crammed into the tiny back seat, hang on to the sides, every muscle clenched against an accident. Harriet commands the driver to hurry, for they are late and she does not wish to miss her train. The samlor driver shrugs, but cracks his whip over his horse's head. His body is smaller and more relaxed than theirs. They watch him enviously as he leans from side to side at corners, shouting jokes and greetings to other passing samlor drivers. On the back of his seat he has hung a pink silk antimacassar; dangling from the roof is a gilded buddha, a coloured portrait of the Royal Family framed in plush, a jasmine garland, the small white flowers intricately knotted on to coloured ribbon. The samlor is his home; at night he parks it in one side street or another, to be in reach both of possible passengers and of the beginnings of the slums in the swamps where his family lives, their shack balanced on a plank laid over the mud. Driven by semi-starvation from the forests in the north after several bad harvests, he has come to make his fortune in the city of Bangkok. Foreign capitalists are pouring in to the country, banks begin to rear higher than the temples dedicated to the Buddha, rich foreigners are in need of servants, cooks and gardeners. Harriet lays her hand on Amy's, her touch a reassurance against the break-neck speed at which they are jolting along. Amy can only nod. The heat and wet gag her like a hot towel, sweat crawls in unmentionable places under her dark dress. She cannot cope with trying to sort out the sights and smells and sounds they are hurtling through.

Bertha is jumping up and down it's here it's here the bus come on. All the other passengers are surging forwards, to grab the best seats, cram the luggage racks with parcels and leave no room for anybody else. No-one likes sitting next to a child on public transport, Julie knows, they fear the whines and the interruptions, sticky fingers on their newspapers, demands for sweets, the lavatory, to be sick. Julie creeps to the back of the bus, where she and Bertha will be well out of the way. Desperate in front of stony glares, she packs their myriad carrier bags underneath their seat and her feet, a rampart to pro-claim to everyone she will not make a fuss or be a nuisance, and that nobody should bother her by sitting next to her. Of course she doesn't mind, she tells the last passenger to climb on the bus who parks himself beside her. He is middle-aged and fatherly, he clucks at Bertha burrowing for sleep in Julie's lap. Julie smiles weakly at him and then dives for privacy into her fat red book.

Harriet and Amy take the slow overnight steam train from Bangkok to the river frontier with Laos. They eat fried rice in a dining-room with brass and mahogany fittings and a vase of flowers riveted to each table. As the train gathers speed, dahlia petals fly in the soup. Later, in the swaying communal washroom, Amy, modestly reaching with her flannel underneath her voluminous dressing-gown, watches a Chinese woman clean her teeth, spitting expertly into the porcelain basin from three feet away. She clutches her pillow in her narrow bunk, missing her usual goodnight embrace from Harriet; the train rocks them separately to sleep. Next day they sit in the bar of the Constellation Hotel in Vientiane, daringly drinking imported French pastis and smoking yellow French cigarettes. Harriet is enchanted by the cultural mix; she exclaims to Amy on the charm of finding wine and croissants in a place like this. They toast each other and their surroundings; they are in the field at last. The bar is long, with a zinc top, on which stand baskets of hard-boiled eggs, a tin calendar with a painting of an elephant. Chinese enamel spit-toons are on the floor. Men stride in and out in a preoccupied manner, glancing at the two women on their own as they pass. In the brightly-lit bar across the street you can taste music like hot and bitter chocolate in your mouth; inside a bamboo cage at three in the afternoon Suzy Cherie sways her hips and breasts. She moves out, among the audience, she dangles her brocade girdle from one hand, her cunt rotating two inches from your hot face and her tiny foot planted indifferently in your lap. Amy and Harriet are equally conscious of the men surrounding and passing them; they raise their chins, lower their voices, tap their cigarettes too frequently on the massive china ashtray.

Julie's neighbour and Bertha are asleep, both with flushed faces and open mouths, Bertha still clutching her hot dog, the man resting his hands under the newspaper spread across his lap. The thick glass windows of the bus cannot be opened by passengers, which makes the sun pressing on Julie's face uncomfortably hot. She feels sticky, and would like to move her legs, but does not want to wake Bertha.

Harriet and Amy have travelled north to Luang Prabang, risking life and limb, they are told, to go there on their own. They ride beneath massing clouds; on either side the hills are green and furry as durian fruit. They sit under a tree half way up the hill on which the little town is built. The soldiers are on parade in their toy-sized barracks far below. The hill is crowned with a chedi topped with chimes made of leaves of tin, as thin as paper, that rustle and tinkle in the gentle wind. Harriet dictates notes on the initiation ceremonies of Buddhist nuns; Amy remembers for her own journal that women do not have souls and must therefore await a higher rebirth. Cocks crow, crickets rustle, lizards flicker. A white staircase snakes down one side of the hill, broad white treads lacy with sun, littered with fallen pods and flowers. On the other side, the steps are steeper, and the balustrade all the way down is a dragon's back. The river encloses the hill on two sides so that they feel they are on an island. The hillside drops with sunshine, the terrace where they sit is shaped like a slice of melon, a formal garden with no-one in it but themselves. Harriet smiles, five thousand pompous buddhas shatter, gold leaves tinkle, cannons thump further away. They have drunk the last bottle of wine in town for lunch; Amy begins to fall asleep. Now the only movements she is dimly aware of are those of sun and shadow on stone, one beetle jumping on another with a buzz and a glint, the only sound the occasional burst of trumpets from the barracks below. Ants run slowly over her skin, in search of crumbs of bread and splashes of wine, heaps of newly-mown grass dry sweetly in the sun. A man is climbing up the steps, she can hear his boots disturb the litter of curled and slowly cracking leaves. He pauses for a moment to survey the two women lying amidst cushions and note-books and baskets, and then she hears his voice addressing Harriet.

– Excuse this intrusion, ma'am. I believe I have seen you at the hotel in Vientiane. My card, ma'am, John Barclay, at your service. You dropped a shawl on your way up here. I have followed you to return it. I beg you to let me know if I can be of any assistance.

Amy opens her eyes. His boots are thick, like a tradesman's she thinks disparagingly, but then her eyes reach his and she knows him for a powerful man, an enemy, whose eyes looking back at her say women alone, say war, say danger, and protection.

Julie takes a chance and wriggles in her seat, slowly, one buttock at a time shifting on the sticky plastic, moving Bertha's weight from one leg to the other, sighing with relief. Her elbow touches that of her neighbour. He opens his eyes and looks at her.

– I'm sorry, she murmurs with contrition for herself, no way to escape speech now it seems: I didn't mean to wake you.

– Not at all, young lady, pardon me, I should say, er, miss, looking at her bare left hand with his moist brown eyes.

– I'm not married, Julie replies defiantly, clutching Bertha closer on her lap.

– Indeed, he says, looking at the sleeping child.

Julie's eyes go back to her book, but she can feel his eyes still on her. Just pretend there's nothing wrong, there's nothing happening. There's no need to get upset, he's only being friendly. Relax. Stop being so suspicious.

John Barclay comes to visit Harriet and Amy in their hotel, a small stone and plaster building in the middle of the little town. They watch the river, flat and brown and muddy, sliding below, and the sun hitting it at evening, a slow dazzle of silver on mud. Green shutters open into their ground-floor room with white plastered walls, sun like a hot cloth on the tiled floor. Their sun-hats hang from the pillar in the middle of the room and their clothes from wooden hooks behind the door. They sit outside, all three, drinking warm tea from a tin teapot, on the little verandah. John Barclay invites them both to dine with him, mindful of propriety, asking Amy as chaperone. His eyes bent on Harriet indicate this, so Amy pulls her rattan chair back a little, into the cool of the shadows that the setting sun cannot reach. John Barclay describes the hotel where he is staying, the other hotel in town, larger than this one, with a stone roof not a thatched one, and run by Frenchmen, not Chinese. He tells them what he will order for dinner: steaks, large and red and juicy. He has a French newspaper brought up from Vientiane; he reads them descriptions of the developments initiated by the French in Indo-China. And they will eat steak tonight, French-cooked steak, the bleeding corpses of the Indo-Chinese, mashed, and minced, and powdered with shot. Amy clamps her hand to her mouth, rises to her feet and hurries indoors, is violently sick. Harriet is indulgent of her companion, gives her smelling salts, takes her to lie down on the high wooden bed. Amy must rest, she is not yet a seasoned traveller, she is unused to the heat.

Julie's companion winks at her. Then, sure he has entrapped her attention, he slowly lifts his newspaper. His prick is as grey as the worn newsprint, long and wrinkled, with a bulbous end; he holds its in one hand to keep it wobblingly erect.

– Go on, he whispers: miss, hold it, sshh now, or you'll wake the little girl.

Julie stares at his prick with fascination, offered to her as business-like as a bus ticket. She can see the veins, purple and tense beneath the skin, and the thick eggy drop of semen trembling on the tip. Yes, very serviceable, she wants to say, but thank you, I've got something of my own a bit like it already, I don't feel like another one now. She is terrified. He is smiling. But will he still smile if she screams for help? He could have a knife in his pocket, anything. Sweat courses under her armpits. She glances around, to see whether any of the other passengers has noticed and will come to her aid. She is paralysed by the fact that they are moving, bumping along through the west London suburbs. Everyone else in the bus is slumped half-asleep. Screaming means shattering the silence, arresting motion, making a fuss, disturbing people, exposing her inability to control an event she is imprisoned by. She has her arms tightly wrapped around Bertha, but she is trying to derive comfort, not give it, and wants to yell at Bertha for recognition of what is happening, as though her child were suddenly adult, as though she were a pro-tecting army. Yet at the same time frantic for her not to wake, not to see what is happening. Surely you do not wish to harm the child? Meaning both of us. The bus hurtles onwards, lurching on its gears through the rush-hour traffic. The drop of semen wobbles. Julie watches it with concentration, somehow, as long as it does not fall off they will be all right. If you walk on the cracks in paving-stones a tiger will get you; keep your fingers crossed when you pass by the idiot boy, he wags his head and dribbles but he will not hurt you. If only Jenny were here now. The man smiles at her and whispers.

– Come on miss, be a good girl now, just hold it, will you?

One two buckle my shoe, three four suck me some more, five six big fat pricks, seven eight copulate, nine ten I hate men.

Amy walks down the winding path towards the river at dusk, veiled and shawled against mosquitoes and the curious gazes of people passing by. Here, the river is wide, with sandspits jutting out into the water. A flight of shallow stone steps leads down to the water's edge, shaded by the overhanging fronds of trees growing on the bank. Here come the women at sunset, to bathe their children and themselves. They do not seem to mind Amy sitting hunched and quiet on one side. They occupy themselves with the children, carefully taking off their patchwork trousers, the black scarves wrapped around their heads, their scarlet sashes fringed with bobbles, their silver necklaces. The women bathe with modesty and grace. They rise, hold their children by the hand, walk down to the river's edge, scoop brown water over themselves with silvered tin scoops, splash the children, laughing. They wade into the river and stand waist-deep, turning round and round, watching the sun slowly set. When they come out, their sarongs cling to them, almost transparent. They reach for the dry sarongs they have brought with them, drop them over their heads, step out of the wet ones, quickly twist the new sarongs around their bodies underneath the arms. Impatiently they call to the children, collect up their bowls, climb the steps again towards the town. Amy stands now on the bottom step, in the dark, smelling the brown water, smelling refuse and jasmine, and far away, in the distance, she hears the boom of guns.

Julie reaches out her hand, not knowing what else to do. For months afterwards she cannot pass the hoarding advertising Baby-cham outside the west London bus-station in Earls Court Road without feeling sick. She'd love a Babycham stop shamming baby wham bam thank you ma'am. At her touch the prick droops limp and small, a few drops of semen blurting on to the newspaper. Carefully, the man folds his paper over and pushes it into his bag on the floor. He is God, giving a signal to the universe; suddenly the bus swings into the station forecourt, passengers wake, stretch, and begin to sort out their belongings, impatient, grumpy. Julie rouses Bertha, giving her a sweet to console her for the abrupt awakening, while her neighbour settles back into his seat and appears asleep once more. Clambering over his legs with her bursting carrier bags, Julie catches sight of a red scarf in the distance, the rescuing army waving its flag much too late.

– Come on Bertha, come on darling, there's Jenny come to meet us.

The morning before Amy and Harriet's departure from Laos, the women of Luang Prabang make offerings to the spirits for their safe return. They bind their hands with crêpe ribbons and place lighted candles between them; they float little palm leaf coracles out on to the river laden with wreaths of flowers and twists of foliage. When Amy wades bare-legged in the river that night, her skirts pulled up around her waist, some of the coracles are still afloat, bobbing against her ankles at the shore. Her legs push the water back in front of her, moonlight spattering her hair, a dark and thickly tangled bush flowering suddenly with silver. Even when she is out of the water the moonlight sticks to her toes, so that she fancies she can trace Harriet's name with one foot in the grass. Harriet stands farther up the bank, calling for her, blocking out the moon, dissipating the creamy froth at Amy's feet. Next morning, in the sun, Harriet's face is furred with gold. They walk in silence towards the waiting samlor, Amy's old straw hat slung from her shoulders by a raffia string, Harriet's red and purple skirt flattening against her legs in the wind. John Barclay is waiting for them by the samlor. He does not belong to this place; he will give them no more time. There's little time for them to do more than simply pick up their bags and climb aboard. He gives them ten seconds for their eyes' farewells, before telling the driver to go. He settles back against the cushions, looks at Harriet and asks her in a kindly tone about the success of her trip.

– Hang on love, just a second, I think I ought to let Ben know I've arrived safely, I'll send him a telegram, it's only fair, he might be worried. When Julie returns from the post office across the road and gets into the borrowed van where Jenny waits for her with Bertha, she sees a women's liberation sticker on the dashboard. Angrily she picks at it.

– You were late, she bursts: why were you late?

Jenny turns her head to stare at her.

– No I wasn't. I was there waiting when the bus came in. What's the matter?

You were not with me when I left. I had to do my leaving on my own. There was a space, between Ben's outstretched hands and yours, through which I had to travel on my own. No-one to tell me what to do, no-one to comfort me. My head down, my eyes lowered as I crept along, my only luggage silence, and passivity.

– Nothing, Julie says: I'm tired, that's all.

That night she undresses slowly, luxuriating in a large room all of her own, in which she can do just as she pleases, Bertha asleep next door, Jenny across the landing. Her clothes are not many, and she enjoys removing them: a rough navy woollen jumper with a deep V-neck, a wide cotton navy skirt reaching below her knees, scarlet tights, flat blue espadrilles. She gets into the wide double bed, pleased at the ample space she can turn and spread her body within, scissoring out her legs under the cool quilt, rolling from pillow to pillow to test their softness, floating between clean sheets that someone else, not herself for once, has washed. Her eyes caress the desk, the bookshelves, now her own, for her own work. The desk has a secret drawer Jenny has shown her how to open by touching a concealed spring at the back. Inside the secret drawer are photographs, of Jenny, Bertha and Claire, and the fat red volume of Miss Amy Sickert's diary.

Julie never went down that part of the cloister leading off from the chapel into the convent. It goes straight for a few yards, and then bends round a corner into blackness. There's a small garden there, and a ten-foot high crucifix. As a postulant, Sister Veronica spent five hours in front of it every day. Now, on her wedding-day, Sister Veronica's hair shows underneath the drift of her veil; it's a dark cloud of seaweed around her pale and drowning face. The prettiest of the other postulants holds her train; the Daughters of Mary, the Imeldists, the Handmaids of the Blessed Sacrament and the Agnesians, their medals on red cords around their necks, toss rose petals in front of the chaplain who enters bearing his God-burden. Sister Veronica kneels at his feet; he bends his red face towards her and whispers that she shall become the angel of God's home and his.

Sister Veronica's hair is cut off with a pair of gold scissors; she lies arms outflung on the cold marble slab. They cover her with a black cloth, they speak of her death to the world, they sing with joy of her rebirth in Christ. The wedding breakfast is shared by all the nuns: meat pies, sausages, bacon and ham.

Fourteenth section

Being on a bicycle is perfect. You are safely in control, setting your own speed, responsible only for yourself, able to accelerate out of trouble, slide up on the inside of traffic queues, beat buses away from traffic lights. Riding at night is best, it is the nearest thing to flying, Julie thinks, as she flees through the silent city. Empty trains rattle over bridges, their din crushing her head; she speeds out from under them and down long hills in gladness, the air streaming behind her like hair, cool on her face after the blazing day, with a hint of wetness.

The smells are different at night, fewer, and stronger. The daily stifling ration of exhaust fumes has lifted, and in its place she catches the suggestion of flowers soaked in heat, of the oil and dirt and barges smell of the river. In the daytime she races through pot-pourri: rotting fruit, sweat, petrol, perfume, dust, garlic, hot bread, rubber, tar, each neighbourhood identifiable by its particular combination of smells. The pavements toss them back at her to be caught when she is already past. Julie's bicycle runs along straight lines from north to south, confined by streets; her body and her head connect to farther places. Sweat curls down her back, and immediately she is flooded with memories of every other time she has been this hot, opening and letting go to sweat, her body coated with water, melting into the air. Lying in a punt with Ben, their hands sticky with picnic food and wine, flat on her back under a black sky and his face, the black silk river sliding underneath, the punt tipping over the edge of the world. Into heat and wet she mixes other memories, triggered by the iconography of particular streets, and tints them like old photographs with fantasies of what she most desires.

She dreams of a house built of wood, cracked and shrunken planks creased with flaking white paint. Aunt Harriet and Miss Amy Sickert have given her a cupboard room under the stairs to sleep in, just large enough to take a mattress on the floor. She lies on it and gazes through the walls made of wire netting to keep mosquitoes out. The garden jungles at her, greenness thrusting fresh tendrils after the beating rains. She lights a mosquito coil and drifts into sleep, sliding through the wire netting into the sharp green world beyond. In the morning she wakes early, the chilly air before the sun is lapping all around her skin where she has thrown off the worn cotton sheet in the night. The house rocks over the pond, its slender wooden pillars thrusting down through lilies and water weeds, a green and patterned floor. Above the pond flash kingfishers and spangled insects; beneath it can be seen the flick and curl of fish. She comes in very slowly from sleep, her body slightly warmer than the morning air registering the difference, every surface taking messages of touch. The coolness is intensely pleasurable, an air sweet and chilly as the wet apples in the garden in Peckham, and Julie loves this especially about it: the subtle changes from warm to chill, the one suggesting the other by contrast.

While the coolness lasts, she stays in her half-sleep, turning over in it like a sea and floating on it, her body slowly becoming the air. And then Jenny enters, and slides between Julie's body and the sheets, holding her lightly at first and then enclosing her, her fingers moving across her skin. Julie's insides dissolve to sweetness, her body touches Jenny's all over, they rush forwards towards each other in an urgent mutually-speaking flow. Words here can be of no use, where the ebb and flow of selves is through the body, that most powerful and delightful game around the other lost and reappearing; now lost, now found in another; now joined as one, now separate. Each moves towards the other in violent waves of desire; each can experience the most extreme openness and acceptance, while the other rushes in headlong like a bee to suck at blossom. They rise and fall around each other, delighted at their capacity to recognise, meet, blur, and overlap, and then distinguish separateness again. They fight and balance as equals, their mutual engagement hurling them to violence and tenderness.

The smallest thing can bring you back. Turning the corner of her own street and slowing down, Julie feels a change in the air; there is a chill under the wide shapes of chestnuts, their green is a sudden weight of darkness, the dusk in the corners by the steps glittering as though with frost. Years ago, coursing on rapid plimsolls through the black streets behind the Elephant and Castle home from piano lessons to cocoa alone in the huge convent kitchen, counting the rows of silent bells strung along the walls in iron curls like notes of music. Years ago, pacing up and down the wide street outside college, trying to make up her mind to face being alone in her room, one of twelve spaced along the corridor sealed away behind black oak doors. If she died in that room, no-one would find her for days. She makes the experiment, and is found.

The front door of the Peckham house is painted gold. As Julie puts her key in the lock she remembers again the convent. Nights when she still wakes up to a black nun crouched at the end of her bed, and when she looks at it, her own face gleaming back. It was Julie who insisted they paint the front door gold. I'm not going to live in this morgue of black paint, this shall be my seventh heaven and you, Bertha, the dirtiest, most ragamuffin angel that I ever saw.

The door is pulled open from the inside. It's Jenny, smiling. She hugs Julie and then looks at her.

– What's up?
– Nothing.

Julie speeds into the kitchen, spilling jacket and bag across the floor, holding her hands towards the flame under the kettle. She shivers.

– It's so cold and dark outside.
– You must be mad. It's so hot out there I came in to get cool again.

Julie shrugs.

– Is there anything to eat?
– Food's in the fridge. Louise cooked. And there's salad, I picked some more lettuces from the garden.

Jenny wipes her earthy hands on her jeans. Her arms and shoulders are brown as eggs, she looks pleased with herself.

– My vegetable love. That's all you can think of, you, lettuces.

Forty thousand of them out there and you're planning to sow more. I tell you, we should have planted flowers as well. We shall have lavender and hollyhocks next year, and dahlias and London Pride, and a weeping willow and an arbour dripping with roses and a pool stocked with carp, and in the middle of it all a fine vast statue of woman in struggle.

– There are loads of flowers out there, you know that. What's up?

Julie falls into a chair. Jenny's words have touched her and tears rise to keep them at bay.

– Nothing. Oh, I don't know, I had a nightmare last night, the nun again.

A few weeks ago Jenny, hearing her cry out in the night had come to comfort her, taking Julie's body into her arms and rocking it until the tears had stopped. She is hurt now, and lets Julie see it.

– Idiot, why didn't you come and wake one of us up?

– You can't tell people every time you're feeling down. Everyone feels awful sometimes. I can't assume my problems are worse than anyone else's, I've got to learn to cope.

– Julie, if you could just hear yourself. Moan moan. I'm nastier than anyone in the whole world. Nobody loves me and I won't give them a chance. Keep away from me. Unclean, unclean . . .

Julie rolls a burnt match on the flowered kitchen tablecloth and mutters.

– Sometimes I wish I were a robot, a nice silver robot all oiled brain and no feelings. Press a button and I will shake your hand but never weep.

– Julie, oh, you fucking idiot.

Julie bangs her hands on the tablecloth, making the match jump on to the floor. Her voice surprises her with its anger.

– I am not mad, I am not an idiot, do you hear?

Jenny's arms wrap Julie.

– All right, you're not, I'm sorry. But there's all this tension between us these days, and when I ask you, you never tell me what you're feeling.

Thou God seest me, into my heart, my secret places. Girls, never do anything that you would be ashamed to let the Virgin Mary see. Your heavenly father knows what His child wants, long before you tell Him. I know what you want, my silly angel, of course you want to get married, every woman does.

– Julie, listen to me. I know what I want. I want you. But I don't know what you want. You'll have to tell me.

We both want the same thing. Is that allowed? Love is a battle, the strongest wins. Is there enough for both of us? My hunger terrifies me; you must be strong enough to cope with me, all my difficulties and my fears. I cannot love someone as weak as myself. There will be rows, misunderstandings, I will be angry, I will damage you. I will leave you unless you are always strong.

– Jenny, oh Jenny, I want you too.

Sister Veronica is asleep and dreaming. Movements contort the tightly-tucked-in bedclothes, a snort or a snore matches the sounds coming from the other rooms on the corridor. She does not sleep in her veil and habit as her pupils might suppose; her flannel nightgown is rucked-up above her cunt and breasts.

Aunt Harriet and John Barclay move in a maze of stone lace alleyways. From his window in the Imperial Hotel, looking down, they can see the secret green of gardens rampant within high walls, a tenuous grid imposed by French development on swamps and banana groves.

The bell clangs in the corridor and Sister Veronica jerks up from her pillow. As her eyes prise themselves open the familiar devil with Harriet's face still squats for a moment on the end of her bed before her wildly ranging limbs and brain return themselves in order. Damp, blurry, hot.

A garden in south London, anywhere. One evening, in particular, like any other. Haggard roses flop along brick walls, their roots lost in a tangle of weeds. The air is damp as earth, grass is cool on your ankles, a blackbird's metallic last notes are drowned by those of the ice-cream van a street away. Julie slumps in a frayed deck-chair, one hand balancing a can of beer on the knee of her jeans while the other, in a tensely separate life of its own, explores the muscle and bone of Jenny's shoulder under the ragged teeshirt thin and soft with age. They wait together, until the colour cools from the edges of flowerbeds, the kids are hauled indoors by Mary and Louise to finish their games in bed, the noise of traffic dwindles to a murmur.

John Barclay hands Aunt Harriet to a rattan chair. The room is dark and dusty, a propellor fan hauling the sluggish air. The flaking walls are washed in faded amethyst and lavender and peacock; the window is square panes of pale strawberry, lime, orange and mauve.

A frieze of ants races madly around the walls at waist-level. The coolest place is on the bed, a wooden four-poster with mosquito nets rolled above it. John Barclay has shut the windows to keep out the clatter and cries of the street. He looks at Aunt Harriet: this is no place for a woman like you. His clichés charm her. After Amy's nervousness, his confidence is as welcome as a feather-bed.

Jenny and Julie sprawl on the bed, talking and smiling; inside one social situation, they wish to change it for another. Jenny gets up to put on another record. Julie stretches out a little more across the bed so that when Jenny returns and sits down again their hands and legs are touching. With men she has lain easily, being hugged and stroked, but this is different, it is up to her, there are no right and wrong places to step, she is frightened of moving forward although she does not want to stay still. They look at one another, and smile.

Sister Veronica is getting up in her cell along the corridor from the boarders' dormitories. Narrow iron bed, white-painted cupboard, chair and table. A palm is slotted behind the crucifix on the wall, the green-flowered china hairtidy holds hairpins and a rosary, an open pot of vaseline stands next to a missal with gilt initials and clasps. The cupboard, when she gropes for the door-handle and opens it, smells of talcum powder, eucalyptus and sweat.

John Barclay gets up from his chair and crosses the room with deliberate steps. He halts in front of an old cabinet like a wide coffin upright on stumpy legs, its teak panels painted with scenes from the Buddha's life. He has bought it from a dealer who pretends he does not know it comes from a ransacked temple. Others will lose their merit and their souls, not they. From the cabinet he brings Harriet a box of red carved lacquer: will you open it, please?

Julie rolls over and faces Jenny, their breaths touching. Jenny puts her arm across Julie, buries her face in her shoulder, gently lifts the hem of her shirt with one finger, slides her hand up the bare skin awake with tension and desire, traces the spine, circles and swoops. Julie moves her own hand lightly downwards, her fingers pass easily under the loose jeans waistband, strain to touch the hair further down. Sister Veronica dresses according to the Rule. She puts on stays and a petticoat, she pulls on woollen stockings and rolls them above the knee. Each garment, each layer as it goes on, reveals a little more clearly the terrible chaos whirling in her room, away from the mapped certainty of the Empire, the mountains of darkest Burma and the teeming Malayan jungles.

John Barclay slides the ring on to Harriet's finger. It is made of silver he bought in India and then had made up in Bali by a silver-smith in a remote village high above the coast. The emerald is huge and soft. It will chip easily. Harriet must learn to move gently, her hand held out delicately, proudly, from her side. She will protect the gem and others will admire it. John Barclay is moved, and passionate. He wants marriage soon, he will whisk Harriet away by train to the wilder south, a honeymoon under the stained-glass tiffany lamps of another imperial hotel by the sea. Then they will travel down to Malaya, to buy a rubber plantation. Time is short, competition is fierce, profits must be assured. Harriet clasps her hands in his. She is totally composed. She knows what he will say; she has rehearsed it before sleep a hundred times. Be mine, be mine, Miss Harriet. And in return I will give you all the splendours of the East, dinner parties with European diplomats, a palace to protect you from the sun scorching the backs of my brown workers, all that your woman's heart could ever desire.

Sister Veronica snips the hair from the mole on her neck, runs her hand over her stubbly shaved head, pats her veil and wimple into place, smoothes her skirts and her scapular into their proper classical lines, and descends the wide stairs to chapel. As usual she arrives in her stall by five forty-five, a figure so familiar to the other nuns that she merges with the chapel furnishings, an unwilling anchorite on her unremarkable rock.

They give each other back the sight and knowledge of their bodies and themselves; they chart each other's flows; each is a moon sucking the other's tides. They are continents which they them-selves map and explore.

Jenny throws up the shabbily-painted window sash and leans out, gulping in the dark. Julie can feel the coolness of the night air like her own breath on the other's naked back. Jenny's body is the stalk of a young plant, her small breasts arch out almost concave to the nipple, her spine is a long curve so tender to look at it is almost painful. Julie's body is a collection of shadows, folds of darkness between flesh and hair, years of swallowing down desire and anger rounding out her stomach. A cool body slides into warm arms under the quilt. I want you to mirror me, to bring me out of confusion and lack of self into recognition of self and acceptance of a pattern I share and shape, fusion that is not drowning. While you are here, having chosen me, I know who I am.

They fall asleep as friends, in a tangle of limbs. Slipping one hand beneath her cheek Julie sleepily sniffs the sweet cheesy smell on it, licks its salty taste, Jenny's cunt or her own, she doesn't know, she doesn't think it matters.

Overnight it seems, the trees in the garden are leafless, or nearly so. They poke up at the thin grey stuff of sky, waist-deep in leaves that blow about the garden, choking it between its low stone walls. Pale brown leaves, and yellow ones, some crisp, some soft, drifts of them blurring the steps to the basement, the divisions between flowerbeds and paths. Distinction belongs to the trunks and branches of trees, every knob and curve intricately clear and black, whipping up at clouds. Jenny's salmon-coloured teeshirt rocking on the line is answered by dried-blood chrysanthemums leaning sideways, battered by winds. The colour seeps out of flowers and drains away. What you notice now are gutters, drainpipes, washing lines coiled around poles and drooping on the grass, plastic sacks once full of manure dumped by the flowerbeds.

The day grows increasingly bright, bouncing off the white squares of the tablecloth, the tiles behind the sink, the taps. The kitchen is far tidier than the garden. Julie takes great pleasure in eating in it. Louise giving the kids their breakfast at the other end of the table means she can enjoy in silent slowness: the sharp colours of posters that you taste like fruit; the clear shapes of china bowls painted in orange and navy-blue and holding wet curls of icy butter, rosy slugs of jam; fresh black coffee tugging against the fatigue behind her eyes.

When she awoke this morning it was to a room full of grey mist, and to a gap left by Jenny going off to school which Julie rolled into, sniffing Jenny's smell and her warmth. She lay lapped in half sleep, watching objects drift towards her, into clarity, the curtains detaching themselves from the window into a greater density of dots, a slow swimming towards blue. Bright grey light began to filter through the curtains from the garden, beyond which she heard the milkman's van across the uneven paving-stones. She surveyed her room: large, square, and untidy, books, papers and objects overflowing from shelves and desk to floor. The room is very shabby, with odd bits and pieces of carpet patched together, faded grubby walls where the damp paints mysterious brown shapes that mushroom day by day, a hole in the ceiling, all not so much concealed as pointed up by bright fabric hangings, plants and flowers, bits of lace. Jenny did not find it a messy or an unpleasant room, Julie remembers; she came into it, and laid her head upon the pillow.

Now, in the kitchen, she almost chokes on the precise edges of colour, and laughs at Bertha climbing up on to her lap. Hugging her and rocking her, for once not irritable with her daughter in the morning, she finishes her breakfast and pours more milk for Bertha and Sam. Mary is standing at the sink, whirling a wire brush over porridge-encrusted bowls; Louise has gone upstairs to struggle with a chemistry textbook.

– Okay, Julie says cheerfully, stroking Bertha behind her ear: I'd better get it over with. I'm going down to the social security office.

– Want some company? Mary asks.

– Please. I'm terrified.

To leave Louise in peace for studying, they take the children with them on the outing. Sam and Bertha are delighted, zigzagging up the street. They hop over cracks in the pavement so as not to summon up the Sandman, they trace complicated relationships to the trees sprouting at intervals behind coiled wire netting with their roots plunged into dog-shit and empty cigarette packets, they whirl three times around the pillarbox. Julie is as happy as the kids, but unlike them, she is shy of Mary, feels that she ought to entertain her, talk, instead of babbling to herself.

It's really autumn. Funny how you suddenly notice it. I smell the smoke from the allotments, of burning cabbage stalks and grass, I chew the day like a rind in my mouth, now sour, now sweet. We enter the park, its black iron railings cold and wet. Dark bushes grow just inside, a controlled harmony of different greens, the leaves speckled and smooth, the stems dusty and dry, mouldy cracked tennis-balls between their roots.

I know each bush by heart from bringing Bertha here, they speak the games that children play, the tunnels and the caves that they construct, endless, bounded only by suppertime, an adult's shouting voice. Mine, I realise; I am the boring adult who drags them off from pleasure, who imposes boundaries. The park is long and narrow, sloping down the hill, on one side terraced houses with box-shaped wooden tops; we see their backsides and the drainpipes bracing them, their little sheds and fences, each back garden a different, loving, careful ordering of colour, space. On the other side the railway leaps along above us, darting between Victoria and Peckham Rye, through the deep greenness of the railway cutting waving with froths of bay willow herb, and then emerging to swoop above the roofs of crumbling factories, above decaying schools and hospitals. We wave at the commuters in the train, and see them seeing us. A small park, two bright dots of children jumping, two women in shabby clothes.

The park has beds of flowers between the faded grass criss-crossed with narrow muddy paths. At one end is the tennis court, and the pagoda where the unemployed men sit, dozens of them, the middle-aged ones, boots resting for weeks on the gravel, the curved back of the bench cutting into the spine, cold hands eking out today's ration of tobacco. Above us the enormous sky is no higher than my head, I am a child too, a mile tall, gobbling at the sky, pillow-fighting with clouds, my feet playing football with the wind. We leave the park through the hole in the iron railings where the nettles swish thick and hairy and the dockleaves wait to comfort us with their cool juice, and bend our heads again to enter the narrow streets. Sam and Bertha clutch at our hands as we cross roads that bend and twist, concealing lorries hurtling to the stalls on Rye Lane to deliver vegetables.

These houses lean together, held up by age that is no longer comfortable. The low pillars on each side of the front door of this one flake with paint; here, the porch of corrugated iron supported by two curls of metal is cracked. Here, a sunset soft with pink and peach and lemon smears a house to life again, the details of the stonework over the bow windows picked out with scarlet and green. Behind a broken wooden fence a tangle of briars that once were roses, and by the door some roses blooming still, planted in old rubber tyres. Here, a small house is complete with battlements and turrets, next to it the glories of Byzantium triumph in red and white tassellated stonework and a stained-glass door with glowing lozenges of colour. Here, we glance at Norman castles, semi-detached, twelve foot of frontage cramming four narrow arching windows. Next to it, three houses in a row are all tinned up, their insides devastated so that squatters cannot move in. A garden is buried under rubbish piling as high as the ground-floor window-sills, and with a slit-eyed cat pale as the rubbish crouching on the top. We look down vistas of jammed-up streets, façades as wide as billboards and the depth of space behind as violently shallow. We peer at shops in short-life properties selling records and stationery, exercise books from India, a handful of thick wax crayons for five pence; the paper sleeves of ancient reggae albums, tall jars of sweets, marshmallows and curry puffs and Turkish coffee pots behind brown-paper blinds. The din of traffic beats upon our heads louder and louder the nearer we get to the lane.

Mary pulls Julie by the sleeve, half-amused, half-irritated.

– Come on, we're there.

The sunlight has dashed outside. They sit in the Social Security office on orange plastic chairs, scuffed and pockmarked with holes from stubbed-out cigarettes. Five chairs for a queue of ten. Prams and pushchairs must be left downstairs along with dogs and shopping-trolleys. Babies are balanced on knees along with shopping-bags and sheafs of forms. Julie and Mary lean against the wall; every time the door opens it cracks them on the shin and another woman enters, pale-faced, pinched, already old. One by one the women vanish to the cubicles from which their voices drift back, angry, shy, complaining.

– No, I'm not married.

– Yes, I have a child.

– No, the father doesn't pay maintenance.

– No, I don't live with a man.

– No, no-one supports me.

– Look, my money didn't come this week, why not?

– But the little boy's been sick.

– No, I don't go out cleaning.

– I don't understand.

Everybody smokes, flicking ash on to the floor as there are not enough ashtrays. Another woman will appear later to clean up. Those who have come along with friends or relatives talk and joke while they wait, gearing up bravado before they approach the officer; others, on their own, wait with tight-lipped faces. No-one can relax properly; you have to watch to see that no-one tries to jump the queue, you'd be here all morning otherwise. A notice on the wall proclaims that only one person at a time is allowed into the claimant side of the cubicle. As though they're frightened of us, Julie thinks: please do not attack the officer, it is not her fault, she is not responsible for all the bureaucracy. But the woman she faces at the enquiry desk does not look sympathetic; she hardly meets

Julie's eyes, her voice drones, her hands play with the forms in front of her, with her cigarette.

Julie, it seems, has been fairly stupid. She should have studied the relevant forms first, to be aware of her rights; she is in an odd position, which perhaps she should not have mentioned, of living in the house of the husband from whom she is separated but not yet divorced; she does not pay him rent and so will not be eligible for a rent allowance. She had better come back and see the social worker next week, very well then, in two days time, and sort it all out with her. Meanwhile, she can read these pamphlets on social security and being a single mother.

She grimaces at Mary as she emerges from the cubicle, tugs a willing Bertha towards the door. The sunshine outside lights on heaps of vegetables on stalls, the season's produce to be carefully costed for possible bargains, on special offers in the windows of supermarkets, on the racks of cheap clothes outside the second-hand shop on the corner. The money from Aunt Harriet's jewellery is long since gone; Julie squashes down a desire for consoling coffee and cakes in the street's one smart café, for a new and fashionable pair of jeans. She sympathises, despite her irritation, with her daughter, who, on being informed that her mother cannot afford to buy her another lot of sweets, begins to whine, dragging at her hand.

– You know what, Mary? Julie surprises herself by saying: I'd like to get a job, really. She has felt shy with Mary previously, fantasising that the other woman is too busy with her political activities to be bothered with her. But Mary has given up the morning to keep her company, and seems to find it bearable. Julie shelves jokes and charm for the moment and tries to sort out her thoughts.

– Yes? Mary prompts: you would?

– It's not just because of the money. That would help, obviously. But if I had a job, I'd be more independent as well, you know. If I was working, I'd be independent of Ben a bit more. Christ, Mary, d'you realise that I've never had a job? I've never worked, Ben's paid for everything right from university days. And I'm still living in his house. First he was my teacher, then he was my husband, now he's my landlord, and he's always paid for everything. I want to earn some money of my own, not just for food and clothes and things, I want to buy things.

– What kind of things?

– Oh, Julie says dreamily, but with one eye on Bertha and the traffic as they cross the road: huge presents for everybody, lovely things for all of you in the house, and for the kids. And a whole lot of new clothes, and all the books I want to read, and a big car, so that I could drive us all out on trips, and some decent carpets for the house. Oh, loads of things – I'd be paying my share that way, she continues anxiously as they arrive back home and sit at the kitchen table with mugs of coffee: I'd feel more part of the house if I had more money, I could do it up, decorate it –

– What's the point of that? Ben can sell it any time he wants to, we don't know when he might decide to. I can't see it's worth our while to spend a whole lot of money on a place we might have to leave at short notice.

The telephone rings, and Mary gets up to answer it. It is a friend from the local anti-fascist committee with which Mary is involved. She flaps her hand apologetically at Julie, and dives into a complex conversation. All Julie's insecurity rushes back. A comrade on the telephone is far more interesting than I am to talk to, she thinks angrily, I can't even sort out what I want.

She leaves the kitchen hastily, ignoring Mary signalling her to wait, and marches upstairs to her room, having first checked that Bertha is happy playing with Sam in the garden. She lies on her bed smoking, flouting the rules in her head. First, says Sister Veronica, the boarders must not go into the dormitories in the daytime, I do not like this habit of young girls lying about on their beds. Second, says Claire, I wish you wouldn't smoke in the bedroom, darling, it discolours the wallpaper and you always forget to bring the dirty ash-trays downstairs again. And third, says God, suddenly popping up from behind the shelves of books across the room, thou shalt not, if thou art a mother, have time to thyself, to think, to consider thy feelings. Meditate only on me; all else is self-indulgence, and sinful. Julie whines at them all to go away, to leave her in peace, and lies back again, one hand curled tightly around her cigarette, the other clenched into a fist at her side.

If only I had a large salary, if only I knew a lot about politics, if only I were beautiful, if only I'd read as many books as everybody else, then I would be powerful, then everybody would love me, then Jenny would never leave me, then Bertha would be happy, then I would find the right political group to get into with the right perspective on things, and then I could start being a revolutionary. I have no time to rest, she thinks angrily, and hurries downstairs again to begin preparing the children's lunch.

Mary, who is still on the telephone, puts her hand over the receiver for a second, and hisses at her.

– Hang on just a minute, can't you? I said I'd do it.

– It's no trouble, Julie says stiffly: I can manage on my own.

And scrubs potatoes, and peels them, and slices them, and chops vegetables for salad, and lays the table, all with the speed of a highly-paid demolition gang. At least there is one thing I can do well, you shall not take it away from me, my servitude. Between that and my half-hour rest period for fantasy, I do very well, thank you.

And that night, lying in Jenny's arms, is rigid, with a dry cunt and a knotted stomach, and cannot believe that anyone wants her to lie back and receive love, and cannot say so, and puts all her wanting into her love for the other, and into her dreams of money and food.

Fifteenth section

Sunday morning, and the feast of the Assumption of the Blessed Virgin Mary into heaven. The principal festival of Barrières-sur-Seine, which holds the Virgin as its special benefactress.

Julie has insisted on cooking lunch for the traditional party after High Mass. She has begun to let herself enjoy French food again. She goes to the cellar to collect bottles of cider, dark green glass misted with cobwebs in the rack on the red-tiled floor. She wipes the bottles and sets them by the fireplace in the salon in readiness. She opens one, and pours herself a drink, wanting to recapture the russet taste, thin and pale gold it looks in the china cup, but sour and then suddenly warm in the stomach. She arranges pâté on a plate, and tastes a bit, earthy pork fat rolling on the tip of her tongue. She slices wide craggy tomatoes and furs them with parsley from the garden, she washes vegetables so fresh and muddy she feels the plot they grew in, sees the black woollen stockings of the widow Mévisse bending over her celery beds, edged with pebbles and scarlet lobelias. The paths dividing the garden's cornucopia into manageable neatness are of white gravel. Crunch crunch go the feet of Julie over them, white espadrilles on the white stones noisy as chewing sugared almonds at a christening party.

Julie has bought frozen chickens, sealed in plastic, from the village grocery shop. Ten years ago, this was a dark and cool place when you entered from the sun in the square outside, smelling of the small golden melons ripening in baskets, the different cheeses stacked on marble shelves in a low cupboard at the back. You proffer your black wire basket for it to be filled with eggs, you hold up an earthenware jar into which Madame Roland ladles fresh cream, thick and slightly sour. On Tuesdays, the fish-woman sets her baskets just outside, heaped with the greenblackblue of mussels, an extra person to chat to as you do your shopping. Today, the village store has a wide glass front, trolleys for self-service. Madame Roland has vanished into the back, busy with accounts; fewer people stop to shake hands with each other and enquire after the health of husbands and children.

Julie breaks the long baguettes into shorter sections so that they will fit into the bread drawer. The village has two bakeries, next door to each other, that compete for the custom of important families like the Fanchots. Long thin breakfast loaves collected every morning, heavier two-pound loaves bought later in the day as they emerge from ovens, galette for Sunday breakfast, brioche when there are visitors to tea, cakes collected after High Mass as a special dessert. Monsieur Fanchot père's favourite cake was always a species of éclair. Two round choux placed one on top of the other, the top one smaller, iced with brown-coloured cream, and surrounded with small brown tongues of cream. Monsieur Fanchot, anti-clerical, delights in explaining the joke to Julie and Claude every Sunday lunchtime. The cake is called a nun, he says gravely, you see the flames – she is burning in hell. Monsieur Fanchot has been dead for years, nonetheless Julie has bought a nun cake in his memory, and from the bakery currently favoured by her mother. She feels today it is important to honour family observances.

While she waits for the chickens to thaw, she begins on the sauce. Wine vinegar from the crock under the sink, hissing over a low flame, mixed with mace. Hot stock drips into eggs and cream. This is the food of her childhood, rich, and fresh, and varied. At Oxford she discovered English food: pork pies, fish and chips, bread pudding, yellow haddock for breakfast on Fridays. She is delighted by it, so different, the contempt of scholars for the mundane task of feeding bodies. They do not seem to notice what they eat, while on the other hand they eat as though starvation followed and preceded every meal. Eight a.m. in the college dining-room, wedged between the hard brown chair and the long refectory table in a sisterhood of greed, hands reaching for a fifth slice of wet white toast to smear it with hoarded margarine concealed from late-comers under inverted cups, marmalade with rare strands of orange-peel caught in the clear jelly. Long thin sausages haloed in grease, cornflakes with white sugar snowed on top. The meal is served by women in green overalls who have been at work since seven. Silently they watch the intellectuals stuff themselves, unmade-up faces shining like the sausages, damp and rumpled clothes picked up from where they were thrown down the night before. The undergraduates leave mounds of debris on their plates; it is the work of other women to clear up after them.

Sister Veronica had explained food to her pupils at convent-school. We eat in silence in order to remember Our Lord, the sacrifice of self, of body, that He made for us. We restrain ourselves from eating as much as we wish, from taking pleasure in food, lest we forget the heavenly food of His body and blood He offers us each Mass. Forget the hours of labour spent in the convent kitchen-garden, the seasons of growth, of ripeness. Ignore the long work of preparation, the washing, scraping, shredding, boiling, the novices dissolving in the thick steam of mutton fat and boiling vats of custard. Call food a miracle instead, remember the loaves and fishes and praise Him, praise Him for carrots tasting of soap, dead ants in the dried apricots, the soggy puddings. Just as at home your mothers produce the miracle of three meals a day out of thin air and love, so here too, we the community say Grace and thank the Lord for all that He provides. Let us not forget we are a family in the convent, in our school. We learn to live together. Sudden loud noises, whether of pleasure or of grief, disturb our harmony, in the day as in the night. Praise be to Jesus sounding from every throat, in silence, lest our lips be tempted to linger on a morsel accidentally over-choice, to seek out other flesh than his.

Further back, further back. Claire holds me in her arms at times dictated by the book, the baby-bible. There is a special low chair, painted white, she wears a white linen apron, a smock that opens easily down the front. She has two of them, gathered from the yoke, one blue, with bunches of grey flowers, the other yellow, pink and blue, with painted wooden buttons. In later years she uses them as dust-covers for the fur coat and the fur cape hanging in her wardrobe. I begged for one of them when I was eighteen and the fashion for second-hand clothes began, I wore it proudly, never realising then why it became my favourite garment. I kept it hanging in my own wardrobe, I wore it again, when I was pregnant with Bertha, and when I was feeding her, and then I used it as a painting-smock, when I moved from Oxford to south London and painted the front door of the house bright gold.

To feed me is her duty; she has read the books which warn of my ill health and emotional deprivation if a bottle is used. She has no choice in the matter, her body is an instrument for the state, the factory where healthy workers breed. She does not care for the emotive side of breast-feeding, it is just a job. The correct amount, the correct length of time the baby sucks each breast. I do not understand that; this is my first love-affair, and I am demanding as all lovers are. She is my world, and I am hers, nothing else matters except exquisite pleasure, mine. She must do what I want, go on fulfilling me. Love is her duty: a mother gives and gives. I snatch at her fat breast, she winces. We glare at one another. Love is a battle now, between the two of us. I suck too eagerly, I choke on love and sweetness. Am I allowed to go at my own speed, am I allowed to suck to satiety? And why not? She feeds me when she, not I, decides I need it, because she, like me, does not recognise that there are boundaries between us. I am enraged, I kick and scream upon her lap, a difficult child to wean.

What I do can never please her, for she, like me, hungers for fulfilment, for perfection. All she is allowed to do is feed us. If we love her, we will eat. We go together to daily morning Mass, both of us begging God for food, more food. Neither of us, the ageing mother, the adolescent daughter, is much impressed with life for women after puberty. We concentrate instead on our eternal hopes. We swallow the Christ, who should be our sufficiency. We are two heretics who get up, sighing still with hunger, we turn away, until tomorrow when we can come back for more. The priest reads the Fathers of the Church on the voraciousness of women. We are just like beasts, wild beasts.

High Mass to celebrate the Assumption of the Virgin to the heavenly table begins at quarter to eleven. It is ten o'clock now, and Julie has let the little pan of vinegar boil dry and has curdled the mixture of eggs and cream. As she flings the back door open, cursing, to let in some cold fresh air and remove the insistent clamour of vinegar, she comes face to face with Suzette Cally, who has her hand upraised to knock.

The nurse sniffs, and smiles at Julie's cursing, and looks around.
– Oh, oh, mademoiselle Julie, what have you done? That's no

way to go about things. You've forgotten everything I ever taught you about how to make a sauce.

Julie frowns with annoyance, tipping the curdled mixture into another bowl.

– Hallo, Suzette, she manages to say: I didn't know you were coming today.

The nurse is surprised, watching her meanwhile open the fridge door to extract some more eggs and begin again.

– But of course I was going to come today, she says crossly: I always do for your mother's birthday, I thought you might need some help.

The little clock on top of the fridge bangs Julie in the face with time, time wasted, time misspent, time to be made up.

– Oh my God, is that the time? she says worriedly: I'll never get everything done before church.

Suzette removes her heavy coat and shoes, exchanging them for the checked nylon overall and pair of slippers she keeps behind the kitchen door. She strides towards the fridge, where Julie stands petrified clutching a wire basket of eggs.

– I'll help you, mademoiselle, you can't do it all on your own, there isn't time.

– Thanks, Suzette, Julie says gratefully: you're quite right, I can't manage all on my own. I'd be glad of some help.

The nurse, who has seen her place in the kitchen threatened, softens again immediately.

– There, mademoiselle, you're tired I expect, sitting up at night like you do. And I wouldn't suppose you'd remember all your cooking lessons anyway after living in England, all those packets and tins of stuff you eat over there.

Julie laughs.

– It's not quite that bad. But it's true, it's nice to be back here, with everything tasting so fresh. What shall I do to help?

– Nothing. You go upstairs and get dressed for Mass, you can't go to church today in those old clothes, it's your mother's birthday, you must show a little more respect. And mademoiselle, she calls after Julie's disappearing back: don't worry about the tea for this afternoon. Marie is coming over in a bit, she'll help me do the tea, we've been to Mass already, the early one, we'll finish everything while all the rest of you are in church.

On her way through the hall, Julie looks in softly at the conservatory. Her mother has fallen asleep again after her breakfast, her bed flooded with the cards that have come for her in the special feast-day post. The family will give their presents later on, at lunch, which Claire insists she will be able to attend. At breakfast she had been quite excited, insisting on a cup of coffee, asking anxiously about the preparations for meals, whether the table had yet been laid in the salon, whether a sufficient number of chairs had been brought down from the grenier. And Julie, realising how much her mother needs the information, does not try to soothe her down, but sits and discusses domestic details so that Claire decides to trust her daughter a little with the organisation and, relaxed, can fall asleep again.

Sixteenth section

Jenny sits on the stone steps in the back garden at sunset pretending to shell peas. She leans her head against the wooden handrail of the steps, watching the sun like a great squashy apricot bursting, and then like a plum, soft and seal-purple, its juice staining the sky and then running down the brick of the houses opposite.

As the colours drain, their last fire sucked by the burning comets in the rose-bed, the sky grows empty and cold, she is a dot in its blankness. The sky blackens, which comforts her, from steely turquoise it deepens into navy. Trees disappear, the darkness wraps her in itself, moist on her skin, to snuff her out, no more smell, or touch, or hearing, to tell her where and who she is. Awaiting Julie's return, and loving Barbara too. Words she can knot together in her diary, like a cat's-cradle game, to describe a triangle whose points constantly shift. Loving Bertha too, trying to protect her from too much pain all at once, knowing she fails.

Barbara's voice is tugging her back towards the house, calling to her to come in, back to the orange lozenge of light that is the kitchen window fighting back darkness, back to all the things that must be done, cooking, and suppertime. She dips her fingers into the peas, rolling them wrinkled and juicy over her palms, sniffing their sweetness. She runs a fingernail down the split seam of a discarded pod, scoring its coarse thick greenness. She will cook them with mint, eggs and cream, she decides, and smells already the starchy sweetness in the dish, the sharp whiff of mint. A dog barks somewhere in the night, puncturing her loneliness. She gets up stiffly, collects the battered enamel colander, the blue china bowl of shelled peas and the bunched newspaper of pods, and goes inside.

Seventeenth section

The parish church, topping a small hill, dominates the village. As you move about your day the spire is always centre, shops, farms, the pump, the school, whirling about it. No need for clocks: the bells divide the day, calling you out of bed into a remembrance of life, the furnisher of food, the mender of roofs. The bells begin to ring for High Mass at quarter to eleven, breaking open doors, bellowing through windows. Julie pulls on her gloves and hurries down the stairs, nearly falling on the steep and narrow bend. Figures scurry from all parts of the village; beaten-up saloon cars curve speedy ruts in the muddy square before the church. Julie is five minutes late; she walks up the centre aisle looking into the eyes of the parish priest a hundred yards away processing in from the sacristy with his retainers, she walks through successive guillotines of the villagers' eyes turned down in righteous prayer but flicking sideways at the jeune Anglaise as she passes by.

The church is vast, cold striking up from the bare stone floor. Its edges are in darkness, pegged by the votive candles twinkling at the shrines of saints, baroque fluttering hearts and ecstatic garments caught in stone. The booming organ ricochets from wall to wall. Far down the nave, two sets of elaborately carved rails separate the sanctuary from the rest of the church, priest from the people.

Julie sits in the Fanchot pew at the far end of the church near the altar. She stares, as she has always done, at the carved choir, and beyond it, at the stained-glass windows behind the high altar. Up and up the eye is sucked, up through the hierarchy of the glittering inhabitants of heaven. Through this rainbow wall you look out at the world; through it, the world transmits itself back to you. Ladders of archangels, cherubim and seraphim; tiers of prophets, saints and martyrs, each in his or her own place, serene. Here too is womanhood in glory: virgins, wives, mothers, widows, every aspect of human female life accounted for, named through its connection with the husband or the Lord. The progression of these categories leads the eye from Eve up further still to where the sin of woman is redeemed, to where the Virgin Mother reigns supreme, she who represents the impossibility that only more than saints achieve: motherhood without the taint of sinful sex, the flesh unassailed and incorrupt. Her finger, sternly and yet tenderly raised, points upwards, out through the roof, beyond the clouds, into the atmosphere farther than any horizon of earth, towards the almighty presence that gives women life and will forgive them for their imperfections.

Latecomers trickle in all through the service. The widow Mévisse settles herself beside Julie, kissing her on both cheeks and smiling with satisfaction at the flowers she arranged last night. Long sprays of gladioli, the blooms bright as crêpe-paper decorations bursting from their vivid green sheaths, grown in the widow's cottage garden up the road from the Fanchot house. The flowers for Julie are inextricable from cabbages, old shoes caked with mud, deliberate cheerfulness despite colds and rheumatism. Madame Mévisse blesses God for widowhood and poverty. She faces her harsh day with dignity, gardening all morning, resting on her back step smiling and chirping to her caged bird. Then she dusts the unused sitting-room with its cold tiled floor and spindly-legged furniture bearing speckled potted plants, dons her grey costume, little hat, grey gloves, and trots down the road to call on her old friend Claire Fanchot. This is one of the few houses in the village where she visits; most of her friends are dead now, more casual acquaintances simply acknowledged on the street with a little bow. Even though lonely, she is careful about where she goes. She enters a farm kitchen in the morning, to collect milk and pay the weekly bill, and Madame Fanchot's salon in the afternoon. And she grows dahlias, great untidy heads of colour flopping above curled and spiky leaves, and gladioli shooting scarlet and purple in abandon over walls.

She whispers, for Julie's benefit, to remind her, the names of the people in the neighbouring pews. Julie hardly hears her, so absorbed is she in her own remembering, finding she has not forgotten a single name, a single face. The postman, the egg-woman, the pharmacist, the cake-maker, the fishwife, the cowherd, the haberdasher, the grocer, the blacksmith, the midwife. Each with his or her special idiosyncracies developed over years of doing the same job. Mademoiselle Lemartin, aged seventy now, surely, and still selling buttons and lace, her birdlike throat pulsing under a choker of velvet, a different colour for each day of the week. Monsieur Gaumelle, the postman, bringing also the newspaper, which he tucks behind the geranium pots on the front window-sill of the house and collecting yesterday's edition that the Fanchots send on to the pharmacist. Here too are the families of the middle and the upper bourgeoisie, the rich farmers, owners of solid wide-fronted houses built of grey stone. Their clothes are expensive and ugly, their shoes are narrow.

Lastly Julie notices the remaining members of the Fanchot family, two of Julie's uncles with their wives, three grown-up cousins with their children, and one of Claire Fanchot's sisters. They will all be coming to lunch and then to tea after the Mass is over; they content themselves now with sipping at her, stretching out their necks from their tweed and linen collars and placing their lips in the air near her cheeks, their heads twisting quickly from side to side. The family is time, is function; over the years she has slotted back into it, been named by it, at the thrice-yearly intervals of school holidays and then at the moments of christenings, marriages, deaths. The family is dead, long live the family. For years the central core has been here in the village, the surrounding towns, consolidating itself with marriages between remote cousins and also careful to refresh itself with new blood as the old grows thin.

Today, the absence of many members proclaims how much all that is changing. Tantes Marie-Cécile and Bénédicte, chained by arthritis to the old people's home in Le Havre eighteen miles away, after the death of Monsieur Fanchot père and the impossibility of further caring for them at home. Claude in Switzerland, immersed in a new project and unable to get away. A dozen cousins and their dozens of descendants scattered through the different provinces of France whose factories and plants summon their specialised labour skills. The train is expensive; condolence over illness is brief, a murmur into the black bakelite ear of the telephone.

The members of the family gathered in church today connect to one another now mainly through God. They are all on their knees, eyes clutching the tabernacle, the words of prayers beating down the anxiety that will keep arising, over taxation, unemployment, the decay of traditional morality and certainty. Forget all that; pray for the infidels, the heathen, and turn your back on darkness. The prayers rely heavily on images luckily pertinent to these farming people: grain, water, shepherd, vine. It is an austere poetry, bony, almost childlike, fleshed out into richness through the private meaning giving it by each individual who participates. The tune of the closing hymn that they sing derives from plain-chant; the voice of the congregation wavers up and down, wind over the words wheat, earth, rain.

French. They are speaking, I am speaking my mother tongue again. But it was someone else, the priest, the pedagogue, who taught Maman the words to teach me to say, the words denoting difference. Say Papa, him up there and you down here. Say please, say thank you, learn to cajole and flatter God, sitting on his knee at teatime and blushing for a biscuit. Lord, listen to me, Lord, love me, Lord, forgive me. You hold my hand as I walk through green meadows, I shall have no demands or wants that you cannot satisfy.

Julie turns her eyes away from the stained-glass window above the altar, away from St Joseph, virgin father too old for sex, a bent staff flowering in his hand; away from St Maria Goretti, who willingly was stabbed to death rather than submit to the sin of fornication; away from St Mary Alacoque who licked the vomit of lepers in her proud, her untouchable virginity; away from Saints Perpetua and Felicity leaping joyfully into the jaws of lions, their newborn babies delivering them to holy martyrdom.

She must not cry, this is no day for grief. Death does not exist: the Virgin Mary simply falls asleep, and then shoots up to Heaven on the arms of angels; she has already risen, and if Julie is good, she will rise too and they will be joined anew, never to part again. How sweetly the priest leads their eyes back up to the stained-glass window above them. There is Julie's mother, executed in glory, strong, perfect, loving, faithful. And the mother only of sons.

I am at convent school again. It is the first of May, the ancient feast-day of St Joseph the worker, the day we dedicate to the Virgin, praising her.

Behind the convent is the garden we are never allowed to enter except on occasions such as this. The lawns slope from the cloister down to the tennis courts. We wear our best white frocks, kept for processions and for prize-giving day. The novices have lent us white-headed pins for anchoring our veils, and flap about us, pulling our wreaths to sit at more attractive angles. The richer our families, the more splendid our clothes, silk and brocade and gauze; if we are poorer, like me, they are only cotton. We parade beforehand for the nuns; they choose the prettiest of us to crown the statue of the Virgin at the climax of the ceremony. I am never chosen: I am lumpy, spotty, shiny-nosed. White does not suit me, anyway.

We walk in twos, behind the nuns, who glide in turn behind the priest. Two altar-boys walk behind him, scattering his path with drifts of flowers: forget-me-nots, lilies-of-the-valley, pinks. Four of the prefects carry the statue, its chipped face gaudy for the ceremony in newly-tinted pink and blue, lurching on a white bier slung on poles. This is our day, the little girls' day, when we sing of pearls, of lilies, of bleeding hearts, of secret soft places visited by God. Only my hands are slimy with heat and perspiration, there is a sanitary towel strapped like a dead rabbit between my legs, my sash is tied too forcefully over my thick waist. I am taller and more developed than anyone else in my class; my dress, which my mother made for me two years ago, strains at the seams across my breasts. I cross the playground towards the procession at an awkward run, arms folded tightly in front of me.

I can smell newly-mown grass, and sweat. On any other May afternoon I could pretend to be out sketching, hiding in the long grass with Jenny, thick fronds of plants meeting over our heads, our faces buzzing with the noise and heat of insects. But the little bell tinkles, and the nuns' voices quaver on. We kneel on the shaved lawn for the final prayers. I squint into the sun and see nothing as the Virgin is finally crowned. In that moment I resolve to talk no more to the Virgin; she is dead as far as I am concerned. I have failed her: I am not beautiful enough to be the daughter who crowns her statue, I am not clever enough to translate a Latin hymn in praise of her and win a prize, I have continual wicked thoughts which she can overhear, which makes her suffer. The Virgin has failed me: she is not strong enough to keep me from confusion and pain, not kind enough to pretend I never hurt her, she is not powerful enough to overturn the law of God. I will take no more part in the stupid interests of women and girls, I will not compete, I will talk only to the Father, to God.

Death exists after all. Today it is Julie who needs a funeral. She needs a place where she can mourn: mourn mothering, mourn herself, losing and lost, still wanting the cradle, she a greedy gobbler of gaps, and of rage. She needs other women now, to witness her loss, loss of childhood, mother and blood. That state called puberty, that is all. Puberty. The word should be larger than that.

Madame Mévisse pulls gently at Julie's sleeve, for Julien is stirring on her other side, anxious to leave now that Mass is over. Madame Mévisse is shy of him, so she smiles apologetically at Julie, helps her collect her bag, gloves, missal and purse. They trail from the church to the soft notes of the organ. Outside, everyone lingers as they always do, to meet old friends again, to greet those neighbours only recognised at church, to show off new babies, to pat other people's children on the head. Julie is enveloped in caresses of wool, of crimplene, of silk. People's eyes poke, prod. So sad, your husband not being here. Poor man, is he looking after the child all by himself? She will miss you, no? Poor motherless child.

Julie blunders past them, past the priest, the lines of altar-boys, her father and her relatives, all staring at her. The road away from the church is dusty and white, gravel chips scattering under her hasty shoes. Through railings, beyond bright bushes she can see the fairground set up in preparation for the evening's amusement. Along the road, workmen are busy tying tricolours to every house, every gas-lamp. Strings of coloured lights bob over her head, the wind swaying them and blowing gusts of flower petals and dust into her face. Away now from the main part of the village, the road is wider, bordered on either side by a deep ditch, lurid green grass thick above mud and sewage. Beyond the banks topping the ditches are the fields, starry with little yellow flowers, where the cows lie panting, their heads under the thorn hedge. Smells of earth, and of manure, of the labour of men, and always the church bells tolling, tolling, trying to pull her back.

The front door is open. She leans against it for a moment, panting after walking so hard and so fast. Claire's voice calls out feebly from the conservatory, setting Julie's heart beating in long slow thumps that pound in her ears.

– Julie? Is that you? Could you come in here for a moment, chérie?

Eighteenth section

Suzette Cally and Marie Baudry step to and fro across the blue and yellow tiles of the Fanchot kitchen floor. Both wear overalls in checked nylon, flat serviceable shoes. They perform complicated operations with their hands, drawing on the skill, timing and delicacy learned from their mothers years before and practised daily. Some of their tasks are undertaken simultaneously and involve split-second decision-making; others follow sequentially upon each other. They peel, chop, slice and quarter vegetables, and then fry, boil, bake and roast them, their knives moving like see-saws, their heavy saucepans summoned from the shelves high above the stove. They separate eggs with a nonchalant single-handed crack, and whisk the whites into stiff gleaming peaks like the clouds outside the window. They heat egg yolks to the correct temperature for thickening sauces; or they beat them with hot vinegar for mayonnaise. They blend flour and butter for pastry until it resembles fine sand, then they add water, an egg, and roll it out dexterously, whipping the dough around and around with fresh butter laid on each time. They purée fruit; they churn egg custard into ice cream; they bed beef on pâté and wrap it in a duvet of puff pastry; they simmer meat juices with brandy and cream. They are a team, working in speed and harmony, no jarring, no mess, no mistakes.

They accompany these operations with a stream of talk, to each other, in silence, words hopping through the menu like the spaghetti letters at the bottom of soup. The coffee grinder needs oil; hand me that knife; more eggs; quickly, give me a cloth. And also they speculate, they concoct, they strain, they mop up the fortunes of Julie, of the famille Fanchot. One who is ill; one who is tired; one who is odd; one who is absent, and missed. They follow the custom of years in the Fanchot kitchen, polishing the black-handled knives of others, carefully carrying delicate china to the washing-up bowl, scouring and polishing floors, reputations, grim little jokes. They are intimate with all family secrets brought from the closet at washday: who menstruates, who sweats freely, who changes most often. They are familiar with the crumpled hopes and faux-pas of waste-paper baskets; they are jealous of pots of jam.

Both these women live in mean dwellings, earth floors covered in cheap patterned lino, one set of crockery rather than four, a lavatory placed outside in the yard, not enough bedrooms. Marie and her husband have been saving for all their married life; if they are lucky, one of the new bungalows on the main road awaits them. Marie handles beautiful old dishes from the factory at Rouen, and polishes crystal glasses, and sighs for the scanty trousseau she had at her wedding day. Suzette, unmarried and full of energy and bitterness, slaps copper saucepans on to the draining-board.

Suzette Cally, the butcher's daughter, used to stand in her father's shop day by day, in the blue-tiled coolness where the blood soaked into the sawdust on the floor and caught you at the back of the throat, and where the joints hung from great shiny hooks above the long marble slab. She sat in the cashier's cubicle, pouring her passion into the noting of livers and hearts and brains, writing out bills and delivering change, as Claire Fanchot picked up her meat for the week, and sniffed in distaste at money, at blood. The cats rooted for offal in the far corners, Monsieur Cally whacked with a chopper at bone and gristle, Suzette rearranged the vase of artificial flowers at the little black grille.

Suzette Cally, debarred by her father's occupation from the select little tea-parties in the Fanchot home, the note of invitation delivered by hand, the hat and gloves donned, the tea from England sipped with murmurs of appreciation, the little fingers upraised. The ladies bend their heads closer together, discussing miscarriages, animal diseases, the children's performance at school, their daughters' possible fiancés. Even when Suzette leaves the village and trains as a nurse, the smell of butcher's blood follows and debars her. What matters is bourgeois blood, the condition of wagelessness; she watches the doctor's wife in her neat suit progress up the road to tea. With a mother who falls sick, Suzette has no choice; she gives up her nursing job in Caen and returns to the Fanchot house as maid, as nurse, as confidante. A reasonable wage, and some old clothes; kindly enquiries after her own and her mother's health; four dinner-services for her to chip away at, to drop, and to break.

The nurse considers herself above the labourers' sons now; no-one else looks at her, failed professional, jumped-up parlour-maid She returned from the boulangerie this morning, clutching the long loaf to her warmer than a baby at her breast. Now she advances on it; the bread shivers before her gleaming knife, dissolving into slices as she looks at it, plop plop, neat little tartines on the cutting-board. Each one she seizes, she smears tenderly with butter and pâté, lays it beside the others on the frilly white cloth in the basket shaped like a cradle.

– Fetch me the soup tureen from next door, will you, Marie? she says to her friend: I want to warm it on top of the stove.

Marie Baudry goes readily next door. The tureen is the one object she wishes to inherit when the Fanchot parents die. Pink it is, and florid, curlicues of china flecked with gold, flirting cupids painted on its sides, a lid wreathed into a knot of flowers with a dragon coiled about the stems. The tureen lives in the largest cupboard in the salon, a plump pink god complacent of its value. Marie walks humbly through the doorway, summoned by the riches of the cupboard, her hands waiting their gratification, her eyes cast down as she calculates the amount of francs, of soup, that the tureen could hold.

Julie is squatting on the floor, in the cramped space between the extended dining-table and the open cupboard doors. She has begun taking out the china and glass needed for lunch. Twenty soup plates, twenty side plates, twenty large plates, twenty smaller plates, twenty dessert plates, twenty fruit plates. Forty knives, forty forks, forty spoons. Sixty glasses, in three different sizes, for water, wine, and cider. Twenty cutlery rests, oblongs of glass engraved with leopards leaping as you tilt the glass. Six sets of serving spoons and forks, three shallow bowls for flower arrangements, ten oval serving dishes, three large platters. She counts, and recounts, she dusts, she wipes.

Waves of grief eddy out at Marie Baudry from the soup tureen.

She backs away, her hands clenched in the pockets of her nylon overall, and bumps into the copper pans hanging from the high stone fireplace.

Julie hears her, and looks up, crouching on the floor with Marie's booty, sniffing.

– Did you know? That my parents are selling up, and going away? Leaving the farm, to go and live with Claude in Switzerland?

– Yes, mademoiselle, says Marie, looking at the soup tureen: I did know, Suzette told me a week ago.

– I didn't know, Julie says angrily, lifting out piles of glazed white napkins from the bottom shelf: Maman only told me just now. I'm the last to know.

– I expect she didn't want to worry you, mademoiselle, Marie says kindly: she must have known it would be hard for you to understand. Mothers, she adds timidly: feel protective about their children, I'm sure you know that.

Julie gets to her feet, holding the pile of napkins.

– This is my home. They've done it without consulting me, I could kill them. Why can't they stay? I'd thought of bringing Bertha over here for a holiday, letting her have a bit of a childhood in the country, like I did, she'd be so happy here. It's too late now.

She blows her nose on the top napkin of the pile.

Marie is scandalised.

– But mademoiselle Julie, didn't you know? A big corporation is going to buy up the land. They have a new scheme for the farmers. A co-operative granary, and a tractor store, and offices, and new bungalows. It's wonderful for the village, it means more money coming in.

Suzette stands in the doorway.

– No-one here can survive on their own anymore, they're all being bought up by the big farming concerns. Your father's been losing money for years. Didn't you know?

– No, Julie says furiously: I didn't know. You needn't tell me, I ought to have written more often, I ought to have taken more interest. But why didn't they tell me before now? I'm not a child anymore.

– But as it was, Suzette points out: you hardly ever wrote. Your mother used to complain about it to the ladies at tea, I could hear her from the kitchen, no news from her daughter in London. You were too busy, she used to say, you had such a rich exciting life in London.

– What do you expect, mademoiselle? joins in Marie: you're

grown up now, you've got your own life, they thought you didn't care.

Suzette, moved by Julie's tears flowing afresh, motions to Marie to be silent. She taps Julie gently on the arm.

– Mademoiselle, I'm sorry, but we must make haste. The guests will soon be here for lunch and we are not yet ready. Will you give me the soup tureen, please?

– Fuck the soup tureen, Julie says: and fuck Claude, and fuck the family.

She has been let down. She lets down the soup tureen in turn, picking it up carefully, holding it up in the air at arm's length, and letting it drop, thump, crack, on to the carpet, where it lies in twenty odd fragments, one for each guest, a bouquet of splinters in pink and purple and gold.

Marie stands frozen, Mater Dolorosa, as though the china splinters had pierced her heart, then she turns around and hurries back into the kitchen.

– They didn't do it on purpose, Suzette says coldly: they didn't do it to hurt you deliberately.

Julie picks up a table napkin and wipes her eyes.

– Nobody ever does, she says wildly: that doesn't stop them from hurting you, that doesn't stop me from hurting them.

Claude, my earliest companion that I remember, the product, I was convinced, of their conspiracy to oust me from their affection. The season of birth propels him into the world in spring, and me into winter-time. I watch him sucking my mother's breast, a greedy baby, she laughs at him, a proper little man. I watch him learning to speak; pig, I whisper to him, but he merely smiles, he loves everyone, even me. He is an active baby, encouraged to walk early, spoilt. He roams everywhere, crawling on fat little knees, a grin on his face as he attacks the china cupboard, the hearth-brush clutched in his hand. Unlike me, crouched plotting behind the sofa, frightened of horses and cows and attacked by nightmares, dazzled by sunlight. He pulls himself upright, he crows with delight. Pig, I whisper, and push him over in the farmyard. His hand bears a deep gash, spouting with blood, and then a metal clip affixed, and bandages. He screams with the pain. Doctor Leroux tells him to be brave, to be a big boy, and Claude stops screaming, rewarded with sweets, and the new word, hero. I like him better as he grows up, I teach him things, I show him my secret places, the forest amidst the redcurrant bushes, the disused earth closet at the end of the garden, I let him play with my dolls. Gradually, when the village boys call him sissy, he learns to despise my games, to beat me at running, because I try less hard than he. He serves at Mass, I can see the muck on the soles of his boots under his frilly white robe as he rings the bell for the Elevation of the Host. I hunch in the front pew, joining loudly in the responses, my knowledge of Latin better than his. I take his side when my father beats him, I moan in the next room into Claude's silence, with pity, with envy, for the male sins that merit such severe punishment, such close attention. We become friends again as he grows up, though at a distance. He shows me a poem he has written, and swears me to secrecy, I write to him, jokes and stories, to cheer him up while he does military service. He takes me climbing, and tells me I am as good as a boy. He has turned out well after all, it does not matter too much that as yet he is unmarried, he has his career to think about. He has always been kind to Bertha, sending her gifts. He has money I envy, he will have the parents I mourn.

– Well, Julie says dully: I suppose if they've decided, that's what they'll do.

Suzette looks at the mess on the carpet.

– I never did like that tureen much, anyway. Come on, your guests will be here any moment. Go upstairs and wash your face, and I'll finish laying the table. And calm down a bit, mademoiselle, all this working yourself up won't do any good. What's done is done.

Julie kicks the fragments of china into a heap with her foot.

Thanks, Suzette, she says for the second time that morning: thanks.

Upstairs, she wraps her mother's birthday presents. A picture from Bertha, done in rich water-colour. No-one can say what it represents, only Bertha knows what mood she is sending to her grandmother. Patches of colour, a blue square, a red one, a green one. And then, as though colour were not enough to state the separation between spaces, texture drawn in with wobbly black lines, a pattern of dots on the red bit, stripes on the green, zigzags on the blue. Julie studies it, worrying. Does Bertha not know what boundaries are? Must there be black, such alarming black lines to divide experience, lest it spill over, and colours merge one into another? She tries not to worry, she thinks of the carpet downstairs, the muddle of colours on silken pile, the fragments of porcelain. She selects scarlet tissue paper to wrap Bertha's present, one of her mother's favourite colours, and ties it with silver ribbon, rolling it up. Her own present has been sewn during evenings of babysitting, hours of labour finally congealing into a sampler. Claire's name, and her birthday date, surrounded by the implements of her various trades: a needle, a saucepan, a screwdriver, a safety pin, a gardening fork, a broom. And then, for Julie like Bertha cannot easily find symbols of feelings outside her dreams, a whirl of primary colours as signature.

Then she washes her face, takes off her decorous church-going skirt and flings it on to the floor, surveys the clothes bought in London in an angry passion of spending. A silver pair of dungarees, a tight black skirt with a slit in the back, an embroidered peasant blouse, a wide dirndl skirt covered in patches and beads. She stands back and laughs, Julie the ambivalent, Julie the anxious to please, Julie the plump in clothes always two sizes too small, Julie the skinny in clothes always two sizes too big, Julie the envious, the competitive, the angry, the miserable. Back go the clothes into the large suitcase. She rummages in the other, and finds the second-hand frock that Jenny gave her for her last birthday, hearing Jenny's voice again, warm, complimentary, teasing. Darling, very incorrect I know, comrade I should say, sister, but you are a beautiful woman, d'you know that? Julie's tongue diving at her mouth, at her breasts, at her cunt, desire growing, ferocious, a festival, like it used to be, until, as always happens now, the memory of Barbara intervenes.

Julie arriving home early, full of good resolutions. I will be calmer, I will be less possessive, I will learn to be less jealous of all Jenny's friends, of her activities that happen without me there, I will get on with my life too. She speeds straight up to Jenny's room to inform her of this, knocks, and enters without waiting for a reply.

The half-drawn curtains shut out the hot restless sunshine and the jungle of green burgeoning up to the sill. One bar of light is solid on the heap of their clothes, touches a leg, slides away up the wall over a string of beads hung from a nail set in a crack in the plaster.

A woman lies on her side in the dimness; the shape of her body indicates that she is smiling, not at Julie, but at her lover, existing for and sensually preoccupied with her. The sheets are warm and crumpled from two bodies distinct in smell and texture. Bony, and soft, dark patches of hair, tenderness, the echo of shouting, the dent of past movement. The outside afternoon murmurs hotly at the low window-sill. Two pot-plants balance on the peeling paint, three flies circle in the middle of the room. Jenny stands naked above the heap of clothes, lingering to feel the sun on her back; stooping slightly as though to pull on her clothes she remains in fact immobile, her body curved like the still of an action shot, a tension created between what the clothes on the floor invite her to do and what the drugging pleasure of her limbs forbids. Then Julie makes a sound, and Jenny and Barbara turn away from each other and see the watcher by the door.

Julie begins to recognise a landscape. She wants to weep for this enormous complete sexuality she fears she will never know again.

The condition of loving is loss. My pain recognises you in the distance, your absence from me. The condition of wanting is found unbearable by me. The condition of woman: lacking desire; and wanting. Being found, wanting. Crouched in the corners of cellars, of bathrooms, of cloisters, stroking away. Poised over breadbins, hands dipping at sugar-bowls, into holy-water stoups. Found out, declared wanting, greedy, and punished: stop it, stop crying immediately. Slake your lust on dry bread, gobble your rosary beads, masturbate on your crucifix, anything that will turn you away.

It is impossible for me to say that I want, since those words define me as lacking so much, as being invisible, as having no speech that is understood. My speech is nagging, is sulks and explosions, silence and tears. Nobody understands that; or if they hear me roar, if I am daring and roar, they mutter how she whines, just like a woman.

Don't let me want. Sell me commodities instead; sell me a silk and lace corset, a vibrator, dieting pills. Don't let me want. If I wanted, who knows what I might do? Get angry, start shouting. Shout about being a woman, in a strong voice, about motherhood, about cunts and breasts and the clitoris, about being a lesbian. Don't let me want; I might start learning how to enjoy myself, I might start wanting more of us to enjoy ourselves. Don't let me work at something I like, lest I demand that you give me more time to myself, for pleasure, for work. Teach me to love on your terms, to wipe up your tears and your arse and your office floors, so that I will be too tired to continue the struggle, so that I will stop thinking of change. Don't let me drag at your tongue, don't let me make you stutter or cause your silence, don't let me force you to listen to me.

Julie sits on the edge of her parents' bed, and pulls the telephone towards her. Careless of how much it costs, she speaks to Jenny again. Late, and fumbling for words to hang on to as she goes, putting one foot forward cautiously in front of the other, she clambers towards Jenny, across the clumsy stepping-stones of words. The epithets of the farmyard, of the playground, of the cloakroom, the forbidden words roll out, the forbidden emotions march: jealousy, rage, love and pain.

Below Julie's feet, the front doorbell rings.

– Fuck, they're here already. I'll have to go. Just remember, you, I'll be home soon, you'd better be there. You won't lose me so easily, I'm coming back. If we're going to go on living together, you'd better start listening to me.

– If I can get a word in. If we've still got a house to have rows in when you get back. There's a board up in the front already, the estate agent came round yesterday.

– What, Julie shrieks: why didn't you let me know?

– Try leaving a telephone number next time you leave for ever. Oh Julie, I wish you'd come back soon, we must decide quickly what we're going to do.

– I think, Julie says slowly: the first thing is to see Ben. We haven't been in touch for ages, I'd better talk to him and find out what's going on. He isn't heartless, he just doesn't think.

How like me, she grimaces as she runs downstairs to greet her guests.

Nineteenth section

At the far end of the convent garden, away from the red brick buildings and the cloister opening out on to swathes of grass, the lawns shaven close as a nun's head end in a riot of bushes, young trees, and thick long grass. And here the world ends, tipping over suddenly down a tiny hill into a ditch wide as the bed of a dried-up stream, full of cowparsley, and docks, and nettles. It is raining, thick drops of water sliding off the glossy green of laurel bushes, down the crinkled runways of horse-chestnut fans, on to the cups of weeds, soaking into the dark earth hidden by newly violent green.

Sister Veronica plunges away from the lawns into the tangle of branches and weeds and long grass, her shoes wet and then sodden, her veil catching on twigs that pluck at her cheeks, at her eyes. Rain soaks in dark patches on to the thick wool of her habit, she smells wet serge steaming, she feels water running down her hands, down her arms under their wide sleeves. Beyond the ditch, half overgrown by brambles and young sycamores seeded by chance in the autumn, she finds the little hut with its tin roof and its crucifix leaning askew from the gable.

She hears the rain drum on the roof, a splash and a tinkle as it bounces off the gutter and pours down the pipe. She squats on the floor of her refuge near the open door, rain misting her face and veiling the convent buildings a quarter-mile away. She smells the earth's freshness again after many years, she counts fifty different shades of green, she sees clouds of tadpoles hang in the scummy water of the little pond.

Harriet and herself, caught in a monsoon downpour while visiting the little ruined temple on the river near Nonburi, take shelter under the trees in the temple courtyard, watching the heavy drops hit the dust on the flagged paths and puddle it rapidly to mud. The trees shake in the wind; in the place of shadows patterning as elegantly as the lace fretwork of the colonnade are sheets of water, grey, and misty, and thick. The two women's panama hats are sodden wrecks, their muslin frocks cling. They run out from under the trees over towards the ruined temple, their feet slipping in mud, their nostrils loaded with sweetness, jasmine, orchids, flame of the forest. Inside, the temple is cool, dust on the tiled floor, faded wall-paintings half-discernible in the gloom. The Buddha still stands at the far end, his left arm raised, his hand curving backwards towards his shoulder; his other arm droops, away from his body, which is bent in the most sensual of walking positions. His head is slightly on one side; he smiles, very faintly. In front of him are withered garlands, for few people visit here now to pay him homage; the monks have built a new temple next to their own quarters, with a roof like a rainbow of coloured glass mosaic, glittering green and blue, with fresh wall-paintings in gold, and with sparkling black pillars.

Amy walks forward a little into the dark of the temple, over the floor strewn with dried-up flower petals and bits of tinsel, and picks up the canister of numbered wooden spills that lies there, to amuse herself by making a prayer, and then shaking one spill out. She picks up her spill, she turns to the bunch of paper tickets hanging from the wall, to find the numbered paper that corresponds to her spill and so read her fortune. Her knowledge of Siamese script is not good; she peers at the faded lettering and concentrates.

Harriet's voice comes from the doorway, where Amy cannot see her, so bright is the sunshine outside poking once more through the rains.

– You need not bother with that. I can tell you.

Amy puts out her hands in supplication.

– Harriet, this is only a game. Soon the rains will be over, we can return to the river and find our longboat again.

– Nevertheless, insists Harriet: it is time that you knew.

Afterwards, they decide to walk back a different way, over the fields of cool mud, past the buffaloes, through groves of palm, past the lush green tips of the rice in the paddyfields. And Harriet is kind, and is brisk. Already she has acquired the manner suitable to her new station in life. She does not omit to say how much she has valued her trusted servant, how important her services have been. The passage to England has been arranged. The convent has agreed to a paying guest, being used to maiden ladies whose families, whose friends can keep them no longer. They have reached the station on the river again; their boat, John Barclay await them. Amy turns over words on her tongue. Generosity. Uselessness.

Sister Veronica is soaked through, already her bones beginning to ache. She bows her damply coiffed head on to her arms, she clasps her hands over her woollen knees, she calls silently on all the gods of Asia who have forsaken her, who deny her a soul, who have exiled her away from their languorous heat, their brightly coloured houses, their complicated meanings of life which she would have understood if only she had been allowed to stay with them a little longer.

When at last the nuns find her, after the rain has stopped and she has missed three Offices in chapel, she is already nearly dead. They find her, and cross themselves, less at her state of bodily ill, than at the place where she has chosen to accelerate death, in the little chapel in the remotest part of the garden where the mystics come for a foretaste of heaven, for a denial of the exile of life. This is the place where Jesus walked with Mary Magdalene on Easter Sunday, where the dreamer saw the lady of the Pearl, where the rose blooms and the lover of the soul is courted, where Eve lives still in innocence. This is the walled garden, where the fountain is sealed up, the place where the Lord Christ takes his rest at noon, where the gimcrack statue of the Virgin lurches with an insipid smile on her ramshackle altar. Over the wall are voices, a tarred main road, a pub, a clothing factory. Further away still, the rubber plantations of the south of Siam and Malaya, John Barclay's chequebook of compliments, Harriet's emerald ring.

Julie has coached the small children in whispers, outside the salon, in the hall. Now they enter, in grave procession along the hallway from the verandah, into the salon where the family sprawls with its guests, leaning comfortably back in a contentment of cheese and breadcrumbs and wine. The first three children bear flowers, deep blue hydrangeas burning like lamps, dark green stalks as sturdy as flagpoles, and above them the great blue globes, massed papery petals each a different shade, from mauve and lilac through sapphire and misty mountain-blue to the deep tones of a midnight summer sea, the blue that encircles the rims of the morning bowls of café au lait, the rich blue of the jackets that the labourers wear on their way to work.

– Tantantara, sing the children, in a fair imitation of trumpets: tantantara, Madame Fanchot.

The fourth child carries the cake, very carefully, her white boots plonking one after the other over the frayed pile of the carpet, her hands clutching the scalloped edge of the thick china dish. The adults around the table look up, and laugh, and applaud.

– Blue flowers, says Claire, with surprise and pleasure: hydrangeas, my favourite, oh Julie, I never thought you would remember, and sits up against her cushions, her eyes bright, defending against tears: you should not, you should not go to all this trouble for me.

The convent cemetery is at the far end of the garden, where the latter joins the little tangled wood that separates it from the wall and the road beyond. The graves are simple mounds of earth, no flowers, no crosses, no inscriptions. The Rule is here triumphantly exemplified: each sister laid to rest in clay and stones pursues in death the logic of her life, anonymity and facelessness. Other, weaker, Catholics need photographs, gold tinsel, florid stone, a railed-off oblong filled with pale green marble chips. In death, as in life, the sisters blush at bad taste and prefer simplicity.

Sister Veronica's grave is deep; the sides are lined with sheets of white cotton pinned with flowers. The cemetery is a peaceful place; cypresses march along it two by two, their regularity exclaimed at by the frivolity of butterflies. Down the beige sand path comes the procession, postulants in ugly short black capes, their hair still showing and their ankles wrapped in the coarse black wool of schoolgirls' stockings; then the novices, fresh-faced in adolescent white; finally the adult nuns in the black and white robes of the fully professed. Six seminarians bear the coffin, draped in white, and behind them Father Rector braided all in black. All of them are singing, with such joy, such certainty, such envy almost, were it not a sin, for the pure soul finally at home. Their voices are not strong; the thin melody, quavering up and down, barely drifts beyond the circle gathered about the grave.

Mrs John Barclay, née Harriet Winterman, rears beneath the cypresses in black crêpe, hung about with ornaments of jet from Africa, her hat nodding with silky black plumes fetched from India, her draperies edged with glistening black fringes twisted in the sweatshops of Singapore, across her face a fine black veil stitched with sequins, black and flashing. Behind it snap her eyes, no less compelling than the sequins. She has no mind these days for anthropological reflections, she does not muse upon funeral pyres or the burial rites of Buddhist nuns.

She notices a smear of mud along the side of one kid boot, dirt clings to her despite the care she has taken to bunch her skirts and lift them clear of the grass on which she stands. Irritated, she lets down her skirts and moves her weight, which is considerable these days, on to the other foot. Then, quivering with the effort not to overbalance, she scrapes one boot against the other underneath her heavy black tent to dislodge the mud.

Her husband is standing by her side; he notices the trembling of the tassels on her breast, the heaving of her shoulders underneath her cape. Surprised at her emotion, nervous lest it spill over, he presses her elbow with his own, still staring straight ahead.

Moved by his concern, Harriet blushes, and arranges her feet next to each other again, one hand going down to lift her skirts free of any more mud. John Barclay has no love for Catholic ritual, as his wife well knows. The missionaries in Malaya exasperate him with their interference with his workers' well-being; their insistence on spiritual as well as vegetable harvests. He has indulged Harriet in her wish to attend the funeral, but he shifts from foot to foot, he glances at his watch.

Who mourns Sister Veronica? None. They are all, except the Barclays, singing as glad as birds at mating-time, their faces blank as the white sheets lining the grave. Father Rector raises his censer for the final time, they all turn around and troop back to the convent. A white butterfly dashes out of the grave where it has been feasting on honeysuckle, and flutters upwards to the cold grey sky.

The cake is in the English style, solid, and heavy with fruit, in order to provide Julie with a firm base on which to spread first a coating of marzipan and then another of icing, pale blue, frilled at the edges with scallops of white. On this crystalline floor Julie has erected pillars and arches of sugar lumps stuck together with icing. Under the central arch topped with a tiny sugar doll she has iced on the floor of the cake the women's liberation symbol: the female sign of the circle and cross, with a clenched fist inside. Around the side of the little sugar temple runs a legend piped in bright scarlet icing: Arise, ye women, happy birthday Maman, and get well soon.

Claire draws in her breath in anger as she reads the lumpy sugar words that her daughter has scrawled across the Virgin's feast.

– Very charming, she says coldly: Julien, chéri, will you cut the cake for me? The knife is too heavy for me.

The other guests crane forwards to see the decorated cake before Julien's expert wielding of the massive knife knocks off the configuration of sugar lumps and slices neatly through the scarlet lettering.

– Ah, le cake anglais, murmurs Monsieur le Curé from his seat of honour at Claire's side: what a treat, madame. I felicitate you. My housekeeper, alas, does not believe in serving the clergy desserts.

He beams at them all, the ascetic young priest, and chews happily, his cheeks bulging like a hamster's, unaware that he is gorging himself on blasphemy.

– It is a nice cake, Julien says tolerantly, noting his daughter's sulky face and wishing to avoid a scene at table: a little heavy, perhaps, the English style, like the plum pudding, eh Julie? But the ingredients are delicious.

He passes fingers of cake down the table to all his relatives, before uncorking the bottles of champagne that Suzette brings in from the kitchen. He pours a measure of creamy froth, pale golden liquid, into each hovering glass.

– Monsieur le Curé, messieurs, mesdames, I give you a toast. My wife: happy birthday, and a speedy return to good health.

They are all on their feet, glasses raised, smiling down at Claire, who blossoms and glows with the adulation, her eyes more sparkling than the fidgeting bubbles in her tulip-shaped glass.

– A sad occasion, madame, the parish priest ventures: I understand that this is the last feast of the Assumption that you will be celebrating here with us in Barrières-sur-Seine. A sad loss, madame, to us all.

Claire's face changes.

– Ah, Monsieur le Curé, you don't know how terrible it feels to be going away. But at least, she says, looking hastily at Julien, to console him for his decision: I shall be with my son again.

She stops, coughing on a crumb of cake. Julie, anxiously watching her, finds it unbearable to notice the thin spotted hands gripping the white linen napkin, the nerve beating on the flushed forehead, the grey hairs thickening at the temples. She pours out a glass of water and hands it across the table, watched approvingly by the priest.

– And of course, Claire says, wishing to divert their attention from her trembling hand: I have my daughter too. You'll come and visit us, won't you, Julie? And bring Bertha next time?

– Yes, of course, Julie mumbles in confusion: I will, I haven't seen Claude for years.

Claire does not wish the priest to know of the divisions within the family. She goes on hastily, as though Julie had not spoken.

– I have been thinking, chérie. There are so many of your old toys here, so many of mine even, things we can't possibly carry to Switzerland, why don't you go through them before you leave? I am sure that Bertha would like to have some of them to play with. My little grand-daughter, Claire explains to the priest.

Julie does not hear his teeth clicking in sympathy, she is too busy restraining tears.

– Things like your lovely carved Noah's Ark? And those old picture books? You really want to give them away?

– Not away, Claire corrects her: I want them to stay in the family. I'd like you to have them. I'd like Bertha to know that her grand-parents haven't forgotten her.

– It's very sad, the priest repeats: a family separated, a home being left behind.

– Never mind that, says Claire, her eyes on Julien's face: no point crying over spilt milk. One has to accept what happens, and get on with it.

– Well, Julien says heartily: perhaps the children will benefit, at least. We have little enough to leave them after we're gone, but meanwhile, they can carry away whatever they like.

– Only what you allow us, Julie mutters to the mirror on the wall opposite her: only what you allow us to want.

She looks at her father.

– I don't want lots of things from the house, she says: not any more. Just a few mementoes, I haven't really got room for anything more, if we move.

– You didn't tell me that, Claire says, shocked.

– But what do you want then? the priest enquires, looking at Julie's ringless left hand, her short hair, her peculiar clothes.

Julien, Claire and Julie all speak at once, and Suzette Cally comes in to clear the plates away.

In the convent parlour, the postulants offer around trays of macaroons and madeira; in whispers, the novices gossip about the death. But Mother Superior glances at the clock. It will soon be time for the nuns to vanish two by two around the corner of the cloister beginning outside the parlour door, the tunnel that swallows them eager up into its candle-lit darkness.

Mr and Mrs Barclay take their leave, John Barclay with barely concealed distaste for these spinsters with their flapping headdresses and their high giggling voices, Harriet with a proud consciousness of her black attire so much more costly than their habits, rough and serviceable. Harriet's goodbyes are gracious, her fingertips extended to the senior nuns. She has been their benefactress, after all, assuring Miss Amy Sickert's welcome in the convent through the payment of a generous dowry, bearing the cost of wedding dress for her reception, and later paying all her medical expenses. The nuns see her go with genuine regret. A source of little extras, butter and cream for the senior nuns' breakfasts, has gone.

The horses nod the Barclay carriage further south, towards wide streets, tree-lined, where the mansion that befits their station in life awaits them. Harriet leans back upon the carriage's velvet squabs. She plans her costume for that evening's dinner with the Mayor and her husband's business partner. Purple, perhaps, with just a touch of white net draped at throat and shoulders. She remembers the white butterfly above the grave and frowns with anger.

Amy in white linen and a broad hat sketching her way slowly around the hundred white temples of the Buddha at Ayudthaya. They sip fruit drinks that taste of macassar oil. She glances at her husband, leaning back upon his cushions, bored, his hair slick with scented grease, his neck spilling over his collar. She seizes his hand.

– My dear, my dear, you have been so good to me. Do you think, the purple and white gown for dinner tonight?

Her husband stares at her, his red face growing redder.

– For God's sake, Harriet, I expect my wife to know what frock to wear for dinner, I give you a generous enough allowance, it is your business, yours alone, to know what pleases me.

All that evening Harriet is reminded by white, the vast snowy tablecloth at dinner glazed stiff as a nun's wimple, the plates like china haloes, the round moon faces of her guests. Later, at night, she wills her husband's body to blot it out, her nightdress billowing whitely around her neck and covering her face while his red face and hands that she cannot see busy themselves with her white flesh.

The older guests have retired to the little conservatory, tidied again to the appearance of a salon, to chat desultorily and to nap, and the children to the garden, where they play with the toys Julien has fetched down for them from the grenier. He seats them astride the big papier-mâché whale made by his father for Julie and Claude years ago, where they squeal with joy, he tumbles boxes of bricks on to the grass, he helps them build toy villages, he catches them as they jump one by one off the well. Claire and Julie lean their elbows on the table in the salon and watch them through the window.

Julie's heart beats with pleasure that her mother has stayed behind to talk to her. She feels rushes of love in her throat as she looks at her mother's body so near to her own, the face turned towards her with interest and with attention, the deep-set brown eyes frowning a little.

– What I can't understand, Claire says, her hands teasing a stained napkin: is why you have to hate men. You go too far, you always did.

– But I don't hate men just because I love women, Julie says: well, I do hate some of them, not all of them. Sometimes it's hard work trying to get anything through to them at all.

– That's it, Claire decides: you've been led astray. You're so warmhearted, you don't always realise. It's because of Jenny.

At least Julie has been named as loving. She throws her arms around her mother and kisses her, to show her she is loved, and to stave off any further criticism.

– But I'm happy, Maman, I'm happier now than I've ever been.

– But you're not happy all the time, Claire says anxiously: I know you're not. It won't last. In a month or so you'll be writing to me saying you're miserable again.

– No-one's ever happy all the time, Julie says, kissing Claire again: and I'm happy now. I'm so glad I came over.

– That's true at least, Claire says, relaxing: at least you've come back to see us. You children, I'm grateful you still come and see us. I didn't expect anything, after you left home. I made up my mind, I had no claims on you any more. You were out of my care, into someone else's. You just have to sit back and let them get on with their lives. You mustn't interfere. They'd only resent it.

Julie holds her mother's hand.

– But I don't want to be that separate from you. My going away again, my living in London, that needn't stop us having a relationship. I know I've got my own life, but I still want to come over and see you, wherever you are. I love you, I still want to see you.

– I don't like your language, Claire says, holding Julie's hand in her own: and I can't help wishing you lived in a different way, but you're my daughter, I'll love you whatever you do. I know you don't like me saying that, you always stop me.

– I like it now, Julie mumbles.

Claire looks at her with affection and with amusement.

– You know, you're so like Tante Lucienne. You wouldn't remember her, she was my mother's elder sister, she died ages ago.

Julie listens and watches her, storing up fresh memories for absence. The vivacity of the hands describing in the air, the soft lines of the face breaking up into smiles, the brown eyes shaded by the eyebrows and the tiny crow's-feet at the corners, the body relaxed and absorbed in storytelling, the stiff crimplene best dress, the bright costume jewellery. Claire wants to please her, Julie realises; she is shy, she turns to her daughter for affirmative nods, she chooses her words carefully, and well.

– And she was always beautifully dressed. Huge white piqué hats, feather boas, that sort of thing. But there she was, with five children, and not a clue about how to look after them. Your grandfather used to send them money from time to time, he was a really generous man for all you say about his strictness, meaning Lucienne to spend it on clothes for the children, or a new bed. But we'd go and see them a few weeks later, and there Lucienne would be with an exquisite dinner service, brand new, another one, and she'd be sitting there, sewing the most beautiful embroidery, and the children so badly-dressed. Still, she adds thoughtfully: they didn't turn out any the worse for it.

– You should write it all down, Julie exclaims: what a lovely story.

– Oh, Claire says briskly: I couldn't do that, it's easy enough telling you like this, but I haven't the words for writing it down, besides, it interests you and me, but it's only about the family, after all.

– Tell me another one, Julie pleads: tell me the one about Oncle Michel.

– He was the black sheep, Claire says, smiling: the bad one, always fighting his parents. He wouldn't learn Latin at school, for example, he refused, that really upset his parents. Then he ran off to north Africa, to Algeria, he refused to go to university. When he came back, he told me amazing stories about his adventures. It was only much later, when I was older, that he told me he'd made them all up from a book he'd bought specially so he could impress me. He'd spent the whole time he was there working in a bank. That picture of the gypsy that hangs in Julien's room, Oncle Michel gave it to me and told me it was a portrait of himself he had done in Algiers. I was so fond of it, I gave it to my aunt one summer when I came to stay here as a young girl. It's a woman, really, dressed in a gypsy costume. Oncle Michel got married in the end, he married a woman twenty years older than he was. But they were very happy together, I think.

Claire stops, and looks at her watch. Immediately, her body stiffens, she glances first towards the conservatory, then out into the garden, and then towards the kitchen door.

– Whatever can I have been thinking of? It's time for tea. Chérie, will you go and get the cups out? I'll help Suzette and Marie.

– Come and sit down again in the conservatory, Julie suggests, helping her mother to her feet: I'll help Suzette, you shouldn't be rushing around so much, not yet, anyway.

– All right, Claire says, sweeping crumbs off the tablecloth with one hand: only don't forget to put out the sugar-tongs, I can't see them anywhere, and –

– I know what to do, Julie says crossly: you don't have to tell me.

Her mother accepts the reproach: all right, all right, I know you do. I brought you up, after all.

Twentieth section

Over the wall the children's voices draw the boundaries of a vast collective garden, chanting rhymes and comments, instructing each other on the penalties of upsetting the delicate balance between group and self. Bertha is slowly getting to know the part of territory they all call hers. Squatting in front of a square foot of brick wall to examine every hairy tuft of grass poking between its crevices, teasing out the hidden meaning of heaps of small stones along the path, finding the connecting angle between the rusty watering-can on the kitchen window-sill and the grating at the bottom of the black pipe that runs down the back wall. If she stands at the top of the garden, with her back to the house, she meets the huge eye of the house whose garden backs on to hers and is caught in a crossfire of bricked-up glances. If she looks away from houses and along the narrow double row of gardens that they sandwich, all the shapes and the light shift to make differences, she is amazed by the earth struggling up from under corrugated-iron sheds and crazy paving, that she can part bushes and touch flesh, hard and stony in places but with green shoots prodding the blackness from below. Bertha crouches in a flower-bed, scrabbling her fingers in soil and dreaming of flying over the sea to bring her mother back. They have pinned up Julie's postcards in the kitchen next to the map of France, a large red drawing-pin fixing Julie in Barrières-sur-Seine. Despite the company of Sam and the other three women, Bertha is lonely. The warm body which hugs her and swings her around in the air has gone. It is the female body she has known best in that way, and it is both too late and too soon for it to be truly replaced by several others. Bertha spends most of her time in the garden. She gets to know the old man who owns the garden backing on to theirs. He was in the navy once, which means he can speak of ships that plunge across the sea towards the East.

Bertha stands on tiptoe against the wall, her hands gripping the weeds that sprout in its crevices, shoes ploughing into the compost heap and her chin propped on top of the wall. Mr Salmon introduces her to the plants in his garden. subjects he calls them.

– Now this subject here, she's a nice little thing, d'you see. Sturdy. She's no trouble. And come next year, there'll be flowers.

Mr Salmon tells Bertha about the trees in his garden and hers.

A hundred years ago, or more, there was a farm on this very spot. He has read about it in a book from the library. Cows they had mostly, to produce milk for the Londoners who would come a long way to fetch fresh cream and eggs from the dairy on the Green. The only trees that mark out the site of the farm now are the walnut tree in Bertha's garden and the mulberry tree in his.

– So where's your mum gone then, and your dad?

Bertha's fingers loosen from the top of the wall.

– It's my bedtime, she says firmly, as an excuse to go.

On her way back to the house she squats in the flowerbed encircling the walnut tree. Its leaves uncurled months ago, from May to June; damp and sticky with the newness of green, they blurred the outline of the branches, the view from bedroom windows. Then, the flowers came: furry tubes like large unruly caterpillars that littered the ground around the trunk. Mr Salmon is doubtful about the walnut tree, he says it is ill, it cannot keep its flowers, which all drop off too soon. Last year, he reminds her, all the walnuts were hard and green, and fell, tiny, in August. It was dangerous, he reckons, to sit beneath the tree at that time, as sharp and pointed walnuts hit your head. He does not think there will be any fruit at all this year. But it has been very hot, Bertha ventures to herself, I shall wait and see. Mr Salmon reckons the mulberry tree in his garden is stronger, its roots growing two hundred years deep in the soil. Extremely large worms roam beneath them, the offspring of

Grendel and her terrible relations Bertha has heard about in bed-time stories. Other worms feed upon the leaves, and then spit out long threads of golden silk that the underground worms will guard, for the silk is valuable, and everybody wants it. The tree itself has many arms that ravel the sky, arms which can toss you into flying. Bertha sits in the hollow between the roots of the walnut tree, her head touching its scar where Mr Salmon says it is ill, a deep gash covered now in fungi and moss. Her hands tunnel the earth between her legs, picking up finally a lump of clay and rolling it into a ball. Slowly, a human figure takes shape, sturdy like herself, for the clay is dryish and tends to crumble if she attempts to elongate an arm or a leg. She sits very still, her body tense with energy spilling only out of her hands and into the figure of clay. Further up the garden she can see Jenny and Barbara sprawling in deckchairs. It is beginning to get dark. She places the clay figure on the garden wall separating the walnut from the mulberry tree, and goes inside.

Bertha shares a room with Sam. Tonight, he is not enough. Uncomforted by the ritual of bath, milk and biscuit, story and good-night kiss, she takes to bed with her three teddy-bears, some building bricks and an alarm clock. It is too hot in the room, despite the open windows. When she first got into bed she had experienced the pleasure of thick cool linen sheets, cut up by Julie from her wedding ones, sliding over her body warm from the bath. Now the heat of her body has transferred itself to the sheets, which have become like another body, twisting around her legs, like the roots of a tree trapping her beneath the earth.

As soon as she closes her eyes the ticking of the alarm clock dominates the darkness. Thump, thump, like the noise of the airing cupboard in the Oxford flat. She is the bellows at the end of the heating pump. She is the pump being worked by the bellows. She is as huge as an elephant filling a skyscraper, yet the skyscraper is only as large as her little finger. She booms and whispers, shrinks and expands. In out, in out, big small, you me.

Ben and Julie's bed in Oxford is wide, chocolate sheets, a white fur rug on top, elaborately splayed headboard of bamboo painted white. The latest thing, imported from Thailand by a shop called Lotus Eaters in the High. A white wicker shelf nailed to the wall on each side of the bed contains their bedtime reading. On Julie's side: Dr Spock, a couple of volumes of lyric poetry, *The Golden Notebook* by Doris Lessing, *Marx for Beginners*, and a novel by Georgette Heyer hidden at the back. The Spock was given to her by Ben's mother, the poetry and the Heyer she bought herself, the other two are presents from Ben. On Ben's side, various journals concerned with historical research, and a pile of science fiction he feels no need to hide. Julie is away for the weekend, visiting Jenny in London. The student Adrienne is insensitive, she sits on Ben's side of the bed, leaning forward to untie the complicated strings of her espadrilles. Ben sits down beside her, slides one arm underneath her legs and the other under her arms, grips her firmly and tosses her to the other side of the bed. She lands deep in the fur, laughing delightedly and waiting for him to pounce on top of her and finish taking off her clothes.

Bertha cries out and opens her eyes. As she focuses on the darkness, she can see Sam sitting up in his bed looking at her. Her mother is not there. Sam gets out of his bed and climbs into hers, lying close to her and putting his arm around her. Bertha, don't cry, don't spoil things, don't wake all the others up. He strokes her, and she strokes him back, hands exploring, speaking. Gradually, they fall asleep.

Adrienne moves her naked arse to and fro across the white fur rug, arching her back and lifting her concave belly into the air. This is what they do in the magazines, grip the fur with your fingers and feet, open your mouth and growl a little, your eyes enticing but turned aside from the viewer, your cunt parting as excitement grows. Seeing Ben remain at the foot of the bed, immovable, still watching her rather than participating, she stops, with the beginnings of anger. What am I supposed to do then? It's up to you, you'd better tell me.

The children dream. Sam wants to be the worm guarding the treasure of Bertha's hollow tree; Sam is the timid dragon sheltering inside Bertha's tree.

Bertha wants to be the tree straddling earth and sky and contentedly sucking both. Bertha is the tree uprooted by storms and crashing across gardens to kill.

Sam is the fresh grass pelted by Bertha's flowers and then her fruit, staggering beneath her strength.

Bertha is the tree-trunk with a secret place caressed by Sam's green grasses, Bertha is the delicate moss stirring inside.

Ben has finished fucking Adrienne. He lights cigarettes for both of them. What do they remember? Only his urgency. Adrienne snuggles up to him, head on his shoulder, mindful that you have to introduce demands with tact and gentleness.

– Let's tell each other our wildest fantasies, she proposes by way of leading up to what she wants to tell him: go on, you begin.

Ben is very stoned. He leans his head more deeply into his silken pillow, shuts his eyes, and concentrates.

– We–ell, first you're lying there, on the top of the desk in my rooms in college. You've come for a tutorial. You'll be much more comfortable up here, Miss Labassecour, I say, spreading you backwards with one hand. Tell me now, this essay of yours on the Industrial Revolution, the movement of productive labour away from families in the home into organised labour on machines in factories for capitalism. What exactly do you mean by women's alienated labour in this context, please explain yourself, Miss Labassecour. You are giggling, of course, in that delightful way you have, because at the same time my hand is inching its way upwards underneath your scholar's gown, up and over the top of your tights, tickling your delectable cunt.

Adrienne stretches out, smiling, to knock the ash off her cigarette into the ashtray on the floor beyond Ben's side of the bed. He leans back into her arms as she comes back into her place; he puts his head on her breasts, and continues.

– So, then I insert a finger, and then two, into your juicy little tunnel, your vulnerable spot, ever so slowly. You're wriggling and crying out for more, of course, but I take my time, it's more enjoyable for both of us that way. You come off over and over again, you're dripping on to the floor in your excitement. But I keep my fingers inside you, they've become a wedge, driving further and further up. And then, when I'm as far in as I can possibly go, *smash*, your flesh is ripping itself apart, mother, you'll never be able to open yourself to another man, ever again.

Adrienne lies clutched in Ben's arms, crying, begging him to stop. Neither of them sees Bertha's face peer round the open bedroom door. Adrienne holds Ben in her arms now, she mothers him, comforts him, as his own tears begin to fall. There, there, revenge, there, there.

Bertha screams her nightmare into Jenny's and Barbara's arms. Sam, woken abruptly by her cries, is sobbing too, in sympathy. Too many grisly fairy stories at bedtime, think the two women, and why doesn't Julie hurry up and come home?

The children are adamant that they are too hot inside to sleep. The adults give in to their demands for sleeping in the garden. Cool night air, lush grass juicy underneath bare feet, toes carefully avoiding bits of gravel, Barbara's torch turning the roses white. Sam and Bertha shiver with excitement, faces popping out of their sleeping-bags to smell the earth, the plants, inspect the moon rocking above the dustbin and the box of broken farmyard toys beside it.

– Goodnight, Jenny and Barbara say firmly from their own sleeping-bags: goodnight.

– Bertha's funny, Sam offers, a gambit to keep the night a little longer: she hasn't got a willie like I have.

– For Christ's sake, Sam, do you have to use such awful words? Jenny protests: it's called a penis, you know that.

– And Bertha's not funny, Barbara says, laughing: she's different from you, that's all. So are Jenny and me. We're all girls, we have a clitoris, and a vagina, and breasts. That's what makes us different.

– I'm a girl, Bertha echoes with satisfaction.

– And now, for God's sake, go to sleep, Jenny threatens: or I'll pack you straight back inside again, and I'll never tell you another story, never.

– Bully, Barbara mumbles.

– Goodnight, they all whisper finally to one another: goodnight.

Sam, who does not know how he feels about being different, who is alone in a household of girls, clutches his penis in one hand until he falls asleep.

Ben lies peacefully in Adrienne's arms, nearly asleep, overwhelmed by the generosity of the arms that rock him gently, so gently. She murmurs to him as he drifts into sleep.

– Darling, it's all right, I have fantasies too, really incredible ones. Vicars and choirboys, black suspender belts, the lot. I feel guilty about them too, sometimes.

She lies awake, smiling gently. They will spend tomorrow together, and in the evening they will eat out somewhere in the country. They will talk to each other about everything, exchange ideas and feelings. He will come to trust her, he will learn to make love to her in the way she wants, he will learn to mother her as she mothers him, and to enjoy doing so. All you need is love. If he has the time.

Twenty-first section

The hooting of many sirens wakes Julie, curled like a grub on the deck, wrapped in blankets. She struggles up into a sitting position, her hair salty and flat, her face cold, and gets up, shedding blankets so that she can walk over to the rail. Cold iron gripped by her hands, drops of water puddling on rust. Rain sweeps across the harbour and blows gently in her face. Mist obscures any view of Southampton. Earlier voyages between England and France were made in the old Normania, ponderous tub fitted up with polished mahoghany, choking with cabins where the bunks wore red blankets and thick white sheets, and where the stewardess, ideal mother in navy-blue and a stream of jokes, brought cups of tea in the early morning, took her tip and vanished again. This boat is lighter, and smaller, glossy with chrome and formica, with a discotheque and numerous boutiques and fewer places to sleep.

Julie's dancing companion of the night before crawls out of his sleeping-bag and comes to stand at her side. She can't remember his name, but it doesn't seem to matter. Both of them concentrate on the mist, willing it to clear, so that they swim towards the outlines of sheds, painting from memory the brown and silver ridges of corrugated iron roofs, the slabs of dirty concrete walls. England at six in the morning, cold, and crumpled, and wet, stretching its yellow cranes to the sky, yawning with factory hooters, with sirens, with whistles and shouts. Home, loved and longed for, even though there are numerous policemen stalking the quays, even though it is raining. She hears English spoken again, she watches chilly men in sandals and shorts marshal their rucksacks, she sees colour arrive with the tops of red buses over a distant fence, she sees battered family saloons parked in neat rows and relatives all waving welcome, she starts thinking of eggs and bacon again, and cups of hot tea.

She pushes her way through the customs hall towards the railway terminus, encumbered by her suitcase, her carrier-bag clinking with whisky, the old-fashioned straw hat given to her by Madame Mévisse on parting.

– For wearing in that garden of yours, my dear, whispers the gardening woman: it wouldn't do for you to be catching the sun.

The train creates time, moving from the coldness of pre-breakfast morning, drizzle over the milk bottles on stone steps and the delivery bicycles leaning against closed corner shops, to the crispness of folded newspapers and the steaming coats of travellers to work, their breath like iron pillars on the chilly August air and their make-up fresh. Moving through drab rows of houses that run along the railway line, that sag beneath the weight of drainpipes and verandahs, the vulnerability of back gardens squatting with faces turned away. A man sits at a kitchen table reading the label on a sauce-bottle, a woman behind a window winds a clock. Two West Indian girls crouch on a damp and balding lawn, braiding each other's hair, serious, patient. She sees them not seeing her.

In London, she changes tubes at King's Cross. At the top of the escalator down to the northern line there stands a blackboard with a message on it scrawled in chalk: due to a person on the line at the Oval, trains will be subject to delay. Downstairs, the platform for trains going south is very crowded, a feel of more than the usual delay. She stands next to a young Indian couple, the father holding his child in his arms. As they hear the train rumbling in the tunnel the people on the platform move together and forwards and the baby begins to whimper in distress. The father holds the child up to his face to comfort it. Sshh, sshh, and the child is quiet. The train doors slide open and the crowd surges forwards, angry people in a hurry trampling on each other's feet, elbowing old ladies like packages and brief-cases out of the way. Julie helps the young Indian mother lift her push-chair into the scrum of legs.

She feels herself jabbed sharply in the back. Turning round, she sees a youth in denims, with close-cropped hair, a chain dangling from his belt, a Union Jack sewn on to his zipper jacket. He elbows the Indian couple and Julie aside, causing the baby to begin whimpering again. The youth jumps on to the train, just as the doors begin to slide together, and yells at them.

– Bloody wogs, too many of you lot here already.

The Indian man sticks his foot in the tube door so that it cannot close.

– Come on, he says urgently: come on.

His wife and Julie push their way with the baby and the folded-up carriage into the packed compartment, standing with their heads bent, squashed up by the doors. The baby crows happily into Julie's face as she tickles it with one finger. Everyone else in the compartment looks away, standing wedged against each other with their eyes cast down, away from three dark faces, away from a badge saying Lesbian, towards the other end of the carriage they strain their ears, where a loud voice shouts all the way to the Elephant and Castle: bloody wogs, bloody perverts, send them all home again.

The others meet Julie at the Elephant with a borrowed van and drive her home. The rain has cleared; it is a mild day now, clear pink and blue streaked sky with a soft air shaking into warmish wind. Julie sitting with a sleepy Bertha in her arms insists that they drive back through the Southwark back streets, not along the main road from the roundabout.

The horrible cages of jerry-built flats with the odd concrete play-space attached are fenced in with wire walls like concentration camps. At the end of every short street the horizon alters, the perspective shifts. Empty half-ruined neo-gothic churches give way to sudden enormous swathes of green housing gasworks, with signs that say keep off, surrounded by miniature art-nouveau terraces, yellow council blocks next to exquisite Queen Anne cottages. The skyscape is a clutter of cranes, factory chimneys, steeples, spires, columns. You can hear tugs still, hooting on the river. Wastelands enclosed in corrugated iron suddenly part, allowing her a glimpse of tree-lined narrow streets of neo-byzantine blocks of houses, each entry with a neatly-painted front door, iron bootscraper, wood and tile porch. The area is a contradiction between time and stone; all the vigour of working locally, small factories and warehouses shrinking the separation between day and evening time, belied by the devastation, the houses and streets laid bare, laid waste.

I know I'm being romantic, glossing with my senses all the

alienation of factory work, the dreariness of cold-water flats. And yet, you can still trace the old communities architecturally, and see their shadow in the clumps of people inside the pub, the crumbling launderette, one to each group of streets, and feel in some ways how it might have been better then than the way we live now, we middle-class intruders, our splits, our isolation from our neighbours and from everybody else. Living here so long, and knowing only two other families and the people in the pub. Hardly what you call a community.

Too late. Most of this is coming down. More people like us will be moving in, only with more money perhaps than we have. Industry is decaying here, or moves away to find cheaper labour elsewhere; the Government cuts back on public spending increasingly; people grow anxious, grow bitter. Just as I did, burning with resentment at my poverty. Constant anxiety about food bills, electricity bills, having shoes mended. Enraged at not being able to afford pleasure in the terms of my class: buying presents for people, rounds of drinks in the pub, going away for weekends. Being a woman meant I swallowed my anger back, denied myself even those pleasures which cost nothing, which depend on being relaxed, on having a little time. I ate too much stodge, I didn't let people hug me, I lost sleep worrying. I forgave Ben for being a bad landlord, for spending no money on keeping this tatty structure from falling apart, I coped, I managed, I made do.

They are back inside the house, sitting in Julie's room. Bertha still clutches her mother in her arms, caressing Julie, pouring upon her three weeks' worth of stored-up embraces. Julie lies back in her chair, getting to know her daughter for what feels like the first time, delighting in being cuddled, cuddling Bertha back. Julie feels strange, as though the afternoon, the outside have come in with her. The room feels light and blowy, she can see beyond the fireplace, out through the bricks and mortar, to the wilderness she has just come from. Their own territory is no longer safely on the other side of the main road from the devastation; down the street the council bulldozers are parked, giant Lego toys for the ecstatic gang of local children. At the top of the street, several lots of council tenants have been moved out, Jenny says, since Julie went away; the fronts of the houses are covered now in bright tin, the insides systematically smashed up so that squatters can't move in.

Ben's letter lies on the floor in front of Mary and Barbara, who are sprawled on the chenille cushions of Julie's bed. Louise, propped up against the marble fireplace with Sam on her knees, draws her toe along the pink and olive-green carpet bought at the local church jumble sale a year ago.

– Julie, what are you going to do, now you're back at last?

– Look in the mirror, see wrinkles, start growing old. Let the mirror crack if it wants to on my old image; let it reflect me stronger these days. Look after Bertha. Look up Ben's telephone number and shout at him. Look up the people in the law centre and see what our legal position is, if we stay here together, if we squat the house. Look at Jenny and Barbara and feel jealous, throw a tantrum or two. See if it works, staying all in the same house. Wait and see.

Julie, Jenny, Barbara, Mary and Louise sit outside in the garden on a rug, plaid wool warm under their bare toes; beyond it the cool tough stems of grass. Their picnic over, everybody sleepy, lolling back, against each other. Julie squints into the sun, at the flowerbed opposite lush with flowers, weeds, tangling with overgrown roses, hollyhocks, irises.

She remembers how, when she was a child, she could become her doll, propped against the edge of flowerbeds. Summer idles past, clocked by the regular gasping of hens. The child passes through space as well as time, clasps flower stems almost as thick as her waist, running with sap. When she rests the side of her face against the stem she feels its hairiness, its green moustaches, and between these prickles, these tufts, the translucent coolness of green, with water surging beneath. The flowerbed is a forest, a jungle undergrowth, offering endless miles to be travelled, endless material for the mind's and heart's occupation. Julie sits very still, hidden by redcurrant bushes. Far away. And the heat.

Now she sits on the wild long grass at the back of the house, on a fat pink silk cushion, and plays this game again. She lies down on the bright green grass, her head on the cushion, and stares face to face with a rose like a monster mouth lipsticked in fifties colours, hot crimson. Plants loom over her head; she can smell earth, and moisture, and green. On either side of her the stone walls are her boundaries. She understands: her world as a basket, lined with pink silk, and holding flowers. Roses, crumpled yellow and pink; the dusty white velvet of marguerites; the tight orange fur at the centre of sunflowers. She is very tiny indeed, a Gulliver doll, lying between stalks thick and black as tree-trunks. A hand picks up the basket, a giant's; she bobs along in her box unable to see the world, only to feel it and measure its size by falling from one side of the box to the other in long lurching swoops, her bones rattling, her heart leaping out of her mouth, as the giant strides along swinging the basket. Six other china dolls in the basket, banging each other, hold on unsteadily. The giant's name is Ben, Brobdingnagian Ben.

Julie sits up, throws away her piece of grass, holds out her arms to Bertha who crawls on top of her, face in her neck, laughing, tickling. She clasps the child in her arms, she rocks her, she rocks the two of them, to and fro, gently, faster, smelling her daughter's warm skin. She watches Louise on the other side of the rug combing Mary's hair wet from the bath, drawing the comb slowly through the dark fronds shiny as sealskin, she watches Mary arch her back with pleasure as the comb buzzes at the back of her neck, flooding her into happy passivity. Barbara and Jenny sit balanced back to back, shoulder blades mutually placed, daisies threaded between their toes. Jenny pulls a daisy rhythmically in and out, humming, as smug as a cat, knees bent, one elbow propping her chin.

– So, Julie says sharply: a decision by all of us. Let's have it, then.

Bertha feels the difference in her mother's tones, the shifting of her attention away from herself. She rolls off Julie's stomach, crawls to the edge of the flowerbed and into it, to sit in the perfumed dark and get drunk on the heavy perfume of late roses. Julie watches her go, and stays in the same position, and continues to rock, a ghost in her arms. Comfort she gives to herself, since everyone else is busy, she bends her head, tasting loneliness trickling from under her eyelids to the corner of her mouth, salty, and warm. She remembers Claire saying impatiently why can't you just get on with it, stop thinking so much. She raises her head and addresses the others, more gently this time.

– Let us hang on, let us hang on, she says, looking at Jenny and Barbara: this is my home, I don't want to leave it.

– Small pleasures, Jenny says dreamily: the taste of egg sandwiches in the sun, sharp shadows on grass, time snatched, a half-hour demanded for pleasure, or more.

– And change, Barbara says, looking at Julie: which you always say frightens you, which has frightened me too, I accept change, I accept seeing you as Jenny's lover. Do you accept seeing me in that way?

– It will be hard, it will be difficult, Julie protests in a loud voice: I am jealous as hell of you both. I insist that you make time for me, both of you.

– Time for your friends too, not just your lovers, Mary says: no longer the door closed each night early on the two of you, always the private joke and the soft conversation. Make a place for each of us too, the only way we shall survive the next few weeks of uncertainty.

– Time to be private as well, Jenny protests: time spent with kids, time spent working, time spent cooking and washing-up. There's not enough time for all I want to do, not nearly enough time.

Louise puts down her comb and begins to dry Mary's hair, drawing her fingers through it, threading it with air and with sun, watching it change and grow light and fluffy and brown.

– So we wait then, until Ben finds a buyer for the house, and then become squatters, do we? What's the point of that? Ben can get us thrown out in no time.

– It's not so much the house, Julie says: although it feels like ours now. It's the people, all of you I don't want to lose.

– We could buy it, Mary says eagerly: I am tired of moving around, from place to place, from squat to squat. I want somewhere secure now, for Sam and for me.

– We could buy it, Louise echoes: between us. No longer Ben's house, but ours, for as long as we want. Julie, what do you think?

– But a mortgage, Julie protests: I have no money, unless I get some crummy job and put Bertha in a nursery full-time. I'm just, she screeches: a mother. I can't buy a house on social security. Families are supposed to have homes, well, I can't afford one.

– We'll buy it, Barbara says: between us. One of us, Louise or me, could probably get a mortgage. The rest of you could pay rent, afterwards.

– No more landlords, Julie says bitterly: can you imagine what that would be like? The power you'd have, to make decisions? Please, Barbara, can I paint the hall green? Please, Barbara, can I sleep with Jenny tonight?

– It was you, Jenny says mildly: who was so keen on communes, a moment ago.

– I still am, Julie says angrily: only there are problems I am beginning to see.

She lies back on the rug, stares up at the dome of sky arching in exact opposition to the curve of her stomach, at the cloudless sky stretching beyond Peckham and Camberwell over the rest of London.

– I want to go out, she declares, spreading her arms and legs wide on the rug: anyone else fancy a voyage out?

– But you've only just got back, Mary protests: what's all the hurry?

– Can't we leave the discussion for a bit? Let's talk about things tomorrow, we'll all still be here.

– Where d'you want to go? Louise asks.

– There's more to life than just this house, Julie declares: I want to get out a bit, I want to go north.

– North, Jenny exclaims in mock horror: they're all cannibals up there, surely?

– Mothers, peculiar, lesbians, women, Julie replies: let's go and see. Let's find somewhere to go dancing. Would you come with me, Jenny? I want to go out.

– I'll babysit, Barbara volunteers: if you like, I was going to stay in anyway.

– Thanks, Julie says gruffly: I know you looked after Bertha a lot while I was away. Thanks.

On her way in through the house, she telephones Ben.

– He's out, says a voice Julie recognises as that of Adrienne: I'm not sure when he'll be back. Who shall I say called?

– Oh. It's Julie here. Hallo, Adrienne.

– Oh. Hallo, Julie.

The wife and the other woman exchange awkward politenesses, which they both would like to convert into other words, but have not yet found the courage to do. When the hell are you going to move out? Adrienne wishes to scream. How dare you assume you have any right to this house? Julie wants to yell in reply.

Finally, Julie says: I'll have to go. Would you tell Ben I'll phone him later tonight? I'd like to see him soon. I'll see you then.

– Fine, Adrienne replies: I'll tell him. See you, Julie.

– See you, Adrienne.

Barbara has bathed the two children and put them to bed. Julie hops into the bath after them and then goes into her own room to survey the clothes hanging in her wardrobe. She selects the graceful black suit unworn since her wedding-day, rummaging at the bottom of her trunk for a pair of black tights and some appropriate shoes. The children admire her choice when she appears in their room, and shout for a story.

As she finishes reading aloud and bends down to kiss them good-night, her body feels like the evening sky, cloudless and light, forked suddenly by jealousy. Bertha looks well; she has not been suffering from maternal deprivation. She babbles of surrogate mothers, she repeats their sayings, she is curled up, rosy, and brown, already nearly asleep.

Julie touches her cheek with one finger. How can you possibly know what is best for them? No rules, except those laid down by experts a long way off; just a series of tussles, and peace sometimes, if you are fortunate. She notes with satisfaction a smear of milk around Bertha's mouth, a crumb of biscuit adhering. Barbara is not perfect, after all. Bertha is sleepy, and cross at having her face wiped with the corner of a handkerchief dampened with saliva.

– No, she protests: don't, I like being dirty. I don't want you to wash me.

Julie is stunned. Here she is, back, taking note of her daughter at last, her cleanliness and her welfare, and she is rejected. She begins to laugh. Bertha immediately takes advantage of the easiness she has not sensed before in her mother.

– Don't go away yet. Stay a bit longer. Tell me a story. I want you to stay with me, not to go out.

Julie hugs her.

– Story-teller yourself. You were practically asleep, a minute ago.

– Tell us a story, Sam shouts from his bed, bouncing up and down: go on, I'm not tired either.

– All right, you wretches. Just a very quick one.

Julie settles herself on the floor in between their two beds.

– Well, she begins: once upon a time there was a little girl called Amy. She lived a long time ago, in this very place. In those days, there weren't nearly so many houses here. There were fields all round Camberwell Green, and a farm. Horse-drawn carriages used to drive out from London for fresh cream and eggs.

– I know, Bertha shouts impatiently: I know that bit. I know all about it.

– Who's telling this story? Julie complains: you or me? Well, anyway, one day Amy got bored just seeing the same old faces every day. She said to herself, I'm going to run away. And she did. She travelled in a boat right to the other side of the world.

Ten minutes later, Jenny speaks from the doorway at the story's conclusion. She is dressed in her best velvet trousers and a crêpe shirt dripping with lace. She pirouettes, smiling, for the children to admire her.

– D'you want to go, Julie? Are you ready?

Bertha curls up again under her quilt, one hand emerging to clutch her mother's on top of the counterpane.

– Don't forget. You promised, you said you would. You've got to do it tomorrow.

– What have you got to do tomorrow? Jenny asks as they climb into the van: it sounded very serious, whatever it was.

– Start writing a book. I said I would as a joke, so they'd let me off story-telling. Now look what I've landed myself with. I'm shit scared I won't be able to do it.

She revs the engine with concentration, and backs carefully out into the road. Jenny is silent until they swing into the Elephant and Castle roundabout and out across the river in an arc of lights, St Paul's like an eager jumping moon away on their right, the oily waters below them dark, two small boats bobbing. Voices float in the night, the sound of a flute pouring music from begging hands under the great railway arch behind them. Strings of lights dance along the promenade in front of County Hall, slung between plane trees, between larger lights. Ahead of them, Parliament burns in silver and the concert-goers stroll over the bridge two by two. Jenny puts her arm across the back of Julie's seat, lightly touching her shoulder.

– Good to be out with you again. What's your book going to be about? D'you mind talking about it?

– I don't know. No, not really. D'you remember this afternoon in the garden? Sam was asking us all riddles.

– What's black and white and read all over? That one?

– Yes. A newspaper. Right? Well, here's another one.

They swoop around Parliament Square and into Whitehall, the trees speckled with light, the offices of the state pale and glimmering. Julie puts her foot down and they rush up the wide avenue as confidently as the tanks of the revolution.

– Well, so what's black and white and red all over? A bleeding nun.

At Trafalgar Square they are caught in a snarl of traffic edging through traffic lights as bright as jellies. Julie casts a disparaging glance up at Nelson's Column.

– My family's still convinced that's a statue of Napoleon, she remarks: well, that's what my book's going to be about.

– French phallic symbols? The pathetic phallusy?

Julie knocks her head briefly back against Jenny's arm.

– Daftie. Well, you could say, yes. D'you remember that notebook I showed you, the one I found in the loft at Ben's mother's house? The one I wanted him to write a monograph on?

– Aimée, was it? Amy? What was her name?

– Amy. I'm going to write a novel about her.

– But you said she went into a convent, Jenny protests: what's the point of that?

– I am beginning, Julie says, swerving violently in front of St Martin's Church and pointing the car in the direction of Soho: where she left off.

– Mind that policeman, then.

They dance in each other's arms in the tiny club, clasped in half-darkness in a hot little communion of sweat and satin and beer, lips seeking each other's ears, each other's necks, hands caressing each other's backs.

– Really, Julie yells above the noise of the music: it's time to let go. Of the house I mean.

She holds Jenny at arms length, lightly, loosely, looking into her face.

– We only came there by chance, after all. It's worked well on that basis. Pragmatically. But it's over now, I can feel it. Time for all of us to move on.

– That might be easier, Jenny admits: I know for me it would, not living with you and Barbara at once. Perhaps I'd better live on my own.

– Let's talk about it again with the others tomorrow, Julie says, turning aside to execute some complicated steps on her own: there's plenty of time.

Ben's voice on the telephone is hesitant, soft. With a shock Julie realises that he is nervous, scared of what she may say. This makes her nervous too, she is not used to this sense of herself with him, she wants to giggle. Controlling it, controlling the urge to soft-soap, soft-pedal, joke her aggression away, she forces a deeper note into her voice, twiddling the coiled flex of the telephone with one finger.

– You could have let us know before now, she says angrily: you're really irresponsible. You've given us hardly any time at all to make plans.

– I'm sorry, love. Things have been very complicated this end.

– I'm sorry, I'm sorry, she mimics him: is that all you can say? I'm not your mummy scolding you, I'm your tenant, fed up with you. You should have given us more warning, you should have given us more time to work out what we're going to do. It's your own daughter, she cannot resist adding spitefully: that you're throwing out on to the street.

– I never intended that. As you very well know.

– What did you intend, then? A nice little payoff? Us to leave, weeping in gratitude?

– Julie, his voice changes, becomes warmer: you've really changed. You sound so strong.

– It's living without you, she says drily.

– I thought, Ben says hesitantly: that maybe, if we met, we could work something out –

– What kind of thing? she says cautiously.

– That depends on you. Are you planning to stay together, all of you?

– That depends on you. If you give us time to talk about it, work out whether we can.

– What about Jenny? he says briskly: don't you want to go on living with her?

– I've told you, I don't know yet. I might decide to live on my own for a bit. Or move to another household.

– You sound a bit uncertain, he says smugly: about your relationships.

– Has anyone ever told you you sound like a pedagogue even off duty? You patronising bastard.

– How was your trip to France? he asks hurriedly: how are your parents?

– Oh, you know, they're all right, more or less. My mother's been really ill, but she's a bit better now. She's pretty depressed about having to leave the farm. They're going to sell it and go and live in Switzerland with my brother.

– Do they want a buyer? he asks jokingly: it sounds just what I'm looking for, a smallholding in Normandy.

– Oh no you don't, Julie says, her voice shaking: don't you dare, you're not to, you're not taking anything more away from me.

– You could live there too, Ben astounds them both by saying: you and Bertha could come and live there too.

– What about Adrienne? she asks viciously: what about Jenny and everyone else? All my uncertain relationships, and yours?

She has a sensation of being forced to run downhill on stilts. Hang on, she tells herself, you'll do better with practice. Emotions, honesty, words, such great clumsy things, clogging her mouth like rocks. How much easier silence is, how much easier the fantasy arguments with Ben practised in front of a mirror years ago. Now she is flailing, awkward, touched by his offer almost to tears and at the same time furiously resenting it. She begins again.

– Let's drop that. It wouldn't work, not in a million years, you know that as well as I do. Lay off my childhood, lay off this house for a bit. Surely you can wait a month or so while we sort things out?

– You seem to forget, Ben says coldly: that it is my house, not yours. You've been living there rent-free –

– And you'll get the profits on the sale, don't you forget. Cosy country retreats, it's all right for some, she says, furious, envious.

– You can't have it both ways, Julie. Either you let me see a bit more of my daughter, or you condemn yourself to being homeless. And I don't know what the courts would say about the kind of household my daughter is living in. A load of lesbians is not the best context for a young child to grow up in –

– You wouldn't, she says aghast: Ben, you wouldn't?

– Listen, Julie, I want to see more of my daughter than I do –

– And I want somewhere secure for her to live, whether I have to squat or –

– You wouldn't, he says: you bitch.

She slams down the telephone, and immediately regrets it. I can't struggle, I can't argue, she thinks despairingly, I just lose my temper and make things worse, I am so envious of his comfortable life, all his money, his security. She bursts into tears, leaning against the hall table, shaking with sobs. She blows her nose, takes a deep breath, and redials his number.

– Ben, listen, it's hopeless, rowing like this over the telephone. Can't you come and see us? Or shall we come and see you?

– I'll come and see you, he says stiffly: if you want, if you think that would help. I don't want trouble, any more than you do.

We've got it anyway, she thinks, as she hangs up the receiver and goes into the kitchen to report to the others: whether we like it or not.

We carry the memory of our childhood like a photograph in a locket, fierce and possessive for pain or calm. Everybody's past is inviolate, separate, sacrosanct; our heads are different countries with no maps or dictionaries; people walk vast deserts of grief or inhabit walled gardens of joy. Tell me about your past, Julie begins to urge other women, and they to urge her. The women sit in circles talking. They are passing telegrams along battle-lines, telling each other stories that will not put them to sleep, recognising allies under the disguise of femininity, no longer smuggling ammunition over back garden walls, no longer corpses in the church and mouths of men.